*Island
of the
Seven
Hills*

Island of the Seven Hills

Zoë Cass

RANDOM HOUSE · NEW YORK

Library of Congress Cataloging in Publication Data
Cass, Zoë.
 Island of the seven hills.
 I. Title.
PZ4.C3418Is3   [PR6053.A824]   823'.9'14   73-20576
ISBN 0-394-49063-0

Manufactured in the United States of America
9 8 7 6 5 4 3 2
First Edition

*Island
of the
Seven
Hills*

Chapter 1

THE FOUR-HOUR flight from London to Malta had been smooth and uneventful, and for that I was thankful. My mouth tasted bitter with the prospect of what lay ahead of me. I wanted no travel sickness to add to it.

Gently, steadily, the plane was circling Luqa Airport. In one moment I would glimpse my beloved island, shimmering like gold in a sea of blue velvet, and as always the glory of it would catch at my throat.

All of Malta is fashioned out of its own yellow limestone. Even in dull weather one has the illusion of sunshine, and on this September day without even a wisp of cloud the sun was throwing light around the sky in a dazzling blaze. Heat would be pouring down onto the baked island. It would bounce off the rock and hang in the still air like an invisible blanket. I knew exactly how it would be down there.

I wore a thin dress, sleeveless, of pale yellow cotton, and had piled my heavy dark hair on top of my head for coolness. However anguished I felt at the loss of my father, I wanted outwardly to appear composed. As never before, perhaps because he was dead, I knew myself to be the daughter of Commander Prescott and wanted to be worthy of him. I had already shed uncontrollable tears in private and would shed more, but in public I would hide my grief.

In one hand I carried huge dark glasses which I planned to put on before leaving the plane. In the other I clutched a letter from Michael Brent, crumpled from having been read so often. It said too much and not enough, that letter, and the very name of Michael Brent tipped my emotions into turmoil, so that it took a conscious effort of will to keep my thoughts from straying down forbidden paths.

Michael, and also Mr. Callus, my father's lawyer, had told me to stay in London now that the funeral had taken place in my absence, but I'd disregarded their advice. For how could I even begin to believe that my stocky, vigorous father was dead if I did not at least see his grave? I almost felt I wanted to see the body before being absolutely sure, but that was a morbid fancy. His grave would be convincing enough: a rectangle of dry, stony soil without, as yet, any headstone to mark it. I must see about that. Nothing ornate. He would not want anything but a plainly carved stone. With his loss, I knew how dependent I had been upon him, even when we were parted by hundreds of miles. Those miles had been put between myself and Michael, not between my father and me. I had not wanted to leave my island home.

The plane tilted, dropping lower, and now at last,

with the familiar catch in my throat, I could see Malta, the smaller island of Gozo to the northwest and tiny Comino, a droplet between the two. I was bound for Gozo, known locally as the Island of the Seven Hills, for it was there my father had died.

The sea was not velvet after all, but watered silk, blue mixing into green, the surface ruffling and glittering. Great bays bite into the cliffs and beaches, making the best natural harbors in the world, and Malta is jeweled with the towers and domes of more than three hundred fifty churches. There are many towns, villages and farms, and all are surrounded by tiny walled fields, the stone walls built laboriously by hand to keep the thin topsoil from blowing out to sea. From the air, the fields in autumn are like brown blankets spread to dry. Blobs of yellow on the flat roofs are pumpkins and melons, put up there to ripen beside the lines of washing quickly blowing dry.

Malta is my second home. I went to school in England and took a course there in hotel management, but for holidays I joined my father in Malta and worked in Valletta after completing my training. When I was three years old, Mother died by drowning, caught by one of those sudden Mediterranean storms when she was out alone in a sailing dinghy. Father and I are very close. I shut my eyes and repeat the sentence silently to myself, correcting it: Father and I *were* very close.

I have to keep reminding myself that he is dead—he also by drowning, which seems incredible. I can hardly believe that when I leave the plane the short, square man with white windblown hair and neat white beard will not be at the airport to meet me. There would be no substitute figure, thank God, for I had told no one I was coming. I wanted to go at once to Gozo, an island that I had

5

visited only a few times, briefly, and scarcely knew. If any of my friends were aware of my plans, they would assume I was making a morbid and useless expedition and would try to stop me. I was in no mood to be stopped. Besides, as I no longer had the right to be with Michael Brent, I wanted to be by myself. I had already accepted our broken engagement. Now I must come to terms with the loss of my father.

I spread out the letter I held in my hand and read it yet again. It was short, but at the sight of that angular black writing the blood-beat hammered in my ears and made my limbs feel heavy as I remembered the passionate letters I used to receive from Michael. This letter was far from intimate, but it was not exactly impersonal. It was sympathetic, brisk and businesslike. It made assertions and assumptions. I had learned to accept both from the writer, but I had loved him nonetheless. I could only hope that my love was dead and not merely dormant.

"Alexa," the letter began:

I am very sorry about your father's death. Shocking bad luck to lose both parents in this way.

As you know, your father was converting a farmhouse near Xaghra for his own use. I suppose you will want to sell the property and I know of a likely buyer. Shall I get in touch with your lawyer in Valletta? I know you used to say he was too fussy, but his reputation is sound.

I am more than willing to help you in any way but I don't advise your coming here. There is nothing you can do now.

With sincere sympathy,
Michael

So he did remember some things about me. I had indeed thought Mr. Callus fussy.

A year ago I had been engaged to Michael Brent and spellbound by him. A young Englishman who lived in Malta, he was dark and strong, broad like my father. His mouth was firm but with a tender quirk, and I thrust away from me now the memory of how it had felt against my own.

Michael had broken our engagement and shattered my world, but I could hardly blame him for falling in love with Noni Jarvis, the daughter of a retired Englishman who had recently come to Malta. Noni was every man's dream of perfection. Golden-brown satin skin, high, full breasts, slim waist, long legs, thick blond hair falling to her shoulders and curling deliciously in wet tendrils when she swam. When my dark hair gets wet it goes into rat's-tails, not tendrils, and though my legs are long I have always been too thin. Huge dark eyes do not compensate for a lean figure.

By now Michael and Noni would be married, and the thought was unbearable.

My ears were bursting as the runway rushed up to meet us. Although I had flown so many times, landing still held terror for me, but today I was almost indifferent. I could think of nothing but the letter in my hand and its writer. Until my thoughts moved to another letter, written by my father's lawyer in Valletta more than a week ago. Ten days to be exact. Poor Mr. Callus: he had cabled, telephoned and finally sent a letter, but I received it only yesterday. It seemed longer ago than that. An age ago.

I had been visiting friends in Bath and there was no one at my small flat in London to answer the telephone or forward mail. So my father was long dead before I knew anything about it. I felt guilty, as if it were my fault that I had been enjoying myself with friends when I should have been mourning at his graveside. I had even been to a party on the very day of the funeral. I felt sick at the thought. But we had lived this way, he and I, in touch only at irregular intervals, perhaps every three weeks or so.

Each of us had almost too much respect for personal freedom, mental and physical. Father would no more expect to be told of every little thing I did than I would expect him to explain his every action. But now that he was dead, surely I owed it to him to find out how it had happened. Accidentally, by drowning, as had been reported? I could not believe it. My father? He had had years of experience in the Navy and, after retirement, an assortment of vessels of his own, culminating with his beloved sloop, a twenty-two-footer called *Francine,* after my mother.

Mr. Callus—and Michael—were both convinced that there was nothing I could do in the Maltese Islands, but I could not remain in London. Perhaps I was making a fruitless, morbid journey, but I thought not. Xaghra, where my father had bought a house, was on the island of Gozo. Michael had moved to Gozo only a week or two before breaking our engagement. I had never visited him there, but I'd heard he lived well. Why shouldn't he? In addition to being a geologist making specialist studies on the rocks of Gozo, which are notably rich in fossils, he writes tremendously exciting thrillers under the pseudonym Mike Villiers. His face stares out from paperback book covers all over the world. Michael had never discussed his earnings in any specific way, but when we were together there seemed to be no shortage of spending money. He enjoyed doing things in style.

I looked down at the piece of paper which I still held

tightly in my hand. My father was too suddenly dead. It is terrible, to have someone snatched away forever, without any warning, any chance to comfort or be comforted. Instinct told me that there was something strange about this drowning, reason confirmed it, and not for a moment would I consider having the farmhouse disposed of without my having seen it. My father must have intended to show it to me when he had completed the renovation. I wanted to see what he had done.

"May I help you?"

The stewardess was bending over me, concern written on her pretty face. It surprised me into a smile. Concern is an emotion stewardesses seldom display in public. And almost never for women. "I'm sorry," I said. "I was daydreaming."

She smiled back and handed me the small bag which I had placed on a vacant seat nearby. I thrust Michael's letter into my bag and slid the enormous spectacles over my nose. Behind the dark lenses I felt less exposed.

The plane had already stopped. I had not noticed the bump of wheels or the screeching roll to a halt on the runway. I was the last in line, last to emerge into dry, scorching afternoon heat, last to reach the terminal building.

As I entered, a short, thickset man who had been waiting by the glass door began walking away, then returned, apparently to look more closely at me. He was barrel-chested, dark-haired and dark-eyed, a description which would fit half the men in Malta. There was a marked intensity about the way he watched me, but I was sure I had never seen him before. After an instant in which our glances locked, he turned and melted into the crowd.

I shook off a feeling of unease. I must be mistaken in thinking that there had been a look of recognition on his face. Certainly I did not know the man, so how could he know me? I had not slept much last night. My imagination was overworking and my nerves were worn raw. There was no reason whatever for thinking that a total stranger had recognized me, and surely no reason for feeling cold in this burning heat.

Formalities over, I fought my way outside and joined a crowd of people meeting friends or flagging taxis. I felt alone and apart, for I was neither resident nor tourist.

Intending to go to Marfa Quay at once, to catch the ferry for Gozo, I started to hail a taxi but my hand fell back at my side and I stared in amazement at an open MG which moved off almost before the passenger had closed the door. I caught a glitter of glass and chrome, the shine of white paint, and the car flashed away—but not before I had recognized driver and passenger. The passenger who had scrambled in at the last moment was the thickset man who had stared at me when I arrived. As for the driver, there was no mistaking Noni Jarvis, Michael's Noni. I was shocked by an onslaught of emotion so violent that it was almost like a physical blow. I ought not to have felt so strongly still about the girl who had taken Michael from me, but the hate remained. She had so many advantages, and now she had Michael too.

Bleakly, I stared through the dusty palm trees and oleanders, seeing myself as I had been a year ago: green as a bay tree, trusting, reasonably attractive, but no match for the girl who was now driving the sports car with such scant consideration for her passenger.

Noni a year ago had been confident, contemptuous of me, and above all beautiful. She was still beautiful, a glance had told me that. The brown shoulders emerging from a white frock were slim and sleek, the fall of pale blond hair silky. In the salt air, sun and wind, it was a minor miracle to keep one's hair so healthy. She was a golden girl, perfect for any travel brochure. No wonder Michael had fallen in love with her. I hoped he was happy, but Michael was a jealous man and with Noni he would have cause to be. I thought of him, dark, tall, immensely strong, a foil for Noni's blond loveliness. Both so attractive; together, a formidable couple.

"May I call a taxi for you? Or give you a lift?"

Voices are important to me. This one was clear and deep. It sounded . . . developed. That was the only word I could think of at the time. As if the man were an actor, perhaps. I looked at him and liked what I saw. He had brownish hair, gray eyes in which concern was turning to amusement as he waited too long for my answer. He was deeply tanned. This was no tourist from England. His chin looked remarkably solid in spite of an uneven scar on the jawbone where a right hook might have caught it. When he smiled, his mouth went up at one corner, showing good teeth.

"Do you always give casual offers of help such careful consideration? It is a genuine offer. At this time of day I am quite harmless."

I laughed and opened my mouth to say that I knew Malta, but then changed my mind and said merely, "Thank you. I would like to take a taxi."

"Sure you wouldn't like a lift? My car is at the airport."

"And you're quite harmless," I finished for him. "But I doubt if you'd be going my way, so I will take a taxi if you don't mind."

He smiled, gave a small shrug and lifted an arm. Immediately, a taxi came from nowhere and swerved to a halt beside us. The driver seemed disappointed at having only one passenger, but one was enough for he talked nonstop over his shoulder, taking his eyes off the road regardless, pausing only occasionally for a reply and driving at terrifying speed. I noticed a St. Christopher badge on the dashboard, indicating a slight difference of opinion with the Pope over the functions of the one-time patron saint of travelers. There was also a small figure of the Virgin Mary with a shiny vase of plastic flowers below it. The driver glanced at the Virgin occasionally, with affection—as well he might, taking the risks he did—but there was humility too, and I found it touching.

When I had lived in Malta, I had seldom used taxis. Dad drove a sporty MG, an older vintage than Noni's, and for my twenty-first birthday he had given me an Austin Mini. With a stab of annoyance I realized that although my Mini had been sold when I decided to go and work in London, Dad's MG would be at our St. Paul's Bay house in Malta if he had sailed to Gozo in the *Francine*. Perhaps, though, he might have taken the car to Gozo. Would I have to get permission from the lawyer to use Dad's car? Mr. Callus would willingly give it, but if I contacted him he would know I was here and would begin to fuss.

I put a hand to my throat. Nausea welled there. Everything was unreal. This could not be me, on such a mission. Only occasionally, for brief spasms, was I aware that I would not see my father again. Most of the time it was as if this journey would end in a meeting. I even stored up anecdotes which I knew would amuse or interest him.

"I met a man at the airport," I would say. "He offered to help me. I must have looked lost . . ."

Suddenly, I realized that I hadn't said goodbye to my would-be rescuer, or thanked him. How churlish of me. I turned to peer through the rear window as if expecting to see him in the car behind, but the car behind was being driven with a crazy panache which was certainly Maltese. I turned back and tried to pull myself together. The chance of my rescuer coming this way was a million to one. Well, about three hundred and twenty thousand to one, anyway, that being about the population of the Maltese Islands last time I'd looked.

I began counting things: carved balconies, men on bicycles, women in black (plenty of these). I even saw some women wearing the *faldetta,* black national dress with huge headgear three or four feet wide. And nuns, also in black, scores of them. We were sisters, these nuns and I, for after all my flat in London was little more than a cell. Since my broken engagement, I had avoided men almost entirely, not wanting to be hurt again. Oh, an occasional evening out, a few kisses. I worked in a smart hotel, the Torridon, in Park Lane, where there was no lack of opportunity for meeting people, but I'd kept men at arm's length and avoided any kind of deep involvement. I was still insecure, I thought ruefully: Look at my behavior when a perfectly ordinary nice man had offered me a lift from the airport. I had shied like a nervous mare. I thrust aside the distasteful thought of my own cowardice, not for the first time, and went on counting. Mules, busses, bars . . .

We whizzed through crowded small towns, with narrow alleys angling away from the main road, the houses elegantly built of that golden limestone, like melting sunshine. Many of the main streets were narrow and congested, yet the people all seemed to be smiling. The Maltese are the warmest, kindest people in the world.

We inched through the town of Mosta, passing the marvelous Dome which never failed to take my breath away though I had seen it so many times. Then on at a mad speed through relatively open country, skirting the blue water of the bay where St. Paul was shipwrecked nearly two thousand years ago. Now it is a giant marina, with all kinds of craft from modest toys through large, painted fishing boats to millionaire eccentricities with enormous superstructures. There were handsome bronzed men and gorgeous girls wherever I looked, and I felt like a death's-head at the feast with my wooden heart, grim mouth and my longing, not only for a lover but for my father also.

Round the bay through Mellieha and we were snaking down that long slope toward the quay, fifteen miles or so from the airport. It was bare and rocky at this end of the island, with parched areas where small lizards darted over the hot stone and only the hardiest succulents grew in weirdly shaped patches. There were few hotels, but the road was new and more hotels would come. The views were marvelous: glittering sea, emerald and navy blue, ribbed with gold where the sun struck, and glimpses across the water of the tiny island of Comino and the larger, higher Gozo.

"Why do you go to Gozo?" my driver asked. "Why do you want to stay with those Scotsmen?" His voice was filled with consternation but he was grinning, looking at me over his shoulder. The Gozitans have no real connection with Scotland, but the Maltese call them Scotsmen for their thrift and industry. Or Irishmen, because they are poor, backward and superstitious.

"I've heard it is an interesting island," I answered evasively. Then, playing the part of a tourist, I added, "Tell me what I ought to see. Have you been there recently?"

14 🍂.

He turned round, the smile smitten from his dark-skinned face as he puzzled over why I should ask such a stupid question. *"Le, skur Le.* No! Why would I go there?"* he asked, mystified.

I remembered that my father had a Maltese friend, a farmer, who had never in his sixty-odd years been more than five miles from his farm. I doubt if he would have covered even those five miles but for the fact that a son had gone to work as a barber in a village that distance away, and very occasionally he visited the boy.

As for the straits which separated the two islands, many natives refused to cross the four-mile stretch of water. There were dangerous currents and a heavy swell. Faith in weather reports was limited and experience taught that storms could be sudden and deadly, canceling the ferry at short notice, perhaps leaving many people stranded on the other side. It was not to be risked. My driver clearly thought that visiting Gozo was an eccentricity for tourists.

We reached the gates to the quay with a triumphant squeal of tires and I got out. The breeze created by the car's rush quickly died and heat enveloped me. In spite of proximity to the sea, the air was still. I paid the driver and bought my ticket for the ferry.

The *Imperial Eagle,* a sizable ferryboat, was swallowing cars one by one. I, and others like me, lined up to get on board. A small knot of people watched the activity from the quayside, Maltese women, knitting as they stood, men idling, children playing with fierce energy in spite of the heat.

The line moved steadily—priests, nuns, a few tourists returning to Gozo after a day spent in Malta, others newly arrived, still journeying, pallidly, to their holiday homes.

Two policemen, wearing sand-colored uniforms and an air of lethargy, watched with indulgent smiles and exchanged jokes with sailors and porters.

Freight coming off the ferry included milk in large modern tankers, en route for Valletta. They joined a procession of cars moving quickly up the quay. Crates of butter, wine and tomatoes were being unloaded, stacked and driven away in waiting trucks. Some were ancient vehicles, privately owned and scrawled with names and slogans from another era and driven barefoot. There was a van called "Jolly Jack Tar" and one with "Hello Sid!" scrawled on the side in gleaming yellow paint.

My father had chosen to live among the Maltese people because he loved them, and he had taught me to love them too. Not that all Maltese are simple peasants or sailors—many are highly educated and cosmopolitan. They have an inbred love of tourists surprising in a nation which has spent centuries in being host to all comers in the past, not always willingly.

In exchange for the goods which had arrived from the smaller island, newspapers and mail were being put on board. There were boxes of groceries, tins of paint, rolls of wallpaper, most going to hotels probably. The Torridon in London, and my job there as assistant to the restaurant manager, seemed very far away, but I would return to my working world. I had asked for, and been given, an extra two weeks' holiday. I hoped it would be long enough.

The barefoot porter who took my bag was dressed in knee-length blue trousers and a faded checked shirt, very clean. He showed me where he had stowed my bag on the lower level, pocketed my tip with a quick *Grazzi* and ran to help someone else. I climbed the narrow companionway to the deck above, moving to the side so that I could still enjoy the activity. One thing was certain: this particular crossing would not run at a loss. The decks were crowded. Dark, chattering Maltese and Gozitans were already buying from a small galley cups of thick, sweet liquid the color of pale fudge. It was tea, heavily laced with condensed milk and greatly relished, though not by me. There were parties of schoolchildren, cared for by nuns, and I spoke to some of them, using my scanty knowledge of Maltese. The few Europeans newly arrived from some cooler climate were pale, tidy and all too noticeable among the predominating, darker-skinned local people.

I leaned on the rail, watching those still on the quay. A man seemed to be waving to me from the third car in line, an open green Fiat. To me? I looked again. He was smiling, his white teeth gleaming, and I realized it was the man who had hailed the taxi for me. So I might as well have accepted that lift. Extraordinary that he, too, should be traveling to Gozo.

He did not look as if he held it against me that I had parted from him with total lack of civility, and now, at least, I would have the opportunity of apologizing. I lifted my hand in an answering wave and felt also a lifting of the spirit. I could scarcely call this chance acquaintance a friend, but to recognize and be recognized made one feel less of a stranger.

"Hello again," he called up from below. He was second in line now.

"Hello!" I called back.

Then, from some invisible place to my right, I heard a voice I knew only too well. "Randal! Hey, Randal!"

The man's eyes moved leftward as he heard his name

being called and identified the caller. His smile was brighter, broader now, and he waved with delighted enthusiasm. "Noni, what luck! Be with you in a minute."

Momentarily, the crowd on my right surged and parted so that I could see a sweep of blond hair, a slim brown arm, waving. It was Noni Jarvis, Noni Brent she would be now, Michael's wife.

Chapter 2

THERE WAS something unbearable about seeing Noni like this, gloriously alive, happy and beautiful, waving to the man she called Randal. The warm moment of kindness, when I felt it good merely to be acknowledged, to be less of a grief-ridden stranger, dissolved. And with Noni on board, I wondered where Michael was. Crossly, I told myself that they were not inseparable, that it had nothing to do with me whether Michael Brent was here with his wife or not.

Somberly, I faced the fact that I was still jealous of Noni, of her looks and of her power, even over this stranger who was nothing to me, and I was shaken by the destructive strength of my feelings. It was shocking that I should feel even a lingering trace of my former jealousy at such a time. It shamed me. My hurt over Michael had made a deep wound, but surely, surely it would not re-open after a year? I must be free of him by now, and therefore of Noni also.

It had taken a long time and much discipline, back in London, to clear my mind of Michael Brent. Now it seemed that even a year was not long enough to slough away all feeling for him, and I knew that I would not willingly have returned to Malta yet. It was too soon.

The final car had been driven aboard. The ferry *Imperial Eagle* thrust away from the quay. I found myself gazing into water that was churning and boiling, throwing up oil and flotsam. I grieved for my father. Death by drowning. Had the water been clear and kind when he drowned? Or had it been murky, thick with oil and muck, filling his mouth, choking . . .

I whirled and pushed my way through the crowd, desperate to get away from the rail and that mesmeric, churning water. But in leaving the side I had come near to the companionway. I saw the man Randal emerge, saw Noni meeting him and reaching for him. They embraced, he hugging her with exuberance, lifting her off her feet, and yet there was nothing in this embrace to which even the most jealous husband would object. I hesitated, wanting to melt back into the crowd and vanish, but over Noni's shoulder Randal saw me.

"Hello!" He grinned and set Noni down upon her narrow, white-sandaled feet.

She turned and I had the impression that she knew who Randal was greeting. With little surprise and even less enthusiasm, in a tone that was unusually flat for her, she said, "Hello, Alexa."

"Alexa!" The man was startled. He looked at me, brows furrowed, eyes full of concern. "Alexa Prescott?"

I nodded.

"Then your father . . . I'm sorry. Truly sorry. When I spoke to you earlier, I didn't know . . ." His nice voice trailed into silence.

"You two have met?" Noni looked puzzled.

"Not really," I answered.

We had moved away from the quay now and were heading steadily for Gozo. Over Noni's shoulder I could see the sea, as smooth as glass, glittering in some places, shadowed in others, beautiful. The beautiful, treacherous Mediterranean. My mother had died in it but I went on loving it, encouraged by my father. Now that he, too, had been claimed, would I be able to keep my love for it?

"We met at the airport, without knowing each other." The man glanced from me to Noni. "Strange as it may seem, I've never met Alexa. You'd better introduce us properly."

"My brother, Randal Jarvis. Alexa Prescott." She flipped a slim brown hand, first at Randal, then at me. Her round, white-framed spectacles had been pushed up into her hair but now she slid them back on her nose. Mine were already in place, screening my sleepless, shadowed eyes.

There is an aggressive, as well as a shielding quality about heavily tinted glasses. I felt Noni's hostility and no doubt she felt mine. The inside of her right cheek was sucked in suddenly, and I knew that she was biting it. I hitched the strap of my tan shoulder bag higher and enjoyed her discomfiture without understanding the reason for it.

For a brief moment I wondered why I had fled to London a year ago instead of staying to fight for Michael. My father . . . Dad had thought it best for me to get away and at the time I agreed, but now I knew how wrong I had been. Noni had brains and beauty in full measure, but she was short on sympathy and kindness. A man needs those too, sometimes.

"How is Michael?" I forced myself to ask the question. If I avoided it, she would know how much I'd cared about losing him.

"He's fine." A slow smile curved her lovely mouth and she turned to Randal. "What were you doing at Luqa?"

"Collecting those swatches of material I've had sent out from London. Had you forgotten I was going for them?"

"Totally. I'm sorry, Ran. I could have got them for you. I've been shopping in Valletta."

So she did not want Randal to know that she, too, had been to Luqa, to the airport. I wondered where her companion had got to, the short, thickset man who had recognized me as I came off the plane and had hurried out to join Noni in her car. And I wondered, vaguely, about those swatches of material. Why would a man want such things?

"Alexa, I'm sorry too about your father. If there's anything we can do to help . . ." At that moment, Noni's mouth looked gentle, but I wished I could see her eyes and read the expression in them. Tension still twitched that right cheek.

Her brother watched her with quiet pride. Clearly, he was fond of her. It was odd that we'd never met, unless he had come out here only recently. I'd met her father, Edgar Jarvis, and remembered him well. A man of great charm.

We passed the small, rocky islet of Comino, going fast, and Gozo seemed to grow out of the water as we approached. As we drew closer, the church on the headland loomed larger, high above the busy harbor, golden spire soaring into blue sky.

I started to take my leave of Randal Jarvis and Noni, for the second time refusing a lift from Randal. I thanked him but was firm, for the simple reason that I did not want to accept a lift when I did not know where I was going. The next thing would be an offer of hospitality which I would also have to refuse. An impersonal hotel would be best for me now, and later I would find my father's farmhouse.

It was not possible to get away at once. The press of people around the companionway was too great and presently Noni, who had been watching the quayside, said, "Look!" She put a hand on my arm, gripped it with her long fingers, then released me and pointed.

I looked. A pale-blue open car, a Triumph I thought, drew up on the quay and a man got out. He was tall, but not so tall as Randal Jarvis. His hair was dark, and even from here the breadth of shoulder was noticeable. He lifted a strong, brown arm and waved to Noni with no eyes for anyone else. How well I knew that gesture.

Any thought I'd had of being able to meet Michael Brent with indifference fled from me at first sight of him, and Noni's soft laughter was malicious. My heart thumped and I felt dizzy, only partly from lack of sleep and food. The heat on the ship, now that movement had ceased, became intolerable. There was a smell of oil, then of gasoline exhaust fumes as cars prematurely started their engines. I felt sick and as if I were floating, and I put out a groping hand. Randal Jarvis, a perceptive man evidently, took my arm and steadied me. When the crowd began moving downwards with a hollow drumming of feet on the steps, he went before me—a cushion to fall on, as he put it. But of course I didn't fall, I got a grip on myself, and by the time we reached the lower deck I'd lifted my head and walked with a sure step.

Randal said, "It doesn't make any sense for you to go alone to your hotel."

"I'm all right now. I'd rather take a taxi. Please."

He shrugged, said, "As you wish," and disappeared among the cars. Noni had already left us. In fact, from the moment she had indicated that Michael was waiting for her on the quay I could not remember seeing her. She must have slipped through the crowds and made her way below, very quickly.

Again I had refused a lift from Randal Jarvis, and again I was aware that I could have declined his offer with more grace. I might have thanked him, invented some excuse, but ahead of me was the ordeal of meeting Michael and I could think of nothing else.

He was waiting at a barrier beyond which cars and taxis did not come. Only vehicles traveling by ferry were allowed beyond that gate, and as a porter had already seized my case and received my nod of encouragement I was on my way, off the *Imperial Eagle* and into the burning sunshine. A car driven by an elderly tourist making heavy weather of it crept along by my side, encouraged by shouts from dock officials, porters, police and friendly fishermen. The atmosphere was relaxed and happy, even more so than at the other side of that four-mile channel of water, and yet I'd thought the dockside happy in Malta.

Randal's car would be next off, Noni's far behind, as she had gone on board earlier. I walked behind my porter, dazzled in spite of sunglasses, with heat striking up from the stone quay through my shoes. I felt travel-stained and weary, and a downward glance told me that my yellow dress was not so crease-resistant as I'd thought.

If Michael Brent did not see me, what would I do? Stop and talk to him, or walk on by? But of course he saw me, and knew me instantly, watching my approach with consternation.

"Alexa!" He held out his hand and I took it. "You shouldn't have come. Didn't you get my letter?" The voice admonished me gently. He was concerned for me and I almost broke then, for the first time since leaving my London flat, but I fought for control and found it. If I could hold out for a little longer, I told myself, an hour, perhaps less, I would be in some hotel room, in complete privacy, and could howl my eyes out if I wanted to without anyone knowing.

There was no one in my life at the moment to care at all what I did, but that, I told myself coldly, was largely my own fault. No one need be friendless in this world, but most of the time during the past year I had shunned social contact, working like a demon during the day, making plans in my free time to have a small hotel of my own somewhere in England.

"Hello, Michael. Yes, I got your letter, but naturally I had to come. There are things I must deal with myself."

He was silent, looking down at me intently. How little he had changed. He was not wearing dark glasses and his hazel eyes were bright and warm. He didn't even have to screw them up against the light. A geologist as well as a writer, Michael spent much time out of doors and always said he was accustomed to the light. He was very tanned and looked tremendously fit.

"I met your wife on board," I said brightly, breaking a silence that was becoming too long.

"My wife! You mean Noni? We're not married. Didn't she tell you?"

Fortunately, I had looked away from Michael before he uttered these shattering words. My porter was stowing my luggage in a taxi. The driver, a large man with black hair fringing his bald head, got in and with great skill backed toward us. Michael glanced at him, then at me, and with a deft movement tipped the waiting porter before I could do so myself.

I was longing to know whether Michael meant that he and Noni were not married *yet*, or were not going to be married. "Really? Noni didn't happen to mention it," I said with a touch of sarcasm.

Michael reddened under his tan. "You don't need Bartola's taxi," he said. "We'll give you a lift."

He and the taxi driver appeared to know each other well, and the man was evidently quite willing to forgo his fare, but I put out a hand in a restraining gesture. "No, thank you," I said to Michael.

I was still mentally reeling from his bombshell. He *wasn't* married to Noni? When I'd left Malta a year ago they were to be married in three months' time in St. John's Cathedral. Noni was a Catholic, her father a devout one I'd been told. My mind whirled. They were not married, but the Jarvis family, too, had moved from Malta to Gozo.

My white wool coat slipped down my arm and I hitched it up again. Goodness knows why I had brought it. I held on to the strap of my shoulder bag, clutching at my belongings as if they were an anchor. I noticed, vaguely, that Randal Jarvis had driven by without stopping, then I glanced back and saw Noni's white sports car bounce off the gangway.

"I must go," I said hurriedly, and in a state of total mental and physical confusion I got into the Mercedes.

"Wait a minute! Where are you staying?"

I did not answer. How could I? I did not know. I signaled to my driver and he moved off. The road was steep leading up from the quay. I turned to peer through the rear window and saw Noni's open car stop. In the driver's seat was the barrel-chested man I'd seen at Luqa Airport. Noni got out and transferred to Michael's car, but first, without haste, they kissed. They might not be married, but they certainly were not estranged. I wondered why it didn't hurt to see her slim brown arms curling possessively round Michael's neck, and came to the conclusion that by now I was numb with repeated shocks and, for the time being, immune. I hoped the feeling would last for a while.

My driver was Mr. Bartola himself, owner of a fleet of taxis and cars for hire, and a useful man to know. He spoke perfect English and asked me, courteously, where I wanted to go.

"I don't know," I said doubtfully. "A hotel, but I haven't booked a room." I could remember little of the island. It was some years since I'd been there, and place-names flew out of my head and floated just beyond reach. There was Xaghra, of course, where my father's farmhouse was, but I didn't want to mention that just now, or go to it yet. I was not ready for that ordeal.

"The Duke of Edinburgh Hotel in Victoria?" Mr. Bartola suggested. Victoria was the capital, in the center of the island, and sometimes called by the native name Rabat. I knew that much.

"Or do you want to be by the sea? The Calypso Hotel at Marsalforn Bay? New, very beautiful, excellent food."

"Is there a hotel at Xlendi Bay?" I asked. That was where my father had moored his boat, Mr. Callus wrote, but not where he had drowned.

"Xlendi Bay?" He pronounced it as if the X were ZH or a soft J, a sound not heard in the English language. "Yes, of course. It is nearly the end of the season. You should be able to find a room. We shall go and see."

He was a kind, friendly man and drove at an even pace, pointing to views which he thought I might enjoy. We were on a new, straight road, wide for a small island with little traffic but ready for a tourist industry which had not yet boomed. Island life had not quite caught up with this sophisticated road. Fishermen sat to one side of the straightest section, with nets spread on the conveniently flat surface of the road while they mended them.

They wore white, open-necked shirts, spotlessly clean, and baggy blue trousers. Their brown fingers, those of the older men gnarled, worked with incredible speed in the fine nets, mending, sliding, folding. There were women helping, too, all clad in black, with longish, full skirts. Most looked up, waving as we passed. Even from the inside of the car, I was aware of an air of busy contentment.

Michael's blue car swept by. Two arms were raised in salute and a horn tooted, gently. Noni's car followed, driven by the Maltese. Or was he Gozitan? The two vehicles dwindled and disappeared into the distance.

I was saddened by the bareness of the island. The earth was scorched and it looked as if crops would never grow again in those brown fields, but here, as in Malta, the parched earth would bloom when the rains came. There had been no rain at all for many weeks, but oleanders planted by the road had been watered and were flowering white and red, with glossy, dark leaves, and everywhere there were clumps and hedges of prickly pear. Goats were tethered in the fields, skinny cats lay sleeping in the sun, and dogs, which all seemed to be of the same shape and size, dozed in doorways. They were dun-colored, medium-sized and peaceable.

On every ridge there seemed to be a village or town, with massive churches and domes and a huddle of square, flat-roofed houses, like golden lozenges baking in the sun. These ridges were the Seven Hills of Gozo. Houses close by had few, if any, windows to the street. They looked into inner courtyards, but by the front doors sat women on wooden chairs, faces turned to the wall, ceaselessly making lace with flying fingers. A few were watching the street and knitting, but most made lace, concentrating on intricate patterns.

We passed a large, modern dairy and soon were in the capital, Victoria. I had a swift impression of grand buildings and humble ones, nearly all constructed from the fantastically beautiful golden stone; modern and ancient shops, palm trees, and high up ahead on our right, perched on its hill, the great bastions of the Citadel, glimpsed between and above the huddled buildings.

I remembered my father taking me to see this fortress, dating from Phoenician times, built long before Rome itself was founded. I could still hear his voice as he laid a hand on the massive stone wall and told me: "A little over four hundred years ago, Gozitans had to sleep within these walls every night. The drawbridge was pulled up and everyone inside was safe from marauding Turks. Nothing could break through these walls. Picture it, Alexa, a straggle of peasants approaching from every direction at night, the torrent flowing out in the morning as soon as the drawbridge was let down, hurrying home and to work in the fields and vineyards, or to go fishing. About four hundred and twenty years ago," he mused in wonderment, as if to himself.

"But that's a long time!" I'd objected.

He had laughed. "Measured in history, young, *young* Alexa, it is a grain of sand on a beach."

I thought now that barring a holocaust the Citadel would surely stand forever.

We turned left and wound downhill, out of Victoria again. I saw a signpost in English saying "To Xlendi Bay" and, totally un-English, a public washplace with women at the spring, beating and rubbing clothes on a slab of rock.

Xlendi Bay I had never seen before. It was breathtakingly beautiful, a great squared-off cleft between cliffs, the sea washing well inland in the deep fjord to a small, sandy beach. It was a natural harbor, with many boats at anchor or moored to a quay. Those out in the bay were a fair size, telling of deep water and deeper moneybags. My eyes searched for the *Francine* but she was not there. I would have to inquire about her.

The headland on the left rose gradually. There were houses and a hotel or two on the ridge. To our right, the cliffs were massively high, with a narrow, climbing path and flimsy handrail. While I gazed upward, small splashes of white, brown and black were winding down tracks or jumping from one perilous foothold to another. It was a herd of goats, and with a sudden, stomach-turning fright I saw that two very small children were leaping alongside the animals, sometimes almost disappearing in the streaming, mottled tide.

"Are they safe?" I gasped.

Mr. Bartola followed my gaze and laughed. "Sure. They herd goats almost as soon as they can walk." He got out of the car and thankfully I scrambled out too, hoping for a breath of cool air. It was hot down here, unbelievably hot. The still atmosphere was beating and throbbing, and under a row of limp palms people were sitting, scarcely moving, waiting for the cool of the evening.

There were several swimmers, diving off the quay and off boats swimming from the flat edge of the headland to the left. I longed to join them, but first I must find a hotel. I looked at the row of buildings along the water-front, small lace and souvenir shops, bars, hotels. Pop music blared loudly from one of the cafés and it occurred to me that there were probably quieter places to stay; airier, too. I hadn't much heart for gaiety.

I consulted Mr. Bartola and he pointed upwards to the ridge on our left. "Try the Hotel Tramonto," he suggested. "It is modern and very good. You will find it cooler up there."

It could not be hotter. By now, my journey from London was beginning to seem interminable.

The Hotel Tramonto was spacious and lovely, with its own swimming pool in the garden. There was a wide terrace running round two sides, with a stupendous view of the fjord from the front and another view of the Mediterranean from the side. Far out on the water I could see two powerboats, their wakes streaking and creaming the intense blue.

I passed people sitting at tables, but even up here it was hot and bright umbrellas provided welcome pools of shade. I went indoors, into the bliss of an air-conditioned foyer, black-and-green tiled, with a tank of tropical fish and massed greenery growing in troughs made from natural stone. Perfect décor.

The girl behind the desk offered me a single room with balcony and bath at a price higher than I wanted to pay, but in the heavenly cool of this place I was in no mood to quibble. I took leave of the cheerful Mr. Bartola, who gave me his business card so that I could hire a car. It did not seem to me at all likely that I would want one, but Mr. Bartola was smiling, knowing better.

I relinquished my passport to the desk girl and walked, heels clicking on the tiles, up three steps to the elevator, following a boy who wore a hotel uniform well suited to the climate—pale gray slacks and a matching short-sleeved cotton shirt with a green T for Tramonto on the breast pocket. He carried my case and led the way to my room. It was as good as the foyer. The balcony gave me a view of the bay, and out to sea as well if I leaned over the baluster. Quiet air conditioning kept the room cool behind pretty shades. Thankfully, I closed the door and locked it, valuing privacy after all the hours of travel. Stripping, I had a bath, planning to go for a swim, but in my white cotton robe I flopped onto the comfortable bed with its blue-sprigged sheets, just for a few minutes, and fell asleep.

Much later I awoke with a tremendous start, hearing shouts. Heart hammering, not knowing where I was for a moment, I stared at a strange ceiling, then stumbled to my feet and over to the window. It was evening. The sun was hanging like a lantern in a gaudy sky, the last rays shafting along the bay. The hotel was well named. *Tramonto*, I recalled, was Italian for "sunset." The shouts I had heard were coming from local fishermen winching a boat out of the water with a cheerful babble of instruction and counter-instruction. Doubtless this was something they did nearly every day, but detailed advice was given and accepted all the same.

The bars along the waterfront down to my right over-flowed with lights, people, gaiety and distant music. In the cooler evening air, Xlendi Bay had sprung to life.

My father hated mourning. I went down to my solitary dinner in a long dress splashed with purple, blue and green and was shown immediately to one of the best ta-bles, a table for two, by a window. A bottle of local wine was brought, well chilled. A deft waiter opened and poured the faintly pink liquid into a glass. He handed me the menu, dark, brilliant eyes flicking over the table to make sure that everything was as it should be. It was.

I'd been in the hotel business long enough to fault a badly laid table at the smallest glance. This one was perfect. If every guest at the Hotel Tramonto was treated like this on arrival, and if the staff could keep up such a standard, it was surprising that there should ever be an empty room, except perhaps in midwinter.

I was still studying the menu when a voice said, "I hope everything is all right?"

It was a highly familiar voice, but not one which I had expected to hear uttering words usually spoken by a headwaiter. Nor was a headwaiter's voice normally tinged with amusement. I looked up at Randal Jarvis in astonishment, glanced at some of the other diners, then back at Randal again. "You work here?"

He grinned. "Constantly. This is my hotel."

My expression of incredulity must have frozen on my face. This man was Noni's brother, Edgar Jarvis's son, and although I knew we had not met before today, I had no wish to be thrown into contact with any member of the Jarvis family. How could I avoid Michael if Noni were anywhere around?

I felt panic-stricken. Randal noticed it at once, and with a swift "May I?" sat in the chair opposite mine. He flicked a finger and another glass was brought. After pouring some wine for himself, he touched my glass with his own and said, "Drink your wine, Alexa. The other members of the Jarvis family are not here. They live in Gozo but not in my hotel." He had read my thoughts.

"Oh . . ." The monosyllable come out in a long sigh of relief, and then I remembered again that Noni was this man's sister. I had been unpardonably rude. "I'm sorry. I didn't mean . . ." I fell silent before Randal's cynical glance.

꙳ 33

"Don't apologize. I live apart from my family because I prefer it that way."

The words were uttered with a sad bitterness which for some reason frightened me.

Chapter 3

So, instead of dining alone that first night, I dined with Randal Jarvis. He made no attempt to explain why he preferred to live away from his family, and if he had not been so intense about it I would not have given it another thought. It was normal, surely, for a man of his age to have made a career for himself, to be married perhaps, but he had made no mention of a wife. He would be about thirty, I imagined, several years older than Noni, whom I knew to be twenty-two.

One of the things which had hurt my pride when Michael broke our engagement was the discovery that Noni, two years my junior and with less experience, was so much more assured. I had spent time training in London and was working in a hotel in Valletta, yet she seemed more worldly than I. It was shattering to discover that another girl, even if she was younger and prettier, had captured Michael with comparative ease. I had been hurt, but also furiously angry—with Michael, with Noni, and most of all with myself for meekly allowing it to happen, for not seeing that it was happening. Wrapped in the security of my father's unswerving affection, I had certainly lacked sophistication. I returned to London partly to acquire a sharper outlook and a tougher hide, along with some specialization in hotel business.

I chose restaurant work because it gave me a complete change. In Valletta I had been working on the management side, in a hotel catering for family holidays and occasional conventions. I was fortunate to find a vacancy in the Torridon in Park Lane and I loved it there. My working life was busy and happy, free time not exactly gay—black-edged as it was with bitter memories and self-contempt—but at least I began to acquire the coveted backbone.

It came to my rescue as I looked across the dinner table at Randal Jarvis and listened to that quiet but resonant voice talking of Gozo, offering to show me the stalactites and stalagmites at Xerri's Grotto, the 4,500-year-old Ggantija Temples, Calypso's Cave, and the ancient cart tracks at Xewkija. He spelled this place-name for me—a necessary precaution since the word is pronounced Shoo-kee-ya.

I thanked him and said vaguely that perhaps I might have time to visit some of the places of interest later. Clearly, this man loved Gozo. His gray eyes glowed as he spoke of the island's long history and a gentle smile turned one corner of his sensitive mouth upward. I found myself liking him, but not trusting him. He was a Jarvis. This excellent table by the window, the concern of the waiter, the proffered wine, were because he was a Jarvis and I was Alexa Prescott. Noni had treated me with indifferent contempt a year ago. Their father, Edgar Jarvis, living at the time with Noni in a flat in Malta, had been too kind, too regretful, over something which was none of his concern. Randal now was somewhere between the two. I found myself wondering where he had been a year ago. Here, apparently, tending his hotel. Yet I hadn't even heard of him. It seemed strange. But he had turned the conversation quickly away from the subject of his family and asked no questions, though I longed to ask somebody, anybody, why Michael and Noni were not yet married.

I refused the offer of brandy with my coffee, and when Randal said, "I'm afraid I have a little paper work to do, but would you like to go out later?" I replied that I thought I would go out at once, on my own, for a short walk, then go to bed early.

I thought he seemed relieved, rather than disappointed. "Yes, of course, you must be tired," he said, with a kind of abstracted, automatic politeness.

As we left the dining room together, I complimented him on the standard of cooking and the deliciously tasty island food. The Tramonto had not made the often fatal mistake of offering only standard international cooking. The chef had also used local products, presented attractively, with interesting sauces; the wine, if lacking in body, had an excellent, fruity flavor. I found the food and wine delicious, and said so. Randal seemed pleased, and we parted.

Out on the terrace it was still warm, but there was the softest of breezes, salty and fresh. A party of six, three middle-aged couples, were laughing a lot, and ordering liqueurs with coffee. A young couple, deeply in love, were sitting at a table by the balcony balustrade, hand in hand and in silence, with coffee and a bottle of local wine before them, untouched. His left hand held her right, their other hands rested on the table, each with a long cigarette, newly lighted, smoldering, the smoke rising almost vertically.

They had their backs to me and I could see only that they were well dressed, he in tight white pants and a pink Swiss lawn shirt, she in a long flowing gown of turquoise cotton. Both were slender and long-haired, and wore beads and chains about their necks. Her head slipped sideways onto his shoulder and his cheek tilted to rest on her hair. The Kings Road was not so far away after all.

My flat in London is in Elm Park Gardens and I have grown to love Chelsea. I thought of it now: the busy streets, brilliant shops, quick scene-changes, the splendid tolerance and lack of convention. Lovely. Great. Living there, one's horizons were bound to expand. Mine had. I felt almost homesick for London. But for the present, until I had inquired into all the circumstances of my father's death, settled his affairs and visited his grave, my home must be here on this island.

Slowly, I descended the shallow, zigzag steps of a path leading toward the deep bay, sounds from the hotel falling away behind me. First I was facing out to sea, then inland as the path turned. A string of lights climbed to the center of the island, along the road we had come down this afternoon in the taxi. Perhaps my father's house was up there. There could be no farm on this promontory for there was rock everywhere. I wondered where the *Francine* was now, and how I could find out about it. From the police, I supposed. Or Mr. Callus might know.

I rounded a sharp bend and came upon a flattened area with a rock bench upon it. A viewing place. There was a man sitting there, smoking. His cigarette glowed in the dark, illuminating a brown face, briefly, but he was looking down at the rock beneath his feet and did not lift his face as I passed. I glanced at him for only a moment and felt foolish for imagining that his was the face of the man who had seemed to be watching for me at Luqa Airport, and who had later driven Noni's car from Mgärr Harbor. I was becoming fanciful. All the same, I shivered involuntarily in the warm night and began to hurry, slipping on the rocky steps in my thin-soled sandals but managing to keep my balance.

Once I stopped to listen but could hear no sound of footsteps behind me, so I continued more slowly. At last I was on the level path by the bay, walking past moored craft of varying shapes and sizes, lighted and unlighted, smells of cooking floating from galleys and snatches of music escaping from guitar and radio. Ahead of me lay the rows of lighted bars and shops which constituted the village at Xlendi. They were thronged with people, noisy with laughter and music. I walked on and mingled, feeling anonymous and liking it.

The lace seller was insistent. A plump, elderly woman with gray hair drawn tightly into a bun at her neck and a remarkably smooth face. With her brown, wrinkled hands, she spread tablecloths, mats and handkerchiefs for me to admire, drew me deeper into her small booth to see knitted goods, exquisitely worked and very cheap—much better, she said, than those in the other shops. I explained that I had only an evening purse with me and a little small change. "No money," I said, spreading my hands.

"You come back?" she asked insistently, and I promised to come back. She let me go then, and as I walked out of the lamplit booth I saw a younger woman with a beautiful, sad face sitting in a dark corner, knitting. I wondered how she could see. As I passed her, she looked up and our eyes met. There was neither curiosity nor recognition in her expression, but I was utterly convinced that she knew me. The sense of being watched had scarcely left me since my arrival in Gozo. Why anyone should want to watch me was a complete mystery. My father would have been known, especially here where he moored the *Francine*, but surely none of these people would know me as Commander Prescott's daughter.

At the quayside I sat down at a table and ordered orange juice. Beneath the hubbub of men and women enjoying themselves I could hear the sea. There was a soft, insistent slip-slap of waves on hulls and harbor walls. Sea gulls rode the little waves, wide awake for any scraps which might be thrown overboard, eyes bright, beaks sharp and curving, cruel as the sea could be. Somewhere to my right, near the roots of a tree, crickets were chirruping. I sipped my drink and tried not to think of the return journey which would take me past the silent man on the stone bench. Perhaps he would have gone by then. An orange juice could be made to last a long time.

I suppose I was hoping subconsciously that I might see Michael in Xlendi, or even that Randal would have followed me, for I was aware of a faint sense of anticlimax as I paid for my drink and rose to go. I had seen no familiar face and a low-spirited weariness crept over me, but as I left the lighted area I was lucky. Ahead of me I saw a middle-aged couple from the Hotel Tramonto, walking slowly up the steep path.

I followed at a distance, quickening my pace only when I saw them approach the hairpin bend where the bench was. To my relief the watcher had gone, but on the rock where his feet had been planted there were several cigarette stubs. Which way had he gone? Up over the cliffs? Or had he passed along the quayside while I was in the lacemaker's shop? It did not matter. His departure meant surely that he had not been watching for me, and so, thankfully, I forgot about him.

When I collected my room key from the desk, the girl broke off a conversation with one of the other guests to hand me a note: "Mr. Michael Brent telephoned." The words were written in English, in black ink.

"No message?" I asked.

"No, Miss Prescott, no message. Mr. Brent merely inquired if you were staying here, so I told him you were. I asked if he wanted to leave a message but he said no." Her English was accented, but good.

"*Grazzi.*" I managed a smile, went to the elevator and pressed the button. As I waited, I reflected that it was extraordinary of Michael to have telephoned and left no message. The cage arrived empty, and as it bore me upwards I told myself that Michael's action in locating me meant nothing. Nothing personal, anyway. He was bound to feel slightly responsible for my welfare, because of my bereavement and what we had meant to each other a year ago. Also, I reminded myself wryly, he knew of a buyer for my father's house, and he had always been an opportunist.

But Michael was going to be disappointed. I was in no hurry to sell. It would seem indecent to hustle onto the market a house which my father had not finished renovating. He had told me little about it except that it was near Xaghra, an inland town northeast of here, in a part of the island I had never visited. Tomorrow I would go and see the house. I dreaded the expedition in a way, because though my father had been living there, the house was unknown—strange to me.

At night, I prefer fresh air to air conditioning. I flung open the door to the balcony and undressed in the dark. The sky was cloudless and stars hung large and close. It was easy to imagine that there might be life on other planets. Life and death. I shook off morbid thoughts and, to my surprise, slept soundly until morning.

English breakfast was offered by the Tramonto, but I settled for orange juice, coffee and excellent rolls, light and crisp. Butter and marmalade seemed to be imported and were of familiar English brands. I sat out on the terrace, dazzled by the golden shimmer of sun on blue water. The sky this morning was pale aquamarine, growing deeper in color every minute. I savored the beauty, enjoying good coffee, and tried to pretend I was a tourist on holiday like the scattering of others on the terrace. I was brought back to reality by the arrival of a pleasant-looking, youngish man who approached my table and said, "Miss Prescott?"

"Yes." It took me a moment or two to realize that the pale suit was a uniform. His hat was flat and peaked and he held it half behind him.

"May I speak to you for a few minutes? My name is Rapa."

I looked at the card he palmed. *Inspector* Rapa. "Please sit down." I motioned toward the second chair at my table and removed from it a book and my huge sunglasses.

If the other guests thought it odd that an English girl should receive a visit from the police, they gave no sign of it, and indeed the man's relaxed easy manner would make it hard for anyone to feel disturbed.

"Will you have some coffee?" I asked, and he accepted my offer.

While we waited for the fresh pot and another cup and saucer, we talked of the island, tourists and the weather. It was all very British. When the coffee arrived and I had poured some for him, he sipped and then said thoughtfully, "You know why I am here?"

"I suppose I can guess. Is it about my father's death?"

"Yes."

As I absorbed this prompt response, fear began curling in my mind. Up to now, any suspicion of foul play had lurked only in my own imagination. Could the presence of this man mean that the authorities, too, doubted accidental death? It hit me with some force that the police had become aware very quickly that I had arrived from England.

"Who told you I had come here?" I asked bluntly.

"Mr. Jarvis very kindly telephoned."

"Mr. *Jarvis?*"

"Yes. Mr. Randal Jarvis, the owner of this hotel."

Astonished, I stared into those deceptively gentle brown eyes. Years of living in sunshine had netted wrinkles at the corners. The hair was dark but sprinkled with gray. He was not so young after all. "Randal Jarvis? Why should he telephone you?" Doubtless my resentment showed. I did not try to conceal it.

Inspector Rapa had no intention of telling me. "Miss Prescott, I knew your father personally. I came to tell you how sorry I am. A man like that, mature, full of life . . ."

I swallowed. "Thank you."

Briskly, he pressed on. "We attended to everything as best we could, in the way your father wished. He is at the British cemetery in Valletta. I expect your lawyer will have told you."

"No. No, he didn't." I did not tell him that Mr. Callus was unaware that I had left London. "I thought my father was buried *here*. He died here!"

I had come to the island full of doubt and sorrow, but sure of one thing: that I would at least be able to visit my father's grave. The disclosure that he was buried in Malta was shattering for me. Yet I ought to have known. Few Protestants would be buried in Gozo, and Mr. Callus would naturally arrange for the interment to be near our house in Malta.

"There is a house here, a farmhouse," I began, and did not know how to continue.

"Yes. The house—do you know much about it?"

"Not really. Only that he was renovating it. After my father died, Mr. Brent mentioned in a letter that he had a purchaser for the house, if I wanted to sell."

The sleepy eyes widened, startled. "Mr. Brent? Mr. Michael Brent?"

"Yes."

Rapa stared at me, inquiringly, almost accusingly.

"We were engaged once," I said defensively, though why I should be explaining Michael's reason for writing to me I could not imagine. Rapa had the gift of eliciting information without even asking the questions.

But now he asked me directly: "Are you going to sell?"

"I don't know. I haven't seen if I like the house. I might want to keep it."

I was watching the Inspector's hand as it rested on the table—brown, relaxed, with squat, muscular fingers. The muscles tensed, the hand twitched, moved to the cup, lifted it. Inspector Rapa drank some coffee. "I don't think it would be suitable for you."

"Why? Is there anything strange about the house?"

"Strange?" The brown eyes which held mine had become alert and inquiring. When he realized I would add nothing to my question, he shrugged massive shoulders, already straining at the uniform jacket. He must have put on weight recently. "There is nothing strange about it. It is a farmhouse, very nice situation, no land of course. Your father planned to live in it for the summer months, he told me, and rent his house in Malta because he found it too crowded over there during the season. Your father said nothing to you about this?"

"Nothing."

Many seconds later: "Perhaps he planned to surprise you when he had completed the renovations?"

"Perhaps." My noncommittal attitude broke in pieces. "I got my surprise earlier."

"Yes, yes." He looked distressed. "I am sorry."

I sat up straighter. "You still haven't told me why you came."

"To offer my condolences. And to say that if at any time you need help, you have only to ask for it."

I took a deep breath and said, "I ask for it now, Inspector Rapa. Did my father die a natural death? Have you any reason to think there was anything strange about it?"

"What makes you ask that?" I was watching him carefully, but he betrayed by not so much as a flicker either surprise at my questions or satisfaction that I should have asked them. He was polite, nothing more.

Harshly, I explained. "A car accident I could have accepted. It can happen to anyone. Or a heart attack. But drowning! My father is—was—a good swimmer, a good sailor. He had respect for the sea. Especially the Mediterranean. You see . . . Perhaps you don't know, Inspector, that my mother died in a drowning accident. She was caught by a storm. But my father—with his skill? I find it hard to believe that he drowned."

"A Mediterranean storm can defeat the best sailor." At my look of scorn, he had the grace to flush slightly.

"Inspector, you are forgetting the British preoccupation with the weather. Our newspapers report storms everywhere, especially in the Mediterranean area during the holiday season. There has been no storm here for many weeks." I waved a hand to take in the bare, scorched hillsides above hot, rocky outcrops. "No storms, no rain, for months."

He sighed and reached for the coffeepot. "More coffee?" he asked politely.

"No, thank you."

He poured another cup for himself. With quiet regret, he said, "Miss Prescott, the fact is, your father drowned. Beyond any doubt."

The breath caught in my throat. "You are telling me that there was an autopsy?"

He nodded. "Always, in such cases. It is necessary."

"Yes, of course." I tried not to think of it. The indignity . . . But my father would not be minding about that by the time it took place.

"Your father's body was washed up on Ramla beach, to the north of the island. You have been to Ramla Bay?"

I shook my head.

"The sand is red in color. Very beautiful. We found red sand on your father's clothes, in the mouth, ears, nose . . ."

I noticed the omission. "Not in the lungs?" I asked.

"No. In the lungs we found sea water, small debris. He drowned, Miss Prescott." He was very gentle again.

I turned and stared at that glittering sea. "No other injuries?" My throat felt tight.

"Some bruising about the face, dirt under the fingernails, seaweed. Where his boat was moored that night, there are rocks underneath, you understand."

I understood. He had gone down, got caught perhaps,

in a cleft in the rock, and had struggled before breaking free too late.

At last, I managed to control my breath and asked, "Where is the *Francine* now? It is not in Xlendi Bay."

"No. We have moored it in the harbor at Marsalforn on the north side of the island. There is a police post at the quayside. We can keep an eye on it there."

"I see."

Sometimes my father drank—not heavily, and mostly wine, but I had to ask the question. "You must have checked the stomach contents?"

"He had eaten a good dinner, drunk a little wine. He had not had too much to drink, Miss Prescott." His grave, sympathetic glance held mine.

"Thank you," I said, breathing the words with intense relief. I could not have borne it if my father's death had been due in any way to his own negligence. The sea had supported him all his life. It had taken his wife from him but he had not lost his love for it even then. Now it had taken his own life, but accidentally, and for that I was thankful. Death must have been quick, and relatively kind. So why did I still feel that all had not yet been explained? The fall. He had fallen overboard. I mused on that. Father was sure-footed on any kind of craft, yet he had fallen. Why? Had he been fishing? Reaching for a line? I was near to tears and could not bring myself to ask any more questions, but I wondered if he had been alone on board.

Inspector Rapa rose, reached into his pocket and brought something out. He laid it on the table. "I thought you might want that."

It was a key. From it dangled a plain buff tie-on label, and on the label, written in neat letters, was the name Prescott. Nothing more.

"The key to the farmhouse?" I asked.

He nodded.

"There is no address."

"It has no address. From Xaghra, take the old road to Ramla Bay. When you are well out of the town, you will see a track going off to the left, between fields. There is a whitewashed stone at the corner. The track winds around and your father's house is at the end of it. It is the only house, you cannot miss it, but it is hidden in a small grove of olive and prickly pear. I shall be happy to drive you there, if you wish."

"You're very kind," I said mechanically. "But I think I would prefer to go on my own."

"You will need a car. We have your father's car, an MG, but we have not yet finished with it. In a day or two we can let you have it."

"Why do you need the car? The *Francine* I understand about, but the *car?*"

Impassively he said, "Even routine examinations, if detailed, take time."

The reply did not satisfy me but I abandoned that line of inquiry. I would learn from Inspector Rapa only what he wanted to tell me.

"There is no bus, to Xaghra?"

"Certainly. The island has a good bus service to all towns." He showed civic pride. "But the walk from the town is long and the day will be very hot. You will need a car. If you do not wish to drive yourself, you can hire a driver. There are taxis, too, in Victoria. One will come here for you. Or I will drive you to Victoria. I am going back there now."

'Thank you, Inspector Rapa. I will go later. This afternoon perhaps."

"As you wish." He rose, and with genuine sympathy he said, "I am sorry, Miss Prescott. *Skuzani.* I wish I could do more for you. Please let me know if I can help. Perhaps when you have seen the house, there will be something more you wish to ask, but I do not think so."

"You have been there?"

'It was necessary for me to go. But there were no messages left for anyone."

Only when he had gone did I realize he had been looking for a suicide note. Suicide! My father? The idea was preposterous. I would have laughed, only I found that I was crying, tears wetting my cheeks, drying immediately in the sun, then pouring again in a stinging, shameful flood. There was no one near me. I waited until the tears had dried, then hurried to the elevator, got into it unseen and pressed the button. My room was tidy and the bed had been made. I flung myself down upon it and cried again. Then I bathed my face and went out onto the balcony to sit there until the ravages had disappeared.

I was thinking about the journey to Xaghra, trying to decide whether to telephone Mr. Bartola and hire one of his cars, or whether for the first time to take a taxi to the farmhouse. I had come to no firm decision when a knock sounded on my bedroom door. "Come in," I called.

It would be a chambermaid, with some task unfinished. I knew from experience how difficult it was to insist that chambermaids clean the rooms during and immediately after breakfast, completing each bedroom and bathroom so that no return visit was necessary until evening, when it was time to turn the bedcovers down.

But this was no chambermaid. From my seat on the balcony I could see the door when it swung open. Randal Jarvis stood there, with a look of grave inquiry on his face.

"I came to ask if everything is all right."

Perhaps, after sending for the police, he wanted to check on their findings.

"You could have telephoned from your room," I pointed out coldly.

He looked startled. "I'm sorry. Do you object to a personal visit?"

"Should I? Any more than I object to being called on by the police?"

Irritated myself, I was in turn needling Randal Jarvis. I had no objection to Inspector Rapa's visit, but I thought I might have been told to expect it. I also wanted to know why Randal had found it necessary to tell the Inspector I was here. My business on the island was private and no concern of the hotel where I happened, by the merest chance, to be staying. I said as much, and by way of reply I received a polite, formal bow and no explanation whatever of his reason for calling the police.

"I am sorry you feel that way, Alexa. I had your welfare at heart. I still have. My apologies for disturbing you." He closed the door and left.

It was a good exit line. I almost called him back.

Chapter 4

THE EMOTIONAL hodgepodge of the morning left me ragged. The sun was climbing to its zenith, burnished in an empty sky. I put on a white swimsuit and robe and went down to the hotel pool. The sea would have been preferable but the pool was nearer. I twisted my long hair into a knot on top of my head, and not bothering with a cap I walked to the edge, dropped the white toweling robe and dove straight in.

I swam slowly, feeling at once the therapy of movement in cool, silky water. I had learned to swim when I was tiny, for my father would not allow nonswimmers to sail with him. He had taught me to love water and I swam whenever I could. Yet he had drowned . . . I rolled over and floated on my back, eyes closed. Through the lids, I saw the red glare of sunlight and I rolled over again onto my face, doing a slow crawl up the pool and back again.

Dimly, I was aware of other people around the pool, lying on loungers, coated in suntan oil, half asleep. Then, while I watched, certain guests stirred slowly, like sleepers in some surrealist ballet. They rubbed their eyes, yawned and, reacting as they did for the other fifty weeks in the year, immediately looked at their watches.

This obsession with midday time had always puzzled me and it did so now. Even on holiday, guests wanted to have lunch at the time they normally ate lunch. Dinner was an anytime meal but lunch was ritual. Not for me. Lunch I could dispense with any day, including this one. But I was thirsty and I wanted a long, cool drink. I dove under the water, swam up the pool and back again, then crossed to the side where I had left my robe. It was gone. In its place were two large feet supporting hairy legs.

When my eyes traveled upward, they confirmed what I already knew. Those intensely muscular legs could belong to only one man: Michael. Michael Brent. He was holding my robe for me, and in his hazel eyes there was pain. Why pain, I wondered, and for a moment I was apprehensive, but whether for him or for myself I did not know. I shook the water from my eyes and shaded them with one hand, holding the rail with the other. We might have been posing for a photograph, he with my robe extended, me half in, half out of the water, reluctant to move or begin a conversation. Why had he come here? Was Noni with him? I glanced past him, half afraid, but there was no sign of her.

With a quick twist, moving slightly away from Michael, I hoisted myself out of the water and turned my back. He put the robe across my shoulders without touching me. I felt that he had been very careful about that. He was

52 🖎.

wearing the briefest of shorts and his body was a deep, even brown.

"Do you often swim here?" I asked abruptly.

Michael shook his head and smiled briefly. "I was working over there." He nodded in the direction of the point away from Xlendi Bay, beyond the hotel. "So I had to pass near here to get back to the bay. I've left my car down on the road at Xlendi but I thought, with any luck, I would find you in the pool."

"And you did."

"Yes."

"So what now?" I unfastened my hair and it cascaded wetly round my shoulders. I had made no attempt to keep it dry and was aware that, thick though it was, it did not look attractive in rat's-tails. I shook it back and left it, aggressively showing Michael that I did not care for his opinion of my appearance any more.

"Nothing, except . . ."

"Well?"

"If you need any help . . ." He stopped and appeared about to rephrase the words, but then he said something quite different. "Alexa, I know things went wrong between us and that it was my fault." He brooded a moment. "Yet in a way it was not my fault. I am as I am."

He smiled, and this time it was a warm, wistful smile, one that I remembered. It had melted my heart in the old days, and could again if I allowed it to.

"I wish I could be two people. And in two places."

He was outrageous. My voice was harsh as I replied, "Don't we all, Michael? Don't we all? But we can't be. We have to choose and you chose."

I began to walk away from him, but he caught up with me. No one could outwalk Michael, with his strong, geologist's legs, accustomed to walking on rough ground, climbing cliffs upward or downward, and edging sideways along impossible, horizontal ledges only inches in width.

"Okay, I chose, and maybe in choosing I did you a favor." There was a stubborn set to his jaw. "But I still . . ." He sought for the right word. When it came, it was not soul-stirring in its originality. "I still *care* for you. I care a very great deal. So if you ever get in any difficulty, I want you to know that you can call on me. I won't get any wrong ideas." He looked discomfited, hearing his own words, and no wonder. The condescension! Yet I did not believe he meant to be arrogant. For some reason he was worried about me.

"You're the second person this morning to offer help if I get into difficulty," I said, swinging the robe off my shoulders and using it to mop my hair. He was watching me. I had a good body even if it was too thin. Long legs, flat stomach, firm muscles. A good body. No so good as Noni's, perhaps, but good enough. He noticed, and remembered, and I was childishly, bitchily pleased about that. At the same time, I disliked myself and felt cheap. I put my robe on again and stopped beside an inviting white table. There were blue chairs at it, and a blue umbrella. I tilted the umbrella away from me so that the chair I was about to sit on was in full sun. "I'm going to have a drink," I said, not inviting him to join me but implying that he could if he wanted to.

He had the grace to ask, "May I?"

"Why not?"

He sat down, snapping his fingers at the same time, and a waitress with beautiful, strongly Arab features, came running on short, sturdy legs. Michael raised his eyebrows at me.

"Orange juice, please."

54

He ordered two, and they came almost before we had started a conversation. The juice was fresh and delicious, with a slice of fruit and a lump of ice floating in the glass.

I thrust my hand into the pocket of my robe, felt for my sunglasses, perched them on my nose and tilted my face back so that it caught the sun.

"If you sunbathe with those on you'll look like a panda," Michael said, amused.

"I shan't be here for long."

At that, he returned to the subject which interested him. "Who else offered help, Alexa?"

I squinted sideways through the spectacles. He was staring at his glass, twisting it round and round. A muscle twitched with tension, near his jaw. He really wanted to know very badly who had offered me help.

"The police," I said indifferently.

"The police!"

"You sound surprised."

"Well, of course I'm surprised. I saw Inspector Rapa's car when I passed the hotel on my way out this morning, but I thought . . ."

"You thought what?"

"Oh, nothing."

"You must have thought something. I've answered your question. How about answering mine?"

"I haven't any answer to give." He paused. "There's been some gossip about smuggling. They might be checking on all hotel guests."

"So far as I know, he talked only to me. Besides, smuggling is a customs matter, not a police matter, isn't it? What sort of gossip has there been? What kind of smuggling?"

"Three questions, not one!" He drained his glass and stood up, laughing. "Darling, on an island, smuggling is every kind and always; it interests customs and police. And often there is no smuggling, only gossip inspired by ill-informed guesswork."

I watched him walk away across the patterned tiles toward the path I had descended the previous evening. He did not look back. On a low, ornamental wall a lizard was sunning itself. It took fright and with the speed of light disappeared into a crack which seemed too small to hold it. When I looked back at the path which led down to the bay, Michael had disappeared also.

🐬.　　🐬.　　🐬.

It was far too hot to eat. I finished my orange juice, tied the belt of my robe and went upstairs. Sunbathing for a while on the balcony, I attempted to read but failed to concentrate. I decided to hire a car and go, at once, to my father's house.

I found Mr. Bartola's card and telephoned his office in Mgärr, half expecting to be told that there was no car available, or that I would have to wait until late afternoon at the very least. But no. There was a small Ford ready for the road, if that would do, and it could be brought over right away.

The prospect of having something to do cheered me greatly and I was galvanized into action. I showered, put on white cotton slacks and a brief pink top and went downstairs. At the desk I bought a map of the island, and a guide, and sat outside to await the arrival of the car. I did not have to wait long and the formalities were minimal. As I drove away, I cought a glimpse of the waitress who had brought orange juice to Michael and me, watching pensively from the dining room window.

Perhaps she thought I was going to have lunch elsewhere, with Michael.

I drove carefully down to Xlendi, then up the narrow, steep road into Victoria, where I stopped to buy gasoline. A skinny black cat was playing near the gas pump. Old Gozitan women were shopping and all of them seemed to be shrouded in black, though the younger women wore colors. Elderly men, very brown, stood about, barefoot, and outside the Duke of Edinburgh Hotel was a knot of Europeans.

As well as cars and ancient buses there were some beautiful little carts, shining with paint and varnish, drawn by horses and mules with polished leather harness. They came spanking along the road, driven with panache, the owners waving whips to friends and calling out greetings. Everywhere there were priests and nuns—so many of them, but then there were so many enormous churches.

It grew hotter and the streets began to empty as people went to lunch or to have a siesta. It was late in the year for afternoon siesta—that belonged properly to high summer—but it was, according to the pump attendant, very hot for September. He glanced critically at the brassy sky. "But no storm yet." He grinned cheerfully.

I was glad to set the car in motion and scoop up a breeze. For part of my journey I went back along the way I had come after landing at Mgärr Harbor, but then I forked left toward Xaghra, which stood on the crown of a hill. All the towns looked large up there on the ridges of the island's seven hills, but I was to learn that they ran long and straggling along the summit, only a few streets wide and not nearly the size they appeared from below. In the old days all of them had been fortified, and there was plenty of evidence, here as in Malta, of the island's long and bloody history. What Mediterranean island had escaped battles in the past? Certainly not Gozo, which had been conquered by Phoenicians, Greeks, Romans, Goths, Saracens and Arabs, to say nothing of later occupation by the French, a Turkish siege, and other small wars.

Xaghra slept. Brown dogs lay sprawled in slumber by the doors of the houses; cats dozed on walls, blinking sleepily. There was hardly anyone about, which was suitable since my guidebook said that Xaghra derived its name from Xaghret il-Ghazzenin, The Idlers' Plateau. I saw signs pointing the way to Xerri's Grotto, Ninu's Cave and the Ggantija Temples, and made a mental note to see all these marvels some other time. I did not feel like a tourist and my heart was leaden with the prospect of visiting, alone, my father's deserted house.

I took the old road, as instructed by Inspector Rapa, and drove out of town. The North African-type blank house-walls, which would have cool courtyards behind their closed faces, thinned and fell away, and I was driving between bare, brown fields, with clumps of prickly pear and a small farm or two where clouds of flies hung over manure heaps. Then there were no buildings at all, and just as the Inspector had said, I came upon a rutted road, no more than a track, with one whitewashed stone about four feet high standing by the corner. I got out to examine it and found that it was deeply embedded, a small monolith. This had not been erected by my father and he would not have whitewashed it; his respect for ancient monuments, however simple, was total. I wondered whose hand had painted the stone, and why. I touched it and almost burned my hand. The air shimmered with heat.

Somewhere a lark was singing, but though I searched

the skies I could see nothing but sun and a blue arc un-marred by even a vapor trail from a plane. A tiny golden butterfly circled and looped past me, and at the side of the lane ants crawled by my feet. I looked over the fields, in every direction. Not a soul in sight. Not even a goat, though herds of these were common enough. I got back into the stifling car, the hot seat sticking to me, and rattled off, lurching slowly over stones and potholes and trailing a cloud of white dust behind me.

I was glad that Inspector Rapa had told me the house was hidden; otherwise I might have turned back, thinking I had taken the wrong road. But a dusty green grove of prickly pear and olive lay in a hollow, just as he had de-scribed it. I could even see pinkish orange fruit among the cactuslike vigorous bushes of prickly pear. From twisted olive boughs, narrow, gray-green leaves hung limp and motionless in the dry heat.

The track turned sharply and with a tingle of excite-ment I saw the house, sturdy, thick-walled and without windows to the front. There was an archway which must have been made originally to take a farm cart. I drove through an open gate and found myself in a yard which someone, my father probably, had made into a beautiful patio, partly in full sun, partly shaded. Here, too, there was an olive tree, old, and with a remarkably rugged knobbly trunk. The branches had been pruned into an in-teresting shape that gave dappled shade, and beneath it was a stone bench by an irregularly shaped pool. Once the pool must have held water but now there was only damp silt at the bottom.

The far side of the courtyard had an arcade with three graceful arches, two broad-based, squarish pillars and a cool, tiled floor. The stone had been sanded to its original butter-yellow and the shaded arcade was charming. A stack of stones was piled at one end, evidently ready for use in some construction project.

The main door to the house lay on my left, a big, wooden door, not new but not, I guessed, the original door to this one-time farmhouse. It was too beautiful—dark wood, carved and studded, with a design of vines, flowers and birds—and must have been rescued from some grander mansion.

I left the car and my footsteps clicked loudly on the square blocks of stone which had been scrubbed clean like the deck of a ship. I moved slowly to the house, eager yet reluctant, and took from my pants pocket the key given to me by Inspector Rapa. Strangely shaped, with a longish shank, it turned without a sound and the door swung open. Before going in, I glanced once more at the courtyard. It was hot and still. Leaves hung limply as if drained of life by the enervating sun. The shade indoors would be a welcome relief.

I was turning to go into the house when I caught a glimpse of a lightweight motorcycle in the courtyard. As if some attempt had been made to conceal it, the machine was tucked in against the wall to the right of the archway, half behind a dusty clump of oleander. I could see the rear wheel, a worn saddle and, behind the saddle, a large roughly woven basket fastened to the frame. Then I noticed something else. Alongside the basket and pointing up to the sky, there was a gun—a rifle, lovingly polished and shining with a wicked glint in a shaft of sunshine.

I stared in fascinated horror while my heart seemed to climb up to my throat and lodge there, pounding. At that moment there was not an atom of courage in my body.

This island was strange to me, alien, not at all like Malta where I knew so many people. Though I had met with nothing but overt kindness, I felt hostility underneath, and I did not like the look of that gun. Acting in panic, I darted into the house, slammed the heavy door behind me and lay back against it, panting, with my eyes closed. When I opened them, I was looking at a long rectangular hall, sparsely furnished as a living room, with stone benches, an olive-wood chest, a few chairs, a desk, books on simple shelves, some cushions and one sea-green rug on the stone floor. I listened. Silence. Where was the owner of that motorcycle? If he too was in the house, I was lost. I had been foolish to shut myself in.

To my right, parallel with the door and where I could not see through them, there were two windows onto the courtyard. On the opposite wall there was a window which had surely been made recently to give a view through olive trees and across a valley which dipped, shimmering, into a heat haze. There were small fields and dry-stone walls. No other habitation nearby, only a tumble of roofs, red-tiled, miles away on the opposite hillside.

By now I was convinced that I had done the wrong thing. I should have gone back to the car when I saw the motorcycle, and driven away. This was a two-story house. Upstairs, the owner of the gun might be waiting for me.

I pulled myself together. Anyone waiting for *me* in the house would have to be clairvoyant, for no one knew that I was coming here today; moreover, a gun strapped to a motorcycle was of no use to its owner and no threat to me.

So perhaps I could investigate without being set upon or blown to bits. It was just possible. Pouring scorn upon myself for my cowardice, I moved away from the door, walked to the middle of the room, and like anyone else entering an empty house (I hoped and prayed it was empty) called out, "Is there anyone at home?"

It was an idiotic question. The owner was dead, the inheritor was myself. Who else could be here? Apart, that is, from the owner of the bicycle. It was time I took another look at that machine.

Deliberately, I walked to the window and looked out. The cycle had gone! Before I could recover from my astonishment, I heard a stuttering start, followed by a steady put-put gradually fading away. I recalled the bend in the lane, close to the house. Whoever it was would already be beyond that, but all the same I ran out and to the corner. I could see a cloud of white dust traveling along the road, and an occasional flash of blue clothing. A fraction of my mind was tinged with disappointment, but the greater part of it flooded with relief as distance grew and stretched between me and that wicked-looking gun.

I decided to continue my exploration of the house, and as it turned out this did not take long. Only a part had been restored. A living room, kitchen, bathroom and one bedroom, all to the left of the courtyard as one entered the gates. The rooms beyond the arcade and to the right of the gateway were in an advanced state of dilapidation.

Outside, apart from the tangled corner where the motorcycle had been hidden, the patio was in good order and everywhere there were evidences of my father's loving, meticulous handiwork. I knew from our house in Malta that he enjoyed creating a home from four walls and had vision and artistry to match his skill. Kneeling on the curved stone seat which he had put in the new window, I stared out over the valley away from the courtyard but my eyes quickly blurred with tears.

The stone was soft and smooth beneath my hands, local stone. When wet, it could be cut like butter; ground down, it made cement which would stick great blocks of itself together again. It could be carved, hollowed, domed, shaped. The stone is one of the miracles of the Maltese Islands and my father believed in miracles. "Never give up," he used to say to me when I was a child. "There might be a miracle somewhere around." Well, I would not give up on my self-appointed task of finding out what happened to him in the days and hours which led up to his death—just in case the accident had not been entirely accidental.

I walked again through the restored part of the house, more slowly this time, enjoying the cool quietness. In the hall which separated living room and kitchen, there was a stone staircase. It led to an upper hall and one bedroom with bathroom *en suite*. All these rooms my father had used. A heavy door from the upper hall led into another room, empty but cleared, and from this room an archway opened into a passage which went off at right angles, above the arcade. There was rubble in the passage and it looked as if no one ever went there. The contrast between the sanded yellow stone in the restored part of the house and the dirty, chipped walls elsewhere was very marked, like plunging from light into darkness.

On the door to the empty room I noticed a large bolt and determined to seal off this small section of the house. With that bolt in its socket the house would withstand a siege, and probably had at some time in its history. There was only one approach to the farmhouse, which could be an advantage or a disadvantage according to how one looked at it. Already, I was wondering if I could live here by myself. If I had not seen the motorcycle and the gun,

I would be happy enough about it. I didn't mind being on my own, normally.

Before bolting the door, I peered through once more. Golden motes of dust danced in the air, but apart from something which looked like a large box lid leaning against the wall beneath the stone window sill there was nothing at all in the room. I went to the window and looked out. Not a breath of wind stirred the air. The olive tree was still. The car, pale blue, sent shafts of light glancing off the metal trim. In spite of the rolled-down windows, it would be hot when I got into it again.

As I turned away, I picked up the lid, I suppose with some idea of tidying it away, and found it surprisingly heavy. Puzzled, I turned it over. This was no discarded item but a canvas stretched on a wooden frame, and on the side which had been hidden there was a portrait in oils of a woman seated on a plain wooden chair. She wore a blue dress with long sleeves and a black shawl, and waited, placidly, with elongated hands at rest in her lap, in an attitude of resignation. Her complexion was ruddy, the mouth small, almost pursed, and the intensity of her expression was disconcerting. It had something to do with the eyes. I looked more closely and saw that one eye was gray and blank, the other finely crosshatched in black. On the wall behind the woman there was a small picture in a narrow black frame, but the subject was dark and understated.

The portrait was signed in white, in rounded, small letters, childlike in their neat simplicity. Modigliani. I was stunned with shock. It looked like an original. But my father could not afford a Modigliani original, so it must be merely a good reproduction. Unless, of course, it did not belong to my father. But then who would leave it here in an empty house? It must be a copy.

I was puzzled and disturbed. The painting struck a false note in this house. I stood staring at it, at the elongated face of the woman, the slanting, almond eyes, the long hands, the deceptively simple painting of ovoid lines. I was holding the canvas carefully in my two hands as if I knew it to be a precious original even while my reason scoffed at the idea.

My eyes went to the window again. There was no sign of life in the patio and inside the house there was complete silence. The last sound I had heard other than the clack of my own footsteps was the measured beat of the motorcycle's underpowered engine. I supposed it was possible that the rider had come to collect or deposit this painting, but more probably he was merely a foraging peasant, gathering olives, whom I had interrupted and frightened off. This was the likeliest explanation but I still held the painting. If it had belonged to my father then it was now mine, or would be mine when the formalities of inheritance were over. If it was not my father's property, the owner would doubtless show himself. Even copies could be valuable, if they were as good as this one.

I went back to the restored rooms, carrying the canvas and looking about me for a safe hiding place. There was none, other than the obvious olive-wood chest. I did not like the idea of leaving the painting in an empty house but I liked still less the thought of taking it to the hotel with me. Puzzling over the lack of cupboards, I laid the canvas down carefully and looked into the chest. It had brass hinges, clean and gleaming with a thin film of oil; my father oiled locks and hinges as a matter of course. Inside the chest were a few clothes, some linen and a couple of wool blankets. I could put the picture in beside them but it would not be a secure hiding place.

Somewhere there must be cupboards for household

goods—in one of the unrestored rooms, probably. And there would be garden tools. My inspection of the other part of the house must have been too cursory, but I was not going back. I had had enough of being here on my own.

First the intruder unnerved me—though probably I had given him more of a fright than he had given me—and then to find a strikingly good picture here in an empty room had been very odd. I admitted to myself that I was afraid. My hands were damp and slippery, and as I lowered the lid of the chest it fell from my grasp and closed with a fearful bang. Watching it happen did not prevent my jumping in alarm and I was ashamed of feeling so panicky. I thought I heard a sound from outside and looked around, half expecting to see someone watching me, or to hear running footsteps approaching the house. But there was nothing, no one. In the end, I carried the picture back to the room where I had found it and replaced it in its inconspicuous position. After all, I had originally taken it for the lid of a cardboard box.

I wiped my forehead with the back of my hand and made for the door, glad to be leaving. Outside, dry, scorching heat enveloped me. How wonderfully cool these houses were, in spite of the baking sun. The thick walls kept them reasonably comfortable even on such a day. I locked the door, put the key in my pocket, went to the car and got in, gasping at the stifling, metallic air inside it.

I started the engine, put the car into reverse and, automatically glancing in the rear-view mirror before moving, caught sight of a man walking quietly toward me. The fresh intrusion did nothing to lessen my already massive nervous tension.

Randal Jarvis knew that I had seen him. My attitude

of arrested movement was eloquent. He stood, hands at his side, looking at me for a moment before coming to my rolled-down window. As he moved from a patch of shade beneath the stone archway into full sun, the light burnished his brown hair to the color of old copper. He wore rope-soled sandals, white cotton mesh shirt, blue pants. Only a faint staining of damp beneath his arms, unavoidable in this heat, detracted from his immaculate appearance.

"Alexa, you should not have come here alone."

I looked up at him, trying to discern what lay behind the searching glance from those gray eyes. He did not sound admonitory, only kind, but I thought he looked faintly worried.

I did not go through the what-brings-you-here routine. I had brought him here. I had no doubt of that.

Chapter 5

"WHY SHOULDN'T I come here alone? Is it unsafe?"

Randal looked uncomfortable. "No, of course not. I only thought that, as it was your first visit since your father's death, you would be upset and ought to have someone with you."

My stomach was churning, but whether from emptiness or nerves I was unsure. Ironically, I said, "Who would you suggest I invite? I have no friends on the island."

He answered stiffly. "I hope you will count me as a friend."

I turned away from him, slid my hands round the hot steering wheel, up and down again. They were grimy, I noticed. "Is Inspector Rapa to be a friend also?" I inquired.

Randal sighed. He placed both hands on the open window and leaned down so that his face was closer to mine. He looked tired, as any *hôtelier* does at the end of a summer season, and he wore an *hôtelier's* expression. His face showed concern, and nothing else.

"You want me to justify having told Inspector Rapa that you were in my hotel. I can't justify it—or explain why I did it. But you said you didn't mind, so why all the fuss? You feel I ought to have warned you, is that it?"

"In a way, yes."

"Do you need warning when the police are about to visit you, Alexa Prescott?"

"No, I don't!" I was furious.

"Okay, okay." He lifted both palms and held them in the air, fending off my anger. "Calm down. It's too hot to rage. Either you object to a visit from the police or you do not. Who called them or why, has no bearing on that. Think about it."

I stared at him, now speechless with fury. He was so —so composed, so sure. But he was right. If I did not object to seeing the police, then I had no reason to be cross that I hadn't known they were coming. Not "they" —one man only, Inspector Rapa. He had been considerate and kind and I had liked him, so perhaps I *was* making a needless fuss. My anger faded. "Point taken," I said, and started the engine again.

"I'm blocking your exit." Randal moved toward the archway. "Give me a moment to turn and I'll lead the way."

I nodded and watched in the mirror. The green open Fiat came into view as he turned it outside the gateway on a flattish, hard-baked piece of ground, maneuvering in the confined space until he was facing up the lane. Then, with a wave, he was off and I backed out and followed the slow-moving cloud of dust, keeping my distance.

This track conferred no benefit on car or driver. We lurched slowly up toward the road and I wondered what one would do if an oncoming car appeared. There were no passing places, merely a dry ditch on our right, and beyond the ditch, boulders. On our left, a wall, intricately made of stones taken from fields, was piled up to a height of about two feet. In places, they were tumbling down and lining the verge.

No one came down the lane so we kept moving, rather too slowly for my liking because I was hot and thirsty. I would have driven faster if I had been on my own, but as things were I had no option but to adopt the pace which Randal set.

As we passed the whitewashed monolith, or menhir, at the end of the lane, I had an almost irresistible desire to turn left instead of right and drive away from Xaghra. It would be amusing to lead Randal Jarvis a dance, and I knew he would follow me. If I had known the island I might have tried it, if only to assert my independence, but as a complete stranger I was bound to get lost. Doubtless, he would find me with humiliating ease, up some blind alley, trapped like a rabbit. It would be pointless and childish, but the temptation remained with me and I was smiling as I meekly turned right and followed Randal into Xaghra, stopping where he had stopped, outside the church of Sant' Anton. He got out of his car and approached me.

"Come and have a drink." His manner was easy and he too was smiling, prepared to forget that I had snapped his head off twice already today. I wondered, cynically, why he kept coming back for more of my rudeness. Perhaps Noni's persistence in her pursuit of Michael was a family trait. I wanted to refuse the drink but it would have taken a superhuman effort, with heat shimmering all around us. Also, I was curious as to why Randal had followed me to the farmhouse. He had given no explanation whatever.

"Orange squash?" I hazarded.

"If you wish. But I could introduce you to something better. A Gozitan special. Very refreshing."

"I don't feel like anything alcoholic."

"At this time of day and in this heat, neither do I."

His tone was dry and I had a feeling that he was laughing at me. Stung, I got out of the car and said with formal politeness, "I'd love a drink, thank you. Where do we go?"

"Over there." He nodded toward a doorway hung with a plastic curtain made of red and yellow strips. The building looked like a private house, one of a row forming one side of the square, but it was a bar. On the wall by the door there were ancient, rusted tin signs advertising beer and cigarettes, alongside newer, brighter signs.

If I had thought about it at all, I would have assumed that the curtain was intended to keep out flies. If so, it had been singularly unsuccessful and served rather to keep them in. As Randal pushed it aside and motioned me to enter, I reeled before a black cloud which circled rather more energetically as hot air wafted indoors from the square. A brown dog stood up, snapped at the flies, then lay down again at the feet of a bright-eyed, youngish man who greeted Randal by name, and nodded at me. He sat near the door and had plainly watched our approach with interest. Now, without any request from Randal, he got up, went behind the lighted bar, where he reached up to a shelf for clean glasses, and bent to take two bottles from an icebox under the counter.

🍃 71

"*Zewg kinnie,* Sur Jarvis. *Sewwa Hekk?*"

"*Iva,* Guis, *sewwa. Grazzi.*"

The barman had offered us drinks. I understood that much, but on either side of the windowless room there were people sitting at wooden tables, speaking in Maltese so quickly that I could not understand a word. Most were men, but there were one or two women with cups of thick, sweet tea in front of them. Conversation ceased as we entered, though there was no feeling of hostility. When I grew accustomed to the gloom, I could see eyes and teeth gleaming in brown faces. Heads bobbed in friendly greeting, and once I heard the name Prescott. My father must have come here, and the local people seemed to know I was his daughter.

Randal exchanged nods with a couple who sat near the bar. They watched, unsmiling, as Randal found space for us on a wooden bench. The man wore the usual blue cotton trousers and white shirt. His companion looked strangely prim and was dressed from head to foot in black —blouse, full skirt and stockings. Her feet were thrust into a modern pair of sandals, the type popularly known as zoris. I'd seen them worn in Victoria by both men and women, though usually on bare feet. I wondered how she managed to keep them on without the thong between the big and second toes, then noticed that she had tied ordinary black shoelaces over her insteps. The result must have been somewhat uncomfortable. I smiled at her, tentatively, but she did not respond. I had the feeling I had seen this woman before, but could not remember where.

"This bar is not at all like the Torridon, is it?" Randal murmured.

I was surprised. "How did you know where I work?"

"Is it a secret?"

"No, of course not. But I don't see how . . ." I broke off as two glasses were put before us, icy cold and misted over. The liquid inside was a brownish pink.

"How I found out?" His gray eyes rested on my face, speculatively, and with a hint of pity which I found irritating. "Well, Michael Brent knows, of course, and Inspector Rapa . . ."

"And you've been discussing me with both of them?"

"I didn't say so. Then there's Mr. Callus. He knows quite a lot about you."

"Mr. Callus! My father's lawyer?" I tried to keep my voice down, but astonishment made it come out as a kind of hoarse whisper.

"Yes. He's waiting for you at the hotel, by the way. *Santé.*" Having dropped his bombshell, Randal tilted his glass at me, and drank.

"Mr. Callus is waiting for me? Here in Gozo?"

"That's right. Drink up. Tell me what you think of this."

"But I ought to go! You're very inconsiderate. And highhanded, not telling me sooner that Mr. Callus is waiting to see me." I felt angry and frustrated, but eyed with longing the cool glass on the table.

"Rather the reverse, I should have thought. What difference would it have made if I had told you at the farm?"

"I'd have gone straight back to Xlendi Bay, naturally."

"Without your drink?"

"But of course without my drink."

"Which you need very badly. You are tired. In no shape to face a lawyer you've been at pains to avoid. Alexa, drink your *kinnie.*"

Momentarily at a loss for words, wondering if I looked as hot as I felt and hoping not, I lifted my cool, cool glass and took a sip. I held the liquid in my mouth for a moment, then allowed it to slide down my grateful throat. It was delicious. A slightly bitter drink, tasting of oranges and something else which I could not define.

"What did you call it?" I asked.

"*Kinnie*. It's a local mineral water, made of oranges and aromatic herbs. I have never been able to understand why it hasn't spread to other parts of the world. To my mind it is the perfect thirst-quencher."

"Perhaps the right herbs only grow on Gozo," I said, taking another sip and then a long drink. I had calmed down and I uttered the words dreamily, without premeditation. Although as yet I did not know it, what had happened to me was that I had already fallen under Gozo's spell. Here, in a strange suspension of urgency, one felt the island to be unique. The hurry of the Western world, even of Malta, only a short distance away, was the bustle of a disturbed ant hill—an aimless scurrying into a state of exhaustion, with nothing worthwhile accomplished. Better by far to sit here and let the world go by.

"You're sure this is nonalcoholic?" I came out of my dream and eyed Randal suspiciously.

"Certain." He grinned. "You're drunk on your first taste of Gozitan life. My hotel is not Gozo. This is Gozo, Island of the Seven Hills. And your father's house is Gozo. He wanted it to be a local house, not a Western villa."

"Yes, I could see that." I frowned. "Have you been in it?" I was thinking of the picture which I had hidden.

Randall shook his head. "I didn't know your father well." A flash of bitterness gleamed in his eyes. "Perhaps he thought of me as a Jarvis."

"But you *are* a Jarvis."

In a flat, unemotional voice which made him sound tired, he said, "Yes, I suppose I am."

I finished my drink, refused another and said, "I really ought to go. You weren't joking when you said that Mr. Callus had come from Malta to see me?"

"No. It's all too true, I'm afraid. I told him I would try to find you."

He got to his feet and reached into the pockets of his blue pants for some coins to pay the bartender, but the man hurried forward and said in good English, "No, no. On the house, Mr. Jarvis, Miss. It is an honor."

At once Randal said, "Thanks, Louis. We appreciate it." He made no attempt to argue, and I was to learn that it would have been futile. The Gozitans are very hospitable, and if they wish to buy you a drink they will not be deflected by any objection or argument. To refuse would be to cause offense.

Outside it was as hot as ever, but the *kinnie* made the heat more bearable. Across the square, a shabby red Mini was parked in a patch of shade. There was a man at the wheel and I thought for a moment he was watching us, but then he bent his head over a map. I could see the bright blue and orange of the tourist's map, the one I had also. Perhaps he was lost.

The sound of an engine and shouts of excitement disturbed the peace of the sleepy town. I had started crossing the square to my car but Randal laid a restraining hand on my arm. A small open jeep roared around the corner and shot past us, revving madly. It was driven by a handsome blond European and with him another man, almost as fair. Both wore swimming trunks and nothing else, so far as I could see. They were deeply tanned, and laughing. In moments they had disappeared but their brief presence seemed to hang upon the air. They were the embodiment of speed, youth and vitality, and I felt a pang of longing for the carefree days I had once known. It took seconds for the torpor of the town to reassert itself.

"Noisy young devils," Randal said mildly. "But happy."

"Yes."

I glanced across the square. The Mini had disappeared during the commotion. The hammer of the jeep's engine died away and silence returned, broken only by the buzzing of flies and a hum of conversation just discernible from behind the bar curtain.

"Well, I'd better go," I said. For some reason I felt awkward and, over-correcting my attitude, sounded gushy when I continued, "Thank you so much for the drink. I feel better for it."

He looked down at me, gravely, and with one finger he momentarily touched my arm. "I'm glad you feel better. Can you find your way back to Xlendi Bay alone?"

"Yes. Easily."

"I'll leave you then. I have another errand to do before I go home. Alexa . . ."

"Yes?"

"Try to believe that you can trust me."

I did not answer. It was a strange thing for him to say.

Randal opened the door of the hired car for me and I got in. As I pulled away, he lifted a hand in farewell salute and turned to his Fiat. I stopped before I left the square—necessarily, as it happened, for the corner was blind—and in my rear-view mirror I saw that he had taken the same route as the jeep. A small fingerpost pointing vaguely in that direction said, "To Ramla Bay." It was an old sign which had once been white with black lettering but now the paint was peeling, and I remembered having read in the guidebook of a new road to the bay. The route taken by Randal must be the old one, but of course I did not know how far he was going. Perhaps not as far as Ramla Bay, where my father's body had been washed up like a piece of jetsam, with red sand in his clothes and in the orifices of his face but not, Inspector Rapa had assured me, in his lungs.

I wanted to see Ramla, but not today. One pilgrimage in a day was enough, and besides Mr. Callus was waiting for me. I drove the little car out of Xaghra and sped along the road back to Victoria, through the capital and down the narrow, twisting way to Xlendi. Goats moved over the rocks in a black and tan tide as they had done when I first arrived here. I stopped the car for a moment to watch as they leapt from one rocky ledge to another. Their agility fascinated me. Perhaps it was not yet time to bring them in for milking, for today there were no children on the cliffside.

Apart from their absence, everything was the same as it had been yesterday. Dusty palms rustled though there seemed to be no breeze; boats lay at anchor as if on a sea of oil; old men and women sat motionless on the benches. Every afternoon in summer, this scene must be the same. Only tourists disturbed the pattern with their restless movement. I started the car again, drove up the winding road to the hotel parking lot and went indoors.

The plunge from brilliant sunshine into the dim interior blinded me, and before I had time to approach the desk and ask for Mr. Callus he sprang from an armchair strategically placed. He must have been watching the door for hours.

"Miss Prescott, Miss Prescott." He shook my hand for too long. Despite the skeletal thinness, his hand felt hot and moist. "I am sorry," he said. "So sorry about your father. I tried to reach you. You shouldn't have come here. Why did you not contact me in Malta? I would have urged you not to come. This is unsuitable . . . a bereaved girl."

There was a round, glass-topped table near the lawyer's chair but nothing on it except an empty ashtray. I saw one of the young waiters leaning on a doorway, watching tables indoors and out. I beckoned to him. "Tea, please," I said. Then turning to Mr. Callus, "Will you join me?"

"Yes, thank you. I was going to suggest . . ."

He had a way of cutting his sentences short, or not completing them, which was unusual for someone in his precise profession. For no particular reason, it irritated me. But then, Mr. Callus had always irritated me, partly because of his fussiness. I looked at him intently. He had not changed much in the few years since I had last seen him. He was tall and thin, his dark hair turning gray at the temples and his skin pale for a Maltese. In spite of the angular thin planes of his face and body, his cheeks were jowled. It was cool in the hotel but the lawyer's forehead glistened with perspiration. Soft, dark eyes rested mournfully on me. For a long time, this man had been my father's friend and adviser, so it was genuine sadness, I knew, and I forced my taut muscles to relax. He had come here out of concern for me, and if I felt hostility it was due to a personal antipathy, nothing more.

"Will you excuse me for a moment, while I wash? I have been out for some time." I displayed rather grimy hands, accepted his assurance that there was no hurry (though he glanced anxiously at his watch) and made my way to the elevator.

It took only a minute or two for me to wash my hands and face and renew my lipstick. My face was stinging and I looked flushed. I applied moisturizer liberally and went downstairs again. Though I had been absent for no more than five minutes, the tea had already arrived. Mr. Callus leapt to his feet, drawing forward an armchair like the one he had been sitting in, covered in floral linen. The pattern was a blend of English wild flowers, buttercups and daisies, tossed among sprays of grasses, all on a pale-green ground. In this black and green tiled room, it was very restful.

"Allow me," said Mr. Callus, and he poured the tea. I added milk and took a sip. It tasted slightly salty but was good. Mr. Callus added a slice of lemon to his and he too took a sip. It was as if, after all his long wait, he could not begin to say what he wanted to say. I found myself watching the tank of tropical fish and I too felt utterly unable to begin a conversation. It was childish of me, but after all he had come here to see me so he must have something to say . . .

My thoughts stopped milling around and settled on that point. Mr. Callus had come to see me and I would wait for him to tell me why.

"I suppose Randal Jarvis telephoned to let you know I had arrived?" I asked the question without any particular emphasis, hoping perhaps to disarm him into answering with a simple yes.

But he did not say yes. He looked completely bewildered. "Randal Jarvis? I don't understand. It was Michael Brent who telephoned, naturally."

"Naturally," I echoed, in flat sarcasm.

But there was nothing natural about it. Why on earth should Michael telephone the lawyer? My thoughts began to whirl again, gnawing at the problem. Then I remembered that in his letter to me Michael had offered to buy the farmhouse through Mr. Callus. Perhaps they had already been in touch about it.

"Did he tell you why he thought fit to inform you that I was staying here?"

Callus got my sarcasm that time. Stiffly he said, "I am your father's lawyer, you are his sole heir. I consider Mr. Brent to have behaved correctly."

I sipped my tea once more, watching the fish weave to and fro in the clear green water and thinking uphappily of my father. I set my cup down and shifted my chair, turning it slightly so that I was not facing the tank. "Michael has behaved correctly and I have not?" I asked lightly.

He flushed, the color running beneath the pale, glistening skin, staining it rapidly. "I did not say that. You have had a considerable shock. Miss Prescott, I did try to let you know, to advise you." He put his cup down.

I relented. "Yes. I'm sorry. I was away from my London address when . . . when it happened, Mr. Callus, and I ought to have called to see you in Malta, but I was anxious . . ." I paused. "I suppose the word 'obsessed' would be more accurate, with the desire to see my father's house in Gozo as soon as possible. After all, it was here that he died."

"Yes. I see that. You have been there this afternoon, I believe?"

"You are well informed."

"When I arrived, Mr. Jarvis offered to find you. He was going that way in any case."

"I see. And how did *he* know where I had gone?"

Callus looked puzzled. "Everyone in the hotel knows where you went. To see your father's house." My astonishment doubtless showed, for he added, "This is a small island. Your father was well liked. Everyone is very sorry for you."

He was right, of course. Foolishly, I had forgotten how things were on the Islands. At first I had imagined I could come here, unknown, and be taken for a tourist, but I was no ordinary tourist and the islanders would know it. I thought of the lightweight motorcycle hidden in the courtyard of my father's house, with a rifle alongside it. I thought of the Modigliani which looked like an original (though it couldn't be), and I wondered how well Mr. Callus had known my father, how much he knew of his plans for the farmhouse.

"Everyone is very kind," I said automatically. Then I said, "Mr. Callus, did my father make any money lately? Suddenly, I mean?" I was thinking of that picture, which he might have bought as an investment.

Callus pursed thin lips and his jowls settled into deeper folds. "He had made a little on the stock exchange, yes. I suppose he thought the farmhouse would make a good investment. Property is always sound. And then Malta is crowded. He wanted a quiet retreat to use from time to time during the season."

In the small silence which followed, I poured a second cup of tea for each of us, and noticed that the lawyer was glancing at his watch again. This time he explained. "I must catch the next ferry. I have my car here." His voice became very earnest. "Miss Prescott, I would like you to come with me. I will drop you at your father's house at St. Paul's Bay and I can help you find suitable daily help."

"Mr. Callus, I am accustomed to looking after myself. If I were to return to Malta I would not require help, but I have decided to stay here."

"I have wasted a good many hours in coming here for you, Miss Prescott."

"I did not ask you to come." I spoke quietly and perfectly politely.

He frowned. "You cannot possibly stay here. If you do not wish to stay in Malta, then you should return to London. I will attend to the selling of the farmhouse in Gozo, and I will do whatever you want with the Malta house. You can rely on me."

"Mr. Callus, you presume rather a lot. I am not going back to London and I am not going to Malta with you and I do not want you to sell the farmhouse."

He flushed again, disconcerted. "But what will you do with it?"

"I haven't decided. Whatever my father was going to do with it, perhaps."

While I had been speaking to the lawyer, the thought crossed by mind that if I really wanted to open my own hotel, the farmhouse might be suitable. It was isolated, but some people like perfect quiet. I would have to find a builder; I couldn't manage that kind of work myself. And everything, really, would depend on whether there was an adequate water supply.

Mr. Callus interrupted my daydream by saying, decisively, "Whether you sell the farmhouse or not, it would be wiser for you to come back to Malta. I can let you have some money, as much as you want, within reason."

I stared at him. I had not asked for money, and he seemed far too anxious for me to return to Malta. He was treating me as if I were a child.

"Enough money for you to return to London if you prefer that. From your father's estate, of course."

I was becoming angrier every minute. Of course any money he let me have would be from my father's estate. And I would be fully entitled to it, in due course. But I would decide for myself about the property and where I would live. "If I did not know better, Mr. Callus, I'd think you were trying to bribe me to leave Gozo," I snapped.

"Bribe? *I* bribe? Be careful what you say!" He was as angry as I—more angry, perhaps. Too late I recalled that he was Maltese, probably unaccustomed to young women making their own decisions without advice from an older male relative, or lawyer. This particular situation might never have arisen for him before. He was being autocratic, but nothing more.

"I am sorry," I said quickly. "I should not have said that."

He stood up, bowed stiffly, and said, "As you are naturally upset about your father, I will accept your apology. I must go now. If you insist upon staying here, it is against my wishes and fully your own responsibility. If you change your mind, please let me know and I will be glad, for your father's sake, to do anything I can to help you. He was my friend." He hesitated. "If you need money, I can advance you some now." It was an inquiry.

"No, thank you. I have enough." The truth was that I had been anxious about my lack of money. The cost of the fare from London had to be met unexpectedly and at a time when my bank account was depleted by holiday expenses. Also, I had bought a new winter coat which was hanging in my closet in London . . . "I have enough," I repeated firmly.

"Very well. But either leave Gozo soon, Miss Prescott, or be prepared to stay for some indefinite time. The weather is going to deteriorate. You know the season. There will be a storm. You may be marooned."

Marooned was a strange, old-fashioned word, but here it had meaning. I knew that. Mediterranean storms severe enough to cancel the sailing of all car ferries and send small craft scurrying for port were not infrequent in spring and autumn, as well as in winter. I had heard of Gozo being cut off for days, but always before I had been in Malta or in England when it happened.

I went with Mr. Callus to the door of the hotel and out into the glaring sun. In spite of suffocating heat, I shivered. I did not like the idea of being cut off, of being a prisoner on this strange island or anywhere else. Instinct told me to run. I almost asked Mr. Callus then to wait for me while I packed my bag. Almost, but not quite. The moment of panic passed. I held out my hand, said goodbye, thanked him, earnestly and apologetically, and watched him get into a large white Mercedes which he had parked in the shade of some shrubs.

Poor Mr. Callus. He had meant well and by my edgy display of suspicion I had deeply offended him. With sadness, feeling that I had lost a friend, I watched him drive away from the hotel.

Chapter 6

THOUGH ADMITTEDLY the afternoon had been too hot for action, I had been sitting in confined places for hours: in the bar at Xaghra, in the car, and here in the hotel with Mr. Callus. Inactivity had made me restless and I wanted some exercise. The choice lay between clambering over the strange rocks or having a swim in the pool, but the thought of that beautiful cool water made a decision easy. I went to my room, changed into a bikini and came down wearing my white robe.

On my way to the pool I saw Randal Jarvis, returning from whatever activity had drawn him away from Xaghra. He drove by me with a wave of his hand and disappeared through an archway leading to the rear of the hotel. I lifted a hand and smiled, feeling glad and sorry at the same time, that he did not stop to talk. I wondered where he had been, and with whom.

The air was sultry, but beginning to cool a little as evening approached. From the moment I plunged into the water my mind stopped churning over the afternoon's events, and thankfully I swam, floated, surface-dived and swam again until I was too tired to do anything but stagger up the steps and out of the water. For the first time since I'd learned of my father's death I was ravenous.

There was no Michael to greet me this time when I left the pool, but as I took the pins out of my hair and let it swing free, blown by the warm wind, I saw two taxis arrive, bringing new visitors. They must have come over on the ferry which would return with Mr. Callus on board, and I realized that it was only twenty-four hours since my own arrival. It seemed far longer.

Two youngish couples, very smart in lightweight travel clothes, got out of one car. Evidently on a second visit to the hotel, they exclaimed at changes in the terrace and gardens and seemed glad to be back. Randal came to greet them, caught sight of me and asked if I had enjoyed my swim, then went to the second car. I was tying the belt of my robe and stopped for a moment as one end of the sash eluded me. A man in a well-cut pale-gray suit emerged from the second car and straightened up. He was heavily built but not fat, and he moved with lithe agility in spite of his bulk. His hair was grizzled, and cut short, which was just as well for it grew thickly in all directions. He wore heavily framed glasses and was smoking a cigarette with a cork tip. Binoculars and a camera were slung over one broad shoulder, and in his hand was a small zipped bag. Since this was the extent of his luggage, I had to admire his mastery of the art of traveling light.

The sun was bowling its hoop out of the sky in a huge, flaming disc, and as the man turned to give me a frank stare of interest a shaft of light glinted on his glasses. For an instant, twin darts of fire stabbed at me, then died. I walked by, giving him no more than the brief expressionless glance needed to take in his appearance.

In the hotel business one becomes accustomed to people, sizing them up in a moment, and this man spelled trouble. He was accustomed to good living—his tailored clothes and handmade shoes shouted that information. If he failed to get immediate attention he would want to know why, probably in a very loud voice. The Tramonto had a high standard, but this man, I fancied, would want to notch all standards higher, wherever he went. Part of his life-style. I was glad I would not have to cope with him.

To my surprise, his approach to Carmela, the girl at the desk, was courteous and quiet. Giving his name as Stark, he received a key and followed the boy to the elevator along with the four other new arrivals. The cage took only six at a time so I hung back, reading an announcement of the horse-racing in the street in Victoria to take place in a few days' time. The elevator hummed discreetly as it rose.

Carmela and I smiled at each other and she greeted me in Maltese, "L'gtodwa t-tajba." We began to talk. She was a good receptionist. Randal was lucky to have found someone so suitable on the island.

"Do you live in Gozo?" I asked her. "Is your family here?"

"No, Miss Prescott. During the season only I live in Gozo, here in the hotel. I am Maltese but I like this island. I am engaged to a man who lives in Victoria. He makes tiles."

"Tiles?"

She nodded and waved a hand toward my damp sandaled feet. "For the floor." Her black eyes gleamed proudly. "He is an artist. He designs for the best builders in Gozo, beautiful tiles."

I murmured something appreciative and went to the elevator, which had returned to the ground floor carrying half a dozen guests, dressed and ready for predinner drinks. I remembered that I was hungry, and took very little time to bathe, dress and make up. I had not brought many clothes with me and I wore the same long purple, blue and green frock. I was gloriously tired after my energetic swim, and completely relaxed.

It was dusk as I entered the dining room. Randal did not join me for dinner but included me in the round he made of all tables, checking that guests were receiving the attention they wanted. He spent a considerable time talking to the two couples who had returned for a second visit, and they laughed a lot. I thought how attractive he looked when he was not on the defensive and felt a twinge of surprise that such an opinion should have sprung into my mind. It was true. Randal Jarvis did seem often to be on the defensive, at least with me. Yet he owed me nothing. We had not met before. He'd had nothing to do with his sister's easy conquest of Michael. It took only two to accomplish that—and a complacent third. Myself. I marveled at my own detachment and thought, sardonically, that platitudes triumphed over poetry; broken hearts did indeed mend, given time.

The waiter advised me on the wine since the local names on the list meaning nothing to me. When the wine came, it was different from the one I'd drunk with Randal the night before—more heady. It tasted like bottled sunshine with a dash of apricot brandy and was entirely, rapturously delicious. I looked at the label and found that it had been bottled at Ramla. It took an effort of will after that to continue to enjoy it, but I managed. My father loved wine. If I had come to the island at his invitation he would have bought this for my enjoyment, and silently I toasted him and all who love the sea.

Mr. Stark came into the dining room, walking slowly but purposefully, carrying a glass of what looked like whiskey and objecting of course to the first table offered to him. He pointed to another table by the window, and the waiter, after glancing toward Randal and receiving an almost imperceptible nod, pulled out a chair for the man, produced a menu and waited, order book in hand, pencil poised. Without looking up, Mr. Stark waved him away with a languid hand, as if he were a fly, and studied the menu.

I started on my veal and lost interest. The immediate next moves were predictable. A complicated order, a complaint—in order to alert the staff—about the first course chosen, grudging acceptance of apologies and a replacement, and then . . . Ah, one never knew what would happen next. Point made, point taken and all forgiven, or continued complaint ending in well-simulated rage. Perhaps even real rage. Mostly, it depended on consumption of alcohol and result thereof. Some people mellowed, some became more belligerent.

During dinner a bellhop came to tell me that there was a telephone call for me. Surprised, I went to the hall to take it and heard Michael's voice asking how I had fared during the long, hot day, hoping I'd been taking it easy and suggesting that he should go with me to the farmhouse. "Perhaps tomorrow? I could take some time off. You'll never find it on your own, Alexa. It's isolated, and unfortunately not the kind of place where you could live on your own. Alexa? Darling?"

He was waiting for my reply. The "darling" did not mean anything. He called lots of people darling. Heat surged through me in a streak of rage and melted again, leaving me icy cool but still angry. Michael thought I was still the green girl I had been a year ago, that I would need him to look after me now that my father was dead, that I could not manage alone. He must think I'd been moping and pining in helpless inertia this whole past year.

With sweet sarcasm I said, "Oh, I don't know. I rather like the position of the house. And my own company. I may decide to live in it."

There was absolute silence. Then a deep-drawn breath. I could picture his tanned face, the mouth slightly open, the eyes wide. "You . . . You've been there?"

"Yes, of course."

"Who took you?"

"No one." Another silence. The amusement must have been easily discernible in my voice as I drawled, "Despite your ulterior motive, my thanks for the offer. You'll have to tell your would-be purchaser, however, that I may not be selling."

Michael laughed, and with the sound of that easy, intimate laughter it was my turn to be discomposed. With savage disappointment, I felt the heart-stirring tug of emotion as the laughter-laden voice I had once loved so much said, "Touché." Then he added, with interest in his voice, "Alexa, why don't we have lunch together tomorrow? Not at the Tramonto, somewhere else. There's a hotel at Marsalforn Bay on the other side of the island, with a good restaurant. Say you will."

Marsalforn Bay. That was where the *Francine* was moored. I wondered if he knew.

"I don't know." To my dismay, my voice wobbled.

"Just to clear the air. To let me know for sure that you've forgiven me." He sounded almost humble.

"On that basis," I said, still uncertain.

"Good. I'll call for you. Twelve o'clock?"

Reluctantly I agreed, and added, "Thank you."

For what was I thanking him, I wondered as I made my way back to my table. I had just given Michael another opportunity to break my heart and return it to me in small fragments. I must be mad.

Mr. Stark was bickering with Randal. Only one voice could be heard, that of Stark. Randal would keep his voice low, the tone steady and firm, and I knew without looking that his face would be devoid of expression other than one of polite attention. In a dining room an atmosphere of hostility could spread very quickly to other guests, could even affect a nervous digestion. I kept my head turned away, sipped my wine and pretended not to notice.

For a woman alone in a hotel, meal times are the worst: toying with food, trying not to eat too quickly, keeping a pleasant and relaxed expression on the face while all the time loneliness sits opposite like doom. No wonder so many women succumb to temptation and take a book to the table. I did it myself, at every meal except dinner. For the evening meal, I was determined to keep up my standards. Like the Englishmen in the old days of colonization, I thought with wry amusement, coming freshly shaved and in evening dress to dine off a folding table in a tent in the African bush.

But this was not at all like the African bush, and when I finished my lemon sherbet I strolled without haste out onto the terrace to take my coffee there. It was still warm, but the air was fresh and sweet and I was enchanted anew with Gozo. Under the mushroom lights lizards ran and crickets chirruped invisibly, a joyous sound. The sky was a great arc of deep blue, shot at the horizon with gold and aquamarine.

I had known the same sky over Malta, studded as this one was with stars so low that it seemed as if one could put up a hand and touch them. They glowed large, faded, winked and glowed again, and their infinity gave comfort. My own troubles on this planet gradually diminished.

I don't know how long I sat there in my cocoon of dreamy isolation. I thought of Michael, briefly, then put him out of my mind. I was tormented by curiosity over his present relationship with Noni and therefore I would not allow myself to think about it at all. I drank my good coffee and planned a stroll down the winding path to Xlendi.

"Good evening."

As I heard the greeting, I became aware of the well-built, well-dressed figure standing a yard or so away from me. Well, Stark was the only lone man in the hotel and I was the only lone woman. It was not so surprising that he should make some approach, but he had not lost much time. "Good evening," I replied evenly, neither inviting nor rebuffing further comment.

"Lovely view." He nodded over toward the opposite headland, taking in the dip into the deep bay and the light spraying upward from the town. I agreed.

He sat down at the table next to mine, neatly avoiding any chance of objection on my part, and thanked the waiter politely enough for the coffee brought in a silver pot from which steam was rising. Well, I had had the same treatment—really hot coffee, well served—and knew that even Mr. Stark would be hard put to fault it. He did not try. His next remark was "Good coffee."

"Yes."

"Have you been here for long?"

He was a trier, I gave him that, and it was not a flirtatious approach. I threw out my cynical thoughts and reflected that Stark could have been made irritable by private worries and now might merely be feeling lonely, as I was. I told him that I had been on the island only since yesterday, omitting any mention of the reason for my visit. He took it, naturally, that I was on holiday, which suited me.

"I've come over from Malta for a few days but I can't say that I like this place. Too primitive for me. I took a taxi from the ferry to the capital back there, inland. Rabat, is it?"

"That is its old name, but now it is usually called Victoria."

"Well, the taxi stopped in Main Square in Victoria, but I took one look at it and sat where I was. The driver suggested this place. I'm told the night life is best here."

"I'm afraid I wouldn't know." I thought of the bars along the waterfront and wondered what Mr. Stark meant when he talked of night life. He should have stayed in Malta.

"The man who owns this place is named Jarvis, isn't he?"

"That's right."

"I used to know someone of that name once . . . I thought he settled out here somewhere. But this one is too young to be the man I knew. Has he any relatives here?" Mr. Stark's voice held only the idlest curiosity.

"I believe he has."

"Do you know them?"

I wondered why Stark was asking *me* these questions instead of Randal. I had no wish to be drawn into any personal gossip. After a momentary pause, I answered no.

It was a white lie, or perhaps wishful thinking. I had met Edgar Jarvis in the past when he lived in Malta but could scarcely say I knew him. Noni I knew only too well. I wished that we had never met.

"Just wondered," Stark said easily.

I recalled that he would have seen Randal exchanging a word or two with me when I came out of the pool before dinner, but that encounter had been casual. An ordinary politeness between manager and guest, from which no one would have deduced that we had sat together in a dim bar in another town that very afternoon. Or that I knew anything about his relatives.

The waiter brought a large brandy, evidently already ordered. "Will you join me?" Stark asked, but I thanked him, refused, and said good night.

I went back into the hotel before leaving for my walk down to Xlendi, and when I came out again Mr. Stark had gone. His coffee cup and glass stood empty on the table. I did not think his stay in Gozo would last long. He was not the type to enjoy a simple life, and I doubted if Xlendi Bay would provide the kind of night life he would appreciate.

The watcher was on the bench again. I smelled the cigarette smoke before I saw him, and my footsteps faltered for an instant. Then I walked on by, not even glancing at him. So far as I knew, he neither moved nor looked up. But as I rounded one of the hairpin bends that the path took in its steep descent to the bay, I saw by the faint glimmer of starlight a sturdy figure running lightly over the rocks toward the roadway which took the easier slope up to the hotel. The plimsolled feet made no sound. It could have been the same man. Then, too, it could have been any one of about a quarter of the men in Gozo. He was a type, as I'd told myself the previous night. Stocky, dark, thickset. Probably he sat there every night, resting.

Xlendi also looked as it had on the previous evening, and I sat at the same table and ordered the same drink, orange juice. In forming a habit there is a kind of security, and that was something I needed very badly. I pulled myself together; my imagination was running wild. In the warm air, with music and gaiety around me and plenty to watch, why should I be jumpy? I began to relax. The nervous edginess which seemed to assail me every few hours began to recede, and I thought how beautiful the yachts were, riding at anchor, with glimmerings of light coming from the cabins and sounds of music and laughter floating across the water.

Whenever I sat down at a table, it seemed that some man came and talked to me. I might have been flattered except that this man, like the last, was hardly in my age group. His greeting, when it came, was formal, and was followed at once by words of condolence on my bereavement, for which I thanked him briefly.

I knew him at once. He had scarcely changed in the year since we had met in Malta and was astonishingly well preserved for a man of his age. What would he be—fifty-five? More? About fifty-five, I decided. Tall, tanned, with thick white hair brushed back from a massive, bony brow and eyes which were still an intense bright blue. It seemed unlikely that he had ever had to wear spectacles, and although he must spend a great deal of his time in strong sunshine there were no wrinkles or crow's-feet around the eyes. His skin was smooth and fine-textured. Perhaps it was from Edgar Jarvis that Noni had inherited her fabulous looks.

"I was exceedingly sorry about your father," he was saying, and his distress seemed genuine. "We saw each other from time to time. Did he tell you?"

"No. No, he didn't." I had not quite succeeded in keeping the surprise from my voice.

"His reticence is understandable, perhaps, in the circumstances." The deep voice sounded soothing and regretful at the same time. "Parents have to adjust to the problems of their children sometimes. Though to read the press, one would think it was always the other way around."

I remembered that I'd liked Edgar Jarvis before, when we'd met. He had been living in Malta then, in a magnificent penthouse apartment in Valletta, with a view overlooking Grand Harbor. "Did you . . ." I steadied my voice. "Did you see much of my father? Recently, I mean? Before he died?"

"The last time was about four days before. He would have made a beautiful place of the farmhouse if he had lived."

I swallowed. "Yes. He had done a lot of work already."

"You have been there?"

He seemed surprised, as Michael had been. It annoyed me. I had come to the island all the way from London. Of course I would go to the house. And as soon as possible. It was my father's home. "Yes, I have been there. I like it very much."

After a fractional pause, Edgar Jarvis said, "Good. Your father would have been pleased. I wonder, Alexa— would you care to join us for tea at the Villa Melita on Thursday?"

"Thank you. It is very kind . . ." I frowned, confused,

unable to imagine why he had invited me, equally unable to think what it would be like to visit Noni's home. But this man had been friendly with my father, and because of it I might learn something from him.

I accepted his invitation, which was for the day after next, and reflected that I had promised to have lunch with Michael tomorrow in Marsalforn. It was entirely possible that he would be at the Jarvises' on the following day. Did I mind? I thought not. Perhaps, subconsciously, I wanted Michael back. I had no certain idea of what I wanted. Emotionally, I was still arid.

Edgar Jarvis left me then, and I watched him walk out of the lighted part of the waterfront to a parked car. He got into the passenger's seat and the car turned to leave the bay. I caught a glimpse of blond hair. Noni had been waiting for her father.

I finished my orange juice, suddenly restless, and walked toward the souvenir shops. They were doing good business. The lace maker called out to me from her booth and I went over.

"*Bonjo.* You have money tonight, madam?"

"No." I shook my head, smiling an apology. "Not tonight. But I will bring some another time."

"Here, on this island"—she waved a hand which was creased all over, like crumpled tissue paper—"evening is shopping time. In London, shops close at night. No?" She laughed then, a noisy, slightly harsh cackle, full of benevolent wickedness. "Come and see," she said. "Come and see what I have. Beautiful lace—tablecloths, handkerchiefs, everything lace. And knitted stoles, jerseys, dresses . . ." She touched the articles in turn as she mentioned them. "And baskets, see?" They were intricately, beautifully woven. It was a traditional island craft. Some of them I knew to be fish traps, but they were suitable for hanging up to hold plants. The patterns were lovely. "And pottery and glass, such wonderful glass, from Mdina."

"Mdina is in Malta."

"Yes. Mdina in Malta. We import it. Look around you, madam. Anything you see that you would like, I keep it for you. You bring the money any time."

"Well, perhaps . . ." I was noncommittal. There were other lace shops and the woman was too insistent for my liking.

Now she wagged a gnarled finger at me. "You come past in the daytime today and you do not stop. Then you would have had money with you but you are too much in a hurry to look at my beautiful lace. No? You look now. I keep for you!"

"Rosa, you are bullying the lady. I won't have it." The chiding voice was laughing but stern. Clearly Randal knew the woman well.

"Ah, Mr. Jarvis, Mr. Jarvis, it is good to see you!" I was not quite convinced by her greeting and neither, I fancied, was Randal. "I not bully. I persuade the lady to look at my lace. It is beautiful. She will like it. She will want to take some away with her when she goes. All tourists want lace."

"Miss Prescott is no ordinary tourist, as you very well know."

"Ah, well . . ." Deflated, she shrugged, and did not deny she'd known who I was and that I was not a tourist. "She will like the lace anyway."

"Probably she has a mountain of lace from Malta."

"Not the same."

The decisive claim that Gozitan lace was not the same as Maltese, the implication being that it was better, amused me. She had intended that I should laugh; her own black eyes were sparkling with fun.

98 🐾

Randal laughed also. "Come on, Rosa, give. One of the very best, mind!"

She knew what he was talking about and ducked under a packing case spread with a piece of old blanket. Producing a battered cardboard box, she took from it several most exquisite lace handkerchiefs, all different and each fine as a cobweb. I had never seen work like this anywhere, neither in Malta nor in London. I bent over it, exclaiming with delight, and at once I was drawn to one which was not covered with Maltese crosses but instead had delicate leaves and flowers in the pattern. The entire handkerchief was of lace and slightly larger than normal —a lovely wisp to carry, floating from the hand. Worthy of Regency England or Renaissance Italy . . . or entrancing Gozo, Island of the Seven Hills.

"Thank you for showing them to me," I said, truly grateful. "If I can afford this one, I will buy it. How much?"

"For you, nothing," she said, her wicked old eyes resting on Randal's face.

There was a bond between these two. He knew how much she wanted for it and he handed over some folding money. I could not see how much but Rosa said, "*Grazzi, grazzi.*"

"No!" I cried. "I couldn't possibly let you pay for it!" I had been trapped into this, and so, I felt, had Randal. "You mustn't!" I protested softly to him. "Really, I couldn't let you."

He looked down at me, his hand on my arm, and at that moment, in some strange way, I felt as if we were alone in the booth, with the soft lamplight glowing around us and muted sounds of water, oars, music and cries of sea gulls coming at us in waves, along with the human sounds from the quayside. Rosa, having achieved her object, was silent. In her black clothes, she seemed to melt into the background.

There was a faint rustle as the handkerchief was wrapped in a piece of crumpled tissue paper, and now Rosa watched us in her silence, standing very still. I threw a helpless glance at her. There'd be no aid from that quarter; the situation appealed to her sardonic sense of humor.

"Of course you could let me," Randal said, his voice so gentle that not even Rosa would be able to hear what he was saying. "Of course you could. I am very happy to give you something you like. I would be delighted to give you half a dozen handkerchiefs." He lifted a hand at my movement of protest. "But I won't, if you'd rather I did not. Have this one, though." He laughed, abruptly, the sound breaking the spell, his face alight with amusement. "How do you know that Rosa and I haven't got a business deal set up? She accosts young women, I rescue them and they leave having bought only one handkerchief. They think they've got off lightly and everyone's pleased. Simple."

"If it were a business deal, you would not be the one to pay," I objected. "And such exquisite work is not come by lightly, or made in a week or even a month."

"Alexa, you appreciate the skilled workmanship, and that will mean more to Rosa and the maker of the hand-kerchief than anything else. Isn't that so?" He had lifted his voice again so that Rosa could hear, and she nodded, showing her gap-toothed smile, bobbing with pleasure.

What could I do? It would have been churlish to refuse the present, so I thanked them both, accepted my precious parcel and left, with Randal's hand under my elbow.

I thought to myself as we walked how little it takes to make a woman feel cherished. A small gift, a hand on

the arm . . . So little, and so much. I liked the touch of
his hand there, and did not draw away from him as we fell
into step and joined the slowly perambulating crowd
along the quayside.

Chapter 7

"HAVE SOMETHING to drink?" Randal suggested.

I shook my head. "I've just finished a glass of orange juice."

"Have another. With me. So that I need not drink alone."

Put like that, I could not refuse. I noticed that Randal drank very little alcohol, and now, when I asked for a Coke, he had the same.

Someone else, not far away, was not so abstemious. Mr. Stark was sitting in the doorway of a bar further along the waterfront and he was very, very drunk. He had two young men and two girls with him. They were dressed in tight jeans and not much else except silvery chains with enormous Maltese crosses. The four had come off a catamaran cruiser which must have been worth a fortune, and they looked as if they had spent the entire summer in the Mediterranean. I'd seen them row ashore earlier in a dinghy, wearing their dark tan, their joy and their confidence like glorious armor. Briefly, I had envied them. Now I did not. They were not enjoying the company of Mr. Stark. They were baiting him, inviting him to come with them aboard the catamaran, then raising miscellaneous reasons why they could not take him, tossing remarks from one to the other so quickly that in his fuddled state he could not follow them. He was explaining, with slow precision, that he had come from Malta "on a matter of business." He sounded pompous and they shrieked with unkind laughter.

"Not pretty," Randal commented, with a sigh.

"Do you get many like that?"

"Every hotel gets the odd difficult guest."

"Oh, I know. And I admired the way you handled him in the dining room, by the way. But I didn't mean Mr. Stark, I meant the two young couples. I saw them come off the *Coralla*." I nodded toward the lazily bobbing catamaran out in the harbor.

Randal looked. "Is that theirs? Expensive job. But hired, probably." He sighed again. "The Mediterranean's full of ritzy floaters in the summer. We get our share of all kinds in Gozo, I suppose. But not many of the wild ones stay here for long. It's on the quiet side. A little short on the razzmatazz."

"Yes. It's a strange island, but I think I'm beginning to like it."

"Good." His eyes glowed.

"Have you always been an *hôtelier?*" I asked. There was something special about him that I'd noticed on our first meeting—a quality which made me think of the stage. He was not theatrical in the word's derogatory sense but he had presence and a charming dignity, in no way old-fashioned.

"I trained as a singer—concert, mainly."

"Oh, that accounts . . ." I broke off, anxious not to be rude.

He composed his features into an expression of mock alarm. "If you'll finish that sentence, I'll brace myself to listen."

I laughed. "I was going to say that it accounts for . . . for the timbre of your voice. It is unusually resonant."

"Yes, well, it would be. At the Academy they worked us very hard and there were hours of practice. One learns to use the diaphragm as well as vocal chords, and the habit stays."

"Why did you give it up?"

He looked away from me, at gently swaying craft on calm water, and for a full minute he said nothing.

Hurriedly, I murmured, "I'm sorry. It is none of my business."

He turned back to me then, and deep lines which had grooved the space between his eyebrows fled as he smiled, but I noticed that his gray eyes remained somber. "I was trying to think how best to answer you. Let's just say that I wasn't good enough. I wanted to be right at the top and I might never have made it."

"I would have thought," I began, and glanced at him. "Are you braced?"

He nodded.

"I would have thought you were the kind of man who would not give up easily."

"Thank you." He flushed slightly. "There were . . . contributory factors. Anyway"—he became more cheerful—"I like being an *hôtelier* very much indeed."

"I'm glad."

It was nice, sitting talking to Randal. He was easy to get along with and didn't expect too much. Unlike Michael. I tilted my face up to the sky to have another look at the fabulous stars, and put a hand up to shield my eyes from the light spilling from a nearby lamp. So I did not see Mr. Stark leave his table and approach ours. I did not even hear him, until he spoke.

"So," he said in a thick voice. "So, Miss Ice-Cool Prescott. You denied knowing Randal Jarvis's relatives." He paused, swaying.

Randal got to his feet with incredible speed and inserted half of his body between Stark and me—the best he could do, since I was sitting at a round table. Stark talked round him at me and the air between us filled with brandy fumes. I leaned back as far as I could go.

"You denied it," he repeated, and laughed. A low, bitter sound, it was. "But earlier I saw you with the old fox Edgar himself, and now you're sitting here with the cub. You're having a busy evening, vixen."

I opened my mouth in astonishment, but Randal was more shocked than I was. In seconds his relaxed, pleasant mood dissolved. He gripped Stark's arm, twisted him around, restrained himself with difficulty from landing a punch on the slack mouth which would have shot the man off the quayside and into oily harbor water, and instead marched him off into the darkness, down a slope toward the small beach.

I gave a quick look around. A few people had noticed, not many. I was afraid. Randal had looked beside himself. I did not know him well enough to know how far he would go, and I was afraid. Not for Stark—I could not care very much what happened to Stark, drunk or sober— but for Randal, who had shown a surprising violence, more than the incident warranted. I followed, out of the light and into the darkness, and after running a little way and seeing nothing more than a few fishermen leaning against a boat pulled up on the beach, and a few cars going up and down the road to Victoria, I spotted Randal coming away from a patch of dark shadow, dusting off the knees of his trousers.

"What did you do?" I asked fearfully.

"I ducked him in the water and I've left him on the sand to sober up."

He took my arm urgently, and in silence, stony-faced, he marched me along the waterfront and turned the corner onto the path which led up to the Tramonto. How different this was from our saunter away from the lace shop. He was stiff, and I, bewildered. I would have twisted my arm away but I had no intention of making a scene here in front of interested spectators.

Sounds fell away behind and beneath us, and we were alone. There was bright starlight, sufficient illumination for me to see the stony, angry face of Randal Jarvis and the bitter set of his mouth.

"Perhaps you'll explain your behavior." I pulled my arm free.

He seemed not to hear my demand but made one of his own. "Is it true that you were talking to my father?"

Bewildered, I said, "Yes, but . . . Why should I not talk to your father? I've met him before, a year ago. He knew my father, and tonight he was very kind to me."

I was going to add that he had invited me to go to his house for tea but I had no time to say another word. Randal let go of my arm and with a brief "Good night" hurried off up the path ahead of me, striding out as if devils were snapping at his heels.

It would be untrue to say that I was attracted sexually to Randal Jarvis, but his company was enjoyable and I had thought I liked him. The arrival of Mr. Stark changed things. The beginning of a friendship had been shattered, probably beyond mending, but it was none of my doing and I simply could not think of the reason. Cross and confused, I climbed the path to the hotel and went to bed, but not to sleep.

I twisted and turned in the hot night, and though I threw off the single sheet which covered me I was still too warm. Occasionally I fell into a troubled doze but most of the time I was wide awake, turning over in my mind the startling events of the evening. My afternoon visit to the farmhouse seemed a long time ago and I scarcely thought of it.

Randal Jarvis must have quarreled seriously with his father. That much was clear and entirely his own business. He had told me that he lived apart from his family because he preferred it that way, and I knew no more except that he was still friendly with Noni. But his reaction to my having exchanged a few words with Edgar Jarvis was alarming. He would go berserk when he knew I was going to his father's house, but I could not imagine why he should object. I'd thought that Michael might not like it, and for my own sake I hoped he would not be there with Noni when I visited. I did not mind seeing Michael on his own, but I still didn't relish seeing him with Noni. Anyway, I would see Michael tomorrow. No—*today*. I glanced at my watch and found that it was a quarter past three. I could ask him if he was going to be at the Jarvises' house on the following afternoon. Then I would at least know in advance about it.

Sleep seemed as distant as ever. I got up and splashed my face and hands with cold water, then went out onto the balcony. I sighed, feeling the terrible isolation which comes to those who sleep alone if they are wakeful in the night. I sat down on a chair and looked at the sea, a ruffled spread of molten pewter. I could not read, for it would have meant putting on the light and I had a hatred of the biting, flying, stinging things that it would attract. So I sat and concentrated on the view.

A milky light washed the sky, too diffused and insubstantial to be dawn, but it was a prelude to daybreak, heralding first light. The sky paled, slowly at first, to a pearly gray, then to aquamarine. When I had watched earlier dawns it was after a night out, never alone, and the time had seemed late instead of early. Now I felt as if I were the only person awake and watching the miracle. But I was wrong.

Beyond the swimming pool a man was running lightly over the great slabs of limestone, carrying a fishing line. He was dressed in the standard peasant garb of pale shirt and baggy pants, and he paused for not a single moment. I could see that he was leaping expertly over small rifts with scarcely any change in the rhythm of his jog trot. It was an economical, medium-paced run, which could be kept up for a long time. Doubtless he went fishing every morning for food, before doing a day's work.

The silence which followed the faint pad-pad of the running man's footsteps was absolute for a few minutes before being broken again, this time with a totally different sound, less mysterious, more intrusive and somehow more frightening. I heard no footsteps at all but there was a small rustle as if someone had brushed against a bush, and the sound was almost beneath my balcony, yet far below, at ground level. I was on the second floor. An early swimmer going to the pool? Not so early as this, surely. Almost stealthily, I rose and leaned over the balcony rail so that I could see the terrace and the doorway to the hotel. A man stood there, looking first to his left and then to his right. I thought he was going to look up-wards and dodged back, but curiosity overcame me and I leaned out again. Now he was taking something from his pocket. With it he opened the hotel door, soundlessly, and slipped inside.

My heart was beating with painful intensity. There had been a secretive quality in the man's attitude but I had recognized him instantly. It was Mr. Stark. Moreover, he was not dressed in the clothes he had worn during the evening. He was wearing sand-colored trousers and shirt. They would make good camouflage against the rocks of Gozo and I wondered what mysterious business had taken Stark abroad in the night. It must have been important. After the treatment given to him by Randal, and after drinking so much brandy, he must have felt like nothing on earth, ready only, I would have thought, to crawl into his comfortable bed. Instead, he must have come back here, changed, and gone out again. Extraordinary. Unless he had not been so drunk as he had seemed.

In the few minutes that my thoughts had been taken up with the runner on the rocks and the furtive Mr. Stark, the aquamarine sky had changed to palest blue, shot with pink and gold. It was exquisite daylight and a cool drift of breeze blew over me. My senses calmed and my thoughts became fuzzy. I was consumed by a need for sleep and I turned, eyes closing already, into my bedroom and almost fell upon the bed. I drew the sheet over me. Momentarily I roused, thinking I heard the click of my doorknob, but it could not be a chambermaid so early. Anyway, I had fastened the latch. It was my habit in hotels. A simple precaution; theft from bedrooms at night was not unusual. Not that I had anything to steal . . . All thought left me and I sank into oblivion.

Not surprisingly, I wakened late and unrefreshed and

breakfasted without appetite on the terrace. My surroundings cheered me. The plants had been well watered in the early morning and in spite of the sun's heat they were moist and fragrant, their leaves gleaming in bright, cool beauty. There were pink and red oleander flowers and even a few carefully nurtured roses. All dead blooms had been cut off by what must be a very meticulous gardener.

I affected not to notice when Randal Jarvis appeared by the dining room window. He was talking to the head-waiter only a few yards from where I was sitting. His behavior last night had been startling in the extreme and I was determined to have it out with him, but I was not going to make the first move. Covertly, I watched until I realized that he had seen me and was preparing to come outside and talk. I was ready for him. The croissant I had half eaten was delicious and the coffee was rapidly putting new heart into me. I poured a second cup and took a sip, by which time Randal was only two yards away. I noticed with amusement that he was nervous and I lifted my face to his, carefully assuming an expression of bland inquiry. I said nothing at all. Not even good morning.

"I owe you an apology," he said abruptly.

"Yes, you do." I spread jam on a morsel of croissant and ate it.

He frowned. "But I'd like to know what you were doing with my father."

"I told you last night. By the way, have you given Mr. Stark a key to the hotel?"

The frown grew deeper. "Certainly not."

"I suppose you don't have a night porter on duty at three-thirty, four o'clock perhaps?" I was pensive.

"You suppose right."

"Yet Mr. Stark entered the front door at about that time, apparently using a key, though I suppose someone might have opened the door from the inside. I thought you'd want to know."

"I assume that you saw him yourself? This isn't just gossip?"

"I saw him." I looked up at my balcony two stories above. "From up there."

"You had a bad night?" He was not sympathizing, he was faintly mocking, and my anger which had been subsiding flared up again.

"Certainly I had a bad night. I'd had a pleasant, friendly encounter with an acquaintance who subsequently turned violent, fought with a stranger and then vented the remnant of his anger on me. Without explanation or reason. The evening turned sour on me. Yes, you could say I had a bad night, but I am beginning to realize I am too easily hurt so think nothing of it."

"Alexa, I'm sorry." He seemed penitent and unhappy.

I was unhappy, too. I looked at him and saw someone else. His sister. Noni. They were not in the least alike to look at or, I suspected, in nature. But Noni came vividly to my mind at that moment, and impulsively I said, "Randal, are Noni and Michael still engaged?"

"I'll sit down if I may." He moved the book I hadn't troubled to open and sat beside me. "You always have a book with you."

"Compulsive reader."

"Alexa, I am truly sorry about last night and I can't explain why I got so mad. Part of it was Stark's boorish rudeness to you, of course, but part of it was . . . something else. All I can tell you is that my father and I don't get on very well and I don't want to be drawn into any of his . . ." He paused again, and finished, "Business deals."

"What kind of deals?" I knew I was being inquisitive.

"Any kind."

Which told me nothing. I went back to my former question. "Noni and Michael," I prompted.

He leaned his elbows on the table and his chin on his fists. The penetrating eyes were steady on mine. "Why do you want to know?"

"Well, I've agreed to have lunch with Michael today. Now I don't know if I ought to."

His expression was unreadable. "Ethics?" There was an edge to his laughter. "Forget them. Others do. If you want Michael back you have to see him, spend time with him."

"I don't want him back!" My voice was full of indignation.

"Methinks the lady doth protest too much." He leaned back and stared out over the sea. "Anyway, who am I to advise you?"

"Noni is your sister."

"Yes. So I'm not exactly impartial. I might not want to see her tied to Michael Brent."

"Then you don't like Michael?"

"I didn't say so—but now that you mention it, not very much."

"Why?" This time it wasn't curiosity. I really wanted to know why Randal didn't like Michael.

I no longer saw Michael clearly. It was as if I viewed him through a distorting lens. The man I knew had become blurred in outline, and indistinct. My judgment had become pretty faulty, too, and I no longer trusted it. Yet I wanted to have lunch with Michael. The attraction was still there and I had to test my resistance. I might discover that I still loved him, which would be awful, but there was an even chance that I might be totally free— the emotional ties finally broken. But either Michael was engaged to Noni or he was not. I wanted to know the score and said so.

"You would have to ask Noni," Randal said, and added quickly, seeing my expression, "I mean that. No one but Noni could answer you. She broke off the engagement, but gave me to understand that it was more of a postponement . . . Oh, hell, it sounds mad. Don't I know it. But my father is at the bottom of it, I suspect. He always is."

Again that bitterness. After a moment he sighed and continued. "I gather that Michael doesn't measure up in some way, so Noni, like the good little girl she isn't, broke the engagement but said it would be on again within the year. That means by Christmas."

I was silent, astonished that any girl would break off her engagement at her father's behest, unable to believe that a man like Michael would accept such a situation.

Rather wearily, very unhappily, Randal said, "If I sound far from big-brotherly, thoroughly disloyal in fact, I am sorry. Actually, I am very fond of Noni."

"Yes. I saw that, on the ferry from Malta."

He nodded. "I wish . . ."

But I was not to learn what it was he wished, for Carmela came to say that he was wanted on the telephone, and Randal, with a murmured word of excuse, left me.

By the time Michael called for me, I was wearing a sleeveless dress of pale biscuit color—a gold chain about my neck the only ornament. My dark hair was coiled on top of my head and I wore pale eyeshadow and bright lipstick. My skin was taking on an even tan and I appeared cool and sophisticated. I was no longer the girl Michael had once known, which would intrigue him.

The telephone by my bedside rang, and Carmela told

me that Mr. Brent was here for me. Without haste, I rang for the elevator and went down. The tiled foyer was no cooler than my greeting, and Michael glanced at me with a touch of wariness as we walked outside together. He held the door of his car open and seemed at a loss for words. Round one to me. I never minded silence, but I recalled that Michael was not often speechless.

We drove off, swinging round the hotel and down to the bay. There was no choice of road; this was the only one. We cruised slowly along, with the harbor on our left, bars and cafés on our right busy with lunchtime trade. I stared about me, remembering the flaring lights and the noisiness of the night before.

"Do you like it?" Michael had been watching me. He had recovered from his slight discomfiture and was the old Michael, his hazel eyes glinting lazily from the brown, brown face, the strong, square hands resting lightly on the wheel.

"Yes, I like it. It is two places, though. One in daylight, another at night."

"You're learning fast. There was a fracas here last night, I understand."

"Who told you that?"

He shrugged his massive shoulders. "News travels. Perhaps you shouldn't wander about unescorted after dark."

I laughed. If he was trying to find out whether I had met Randal by appointment or accident, he would learn nothing from me.

On the hill out of Xlendi and up to Victoria we achieved a remarkable speed, but even Michael had to slow down for the narrow roads through the town, where house walls jutted into the street and people pressed their backs to the walls to avoid the traffic. We caught up with a small cart pulled by a mule. The driver did not even look around. A car growling with impatience behind him meant nothing. For generations, he and his forebears had driven mule carts along this road, returning from the fields to a small stone house at the edge of town for the midday meal. The advent of the motorcar was not going to change his habit.

I relaxed and said mildly to Michael, "There's no hurry, is there?"

He turned to look at me, sensing my change of mood, hearing the alteration in my tone of voice, and smiled. "No, there's no hurry. Alexa, you're still the same. Peaceful to be with."

"Not as peaceful as I used to be, Michael. And not at all the same. I wouldn't want you to be under any misapprehension about that."

The road widened. He drove round the mule cart. "That sounds like a warning."

I shook my head. "Since we're no longer involved, there can be nothing to warn you about."

We wove through a square and down a street I hadn't seen before, passing many Capuchin brothers crowded along the road, mostly young, all dressed in loose brown robes tied at the waist.

The road led downwards through a sloping valley and the sea shimmered ahead of us like blue grass. The hills on either side were bare and brown, terraced steeply into small fields, each terrace built up painstakingly with yellow rocks. From my knowledge of Malta, I was aware that when the rains came the fields would turn green almost overnight. High on the conical hill to our left there was a figure of Christ, a modern sculpture with clean lines.

"Michael, stop. Let me see the statue."

He stopped for a moment, but then said, "You will see it better from the hotel in Marsalforn."

"It's new, isn't it?"

"Fairly new. Nineteen sixty, I think. It's by the Gozitan sculptor Wistin Camilleri. There used to be a wooden cross there and the statue has taken its place."

"Does the hill have a name?"

"Two names. The old one is Il-Mezuq; the new name Is-Salvator, The Savior."

We could see Marsalforn Bay now, a marvelous circle of brilliant blue, ringed by hotels and houses. There was a swimming pool and a harbor packed with yachts and fishing boats. As we drove round to stop before the Calypso Hotel, I saw the *Francine*. My eyes flew to her. She rocked gently at her moorings, and looked—anonymous. Michael had given no sign that he knew my father's boat was here, and there were other, similar twenty-two-footers in the bay. I said nothing.

A church clock sounded one o'clock, a deep, full note. "All these churches!" I exclaimed. "There are so many of them, and all huge. How do they manage to maintain them all?"

Michael opened the car door for me and looked up at the church tower, his eyes nearly as golden as the stone. "You'd wonder, wouldn't you? They are a devout people, the Gozitans."

He had spoken seriously, almost reverently, and I thought that Michael, too, had changed in the year since we'd last been together.

Chapter 8

THE HOTEL was bigger than Randal's Tramonto, though not quite so new, and we had a window table with a perfect view across the bay and into the hills. Apéritifs were brought at once, and we sat contentedly sipping.

The Maltese think nothing of Gozo apart from appreciating the fertility of the island during the growing season. Even the British who have settled in Malta seldom trouble to cross the straits, preferring the more sophisticated pleasures of the larger island. Yet Gozo has a charm of its own, and now that I was overcoming the strangeness and beginning to understand the character of the people, this tiny island of only twenty-six square miles was taking hold of my heart.

Michael was right. The statue of Christ looked magnificent from this dining room, and the wide curve of bay and buildings, pale and gleaming, washed by cream-edged blue water, drew and delighted the eye.

"You bought a house in Gozo just two weeks before you broke our engagement. Why was that? I don't think you ever told me." I had decided on a direct approach and met Michael's steady glance quite calmly. He seemed almost to have been expecting my question and I remembered his magical quality of intuition, of anticipating my needs. How could I forget it? One excludes unwanted recollections from the *surface* of the mind but they lie buried, ready to spring to life at a glance, a touch.

Michael touched me now, his strong, brown fingers lying over mine, gripping them, withdrawing slowly, reluctantly. "I had met Noni," he said. "And I was bewitched. I can describe her effect on me in no other way. Edgar Jarvis had already bought his Gozo house and was preparing to move from Malta. I moved first." His mouth set in a bleak line. "I treated you very badly, Alexa. I'm deeply ashamed."

I was silent, full of emotion. At the poolside on the Tramonto grounds, when Michael had said he still cared about me, he had added, "I am as I am." This was true of all of us, but I was no longer the naïve girl he had broken off with a year ago.

A waiter brought menus. As I opened mine, I said to Michael, "Why would anyone like Edgar Jarvis come here to live?"

"I don't know. A whim, I suppose. And your father?"

I laughed. "The same, I suppose. He was a refugee."

Michael looked up, startled.

"From tourists," I explained, and we chose from the menu. While we lunched, Michael talked of the thriller he was writing, dismissing it too modestly as "just another one, the mixture as before."

Yet it would be his fourteenth thriller, and he had also written two scholarly works on his subject, geology. He was a man who loved to work and his record was impressive. When I said so, he shrugged. "They sell quite well and Gozo is a tax haven, but I don't make as much as I'd like." He was frowning, abstractedly, and I wondered if this was a subconscious reference to Edgar Jarvis's opinion that Michael "did not measure up." Perhaps the Jarvis gauge was purely financial. It would not surprise me.

"Anyway, writing profitable fiction takes up so much time that I lack time for geological research. This island is a geologist's paradise, Alexa, but hotels are being built right on top of evidence of past history, destroying it forever—while I waste my days creating characters who never existed at all."

"Who is to say which is the more valuable—bringing knowledge to a few, or pleasure to many?" I asked lightly.

I meant only to make a consoling remark but Michael looked disapproving before laughing and laying a hand briefly over mine. "Alexa the peacemaker," he said. "You haven't changed. More coffee?"

"No more. It was perfect, but I've had more than enough."

"Then, if you would like to, let's walk round the bay."

I felt that the *Francine* was waiting for me. But I did not know if I had enough courage today to board her. I had seen the police station and supposed I could get permission. I wanted to go, but dreaded it. So we might as well walk around the bay, and I said that I would like to.

Fierce heat beat down upon us but there was more air

here than in Xlendi—the bay was not enclosed by high cliffs and was much wider. There were some very smart houses, with painted shutters, carved stone balconies bright with tubs of flowers and cages of singing birds, and iron scrollwork for ornamentation. Doors stood open so that we could see inside, to rooms equipped with modern furniture. Nearby, there were tiny houses which must have looked for centuries as they did now. Some even had goats accommodated on the ground floor. I could see them peeping at us from between roughly nailed wooden slats, their hooves drumming as they moved around. We caught a glimpse of beard, horn and golden eye as they jostled for a viewing position.

"Do people live over them?" I whispered to Michael.

He grinned. "They do. Immune to the smell of goat, probably. They spend their days in the room above the animals and sleep on the top floor. Or on the roof. Most have roof gardens, though not many could rightly be called gardens. Look!" He turned me round so that across the bay we could see the large, modern hotel where we'd lunched so well. On the roof were lines and lines of washing, blowing in the wind.

"Very practical," I commented.

"Exactly. Land is too valuable here for people to own more than the area occupied by the four square walls. Unless they're farmers, that is."

Which brought us neatly, of course, to the farmhouse. Michael was very accomplished at steering conversation in the direction he wanted.

"Alexa, I've never been inside your father's place. Would you show it to me?"

"But I thought . . . Michael, how can you possibly have a purchaser if you haven't been inside it?"

"Gozitan farmhouses are all much the same and my

friend likes the position. That's the important thing. Wonders can be done to the interior with this soft stone. Without benefit of an architect, too. All a local builder needs is time. Too much time for my liking. My own place is far from finished after a year, but I work on it myself sometimes and one learns patience here."

"Even you?" I teased. Michael had not been noted for patience in the past.

"Even I. You haven't answered me about seeing the house."

"I suppose I could show it to you sometime."

"Today." He was insistent.

"Why today? It is so hot." The wine had made me sleepy. We had come to an esplanade and there were seats beneath the palm trees. "Let's sit here for a while."

Michael hesitated and covertly glanced at his watch.

"Unless you are in a hurry?"

"Not at all." His hazel eyes gleamed at me. "This is much better than writing."

"Tell me about your house," I said.

"It's an old one that I'm renovating as I've explained, and it's up on one of the hills, near Zebugg. It has five rooms, one quite large, and a small courtyard, Gozitan style. It's nice. You must come and see it."

I murmured something noncommittal and we fell silent. It was almost too hot to talk, so we sat and listened to the surge of waves. The sea bubbled up through tunnels in the soft rock, making eerie sounds, and then gurgled and rattled small stones as it receded. Further along, Michael told me, there were salt pans, shallow oblongs carved out of the rock, where sea water lay until evaporated by the sun, leaving salt behind. "The Turks used to land at Marsalforn centuries ago to take on stores and salt. And women, if they didn't hide quickly enough."

But I was not in the mood for history. I listened to the sea, and thought about my father who had died so recently.

"I will show you the farmhouse," I said to Michael, "if you will wait while I go out to look at my father's boat." He was very still. "You know it is here, then?"

"Yes. I saw it." I looked at him. "Didn't you know it was here?"

"The whole island knows. But it is still in the care of the police."

"They can't refuse to let me see it, can they?"

"Probably not. But are you sure you want to go?"

"I'm sure," I said. I'd had time to decide that during lunch, when my eyes had kept straying to the familiar sloop, and while we'd walked I had plucked up sufficient courage for the ordeal.

We went back to the police station. The sand-colored uniform was by now familiar to me and I was becoming accustomed to the relaxed, friendly attitude of the police.

They were watchful and doubtless efficient, but not at all aggressive. A man stood aside to allow us to enter the building. Another one listened to my request, glanced curiously from me to Michael, and went to an inner room where we could hear him repeating my question to an officer. The officer telephoned and we heard him ask for Inspector Rapa. In a few moments, he came out himself and said with great courtesy that we could go out to the *Francine* if we wished. He would send someone with us, to row us out, but the *Francine* must not be moved from her mooring at present. He added that Inspector Rapa himself would take me if I could wait until tomorrow morning at about ten o'clock.

"It might be better to get it over now," Michael urged, gently. I wavered, then shook my head. "Please tell Inspector Rapa that I would be grateful if he would take me tomorrow. I will be here at ten o'clock."

The officer was impassive as he nodded, but I thought he seemed pleased as he returned to his room.

As we went out again into the bright sunshine, Michael asked, "Is there anything wrong?"

"Nothing at all."

"Won't it be more distressing for you to go with the police, instead of with a friend?"

"The reverse, I think. Anyway, I did not ask you to come out with me, Michael. Only to wait for me while I went."

He looked startled. I had gotten under his skin and I wondered why. He had casually assumed that I would want him to come with me to the *Francine*, but with Michael, of all people, I wanted to avoid any situation where I might become emotional. I could have gone alone, but not with Michael. Inspector Rapa, I knew, would be matter-of-fact enough for me to be able to cope with my feelings.

Michael's ill-concealed frustration puzzled me. I could not imagine why he should look so put out. A visit to the *Francine* had not been on the agenda anyway. It was the farmhouse he was interested in.

"Come," I said. "We'll go to the farmhouse if you like."

The gloom lifted from him at once. "Great," he said, and took my arm to walk me back to the car.

🐦   🐦   🐦

Michael took me to the farmhouse by a different route, up a steep hill from Marsalforn to Xaghra, passing the end of a narrow, winding road which led down to Ramla Bay and turning right toward the farmhouse before reaching Xaghra. He did not hesitate for a moment, but whisked the car neatly round the white monolith to jog down the dusty, rutted track.

"I thought you hadn't been to the farmhouse." I was surprised at his knowledge of the location.

"I haven't been inside it." Michael turned to look at me. "But I've been down this track before." He laughed. "Alexa, darling, I don't think there is any vestige of a road that I haven't been along in the whole of Gozo. And I've walked or climbed in most of the places where there *aren't* any roads."

We reached the gateway, and after a moment's hesitation he turned the Triumph in through the arch and parked it almost exactly where I had parked my Ford.

The first thing I did was glance into the tangled corner where the lightweight motorcycle had been. I remembered the gun strapped to the frame, and half shivered in spite of the heat. There was no machine there today and no one about. We sat for a moment. Insects hummed and shimmered in the hot, still air. I could hear a goat bell tinkling in the far distance.

Michael put a hand over both of mine as they lay on my lap and I could feel his eyes on my face. They were probing, asking what it meant to me to be in here with him. It was a question I was not prepared to answer. The nearest person was probably a couple of miles away so we were very much alone, Michael and I.

My scalp prickled. Quickly, I got out of the car and walked to the shade of the twisted tree. Trying to recover what poise I possessed, I brushed a few fallen and shriveled olives from the stone bench. They fell with a dry, rattling sound.

I turned to smile at Michael. "Don't you think the

courtyard is charming? It makes a beautiful patio. Look, there is even a pond, but no water." I pointed, unnecessarily. The shape of the pond was quite visible and I was overdoing the small talk.

"There must be a well," Michael said. "All these isolated farms have their own water supply. How much water there is available, is another matter." He moved to a corner of the garden, pushed aside a bush which grew behind the stone seat and revealed a low, circular wall.

The stone had not been cleaned up and I hadn't even noticed it on my previous visit. There was a wooden cover, not new but sound enough. Michael lifted it, and beneath there was one iron crossbar cemented into place. Suspended from it, by means of an S-shaped butcher's hook, dangled a bucket. Coiled neatly round another hook, on the inner wall of the well, was a nylon rope with one end attached to the bucket by a metal ring. There was no winch of any kind, which surprised me.

"I don't understand," I said. "There are two bathrooms in the house, and a kitchen. I thought water had been brought in."

"It may have been. Or the taps may be there in readiness. Did you turn them on?"

I shook my head. "I wasn't here for long."

"Sometimes one well is used for drinking water, another source for washing, and the washing water might be more salt. But here you are some way from the sea, and I should imagine the water will be the same even if it is piped into the house. Gozo has good supplies of fresh water. Better than Malta."

From opposite sides of the well we peered down into the black depths but could see nothing. I picked up a small, clean stone and dropped it. It seemed a long time before we heard the splash, yet it could have been only two or three seconds at most. We straightened up, and I moved away while Michael replaced the heavy cover.

"In any case, you have water," he said cheerfully. "But you won't think of living here, will you? It's far too isolated for a woman alone. I would be worried about you."

We faced each other across the low wall and I said, rather brusquely, "It's too late for you to start worrying about me, Michael. Anyway, I thought I might open a hotel."

"*Here?* Darling, no one in his right senses would come here for a holiday. What would he do?"

"It's quiet and peaceful," I said, defensively. Michael would not get me to give up this house to his client for a long time yet. Here my father had worked before he died, and here I felt close to him. It would be brutal to abandon the house without living in it at all, when he had spent so many hours lovingly restoring the old rooms.

I looked at the front door, that massive door, and suddenly made up my mind. My money was dwindling and the Tramonto was expensive. I would move in here soon and stay in the house. With that door bolted and the one in the upstairs room similarly fastened, I would be perfectly safe. There was nothing to steal and no reason why anyone should want to break in. Pensively, I recalled my first visit, when I had seen the motorcycle and the gun. The likely explanation was that the weapon was a shotgun and not a rifle, and that it had belonged to some peasant, perhaps on his way to shoot birds. He might have paused to have a look around, maybe to pick a few olives.

The picture, the copy of a Modigliani, was the only thing in the house worth stealing. If indeed it had any value. For some reason, I found myself hoping that if Michael went into that upstairs room he would not notice the canvas leaning against the wall. Probably I could keep him from going in there. After all, it was my house, my prerogative to say where a visitor could or could not go.

Brave words I spoke to myself, and perfectly reasonable, but I doubted if I would be proof against Michael Brent's guile and determination if he really wanted to go through that upstairs door.

While I unlocked the front door myself, refusing to hand over the key, I was thinking hard. There was no reason at all why I should mind about Michael or anyone else seeing the picture. One thing I knew for certain: if it belonged to my father, he had come by it honestly.

I paused to stroke the dark wood of the door with its detailed carving of flowers, vines and birds. Then we were inside the long, beautiful room with its clean, golden stone, the new window looking outward, the enormous chest and the one lovely sea-green rug.

Beside me, Michael whistled. "He really has made something magnificent out of this, hasn't he?"

I nodded, a lump coming to my throat and pride swelling within me. It was delightful to be able to show this to someone who appreciated the work which had gone into it. My lonely year had made me forget the joy of shared experience. I turned and looked at my father's desk, meticulously tidy as always. Suddenly, with leaping fear, I noticed something different, and my pleasure in coming here vanished. A chill moved down my spine and up again. Like a finger, it lifted the hair on the nape of my neck. The picture, the Modigliani, was hanging over my father's desk, perfectly in position.

The woman's strange eyes stared back at me as I looked at her, and I wished she could speak, to tell me who had crept into the house in my absence, brought the picture from that empty room upstairs and hung it here on the wall. And how they could possibly have got in. Did someone else have a key? I wondered if that was where the picture normally hung. It seemed likely. My father would have enjoyed glancing up at it when he sat at his desk. There must have been a hook there the last time I'd been in the house. I racked my brain and could not remember seeing one, but then it was not something I would have been looking for.

"That's a very striking picture." Michael had seen me staring at it, of course. He walked closer, and in surprise he added, "It's a copy, not a print. Remarkably good." He turned to me and slowly he said, "At least, I suppose it's a copy."

I quelled my shivering nerves. "Of course it's a copy." I laughed, but was not much amused. "My father could never afford a Modigliani. You know that."

"Quite." The response was made with total absence of feeling. Michael took three paces to the right, then six to the left, without taking his eyes from the picture. "Hm," he said, and turned away. "I don't know much about art and I admit I prefer a landscape to a portrait any day. Now, show me the rest of the house, darling. If it's all as lovely as this, I'm not surprised that you feel like moving in."

He took my arm and we went together through the other rooms. The bolt on the upstairs door was still in position as I had left it. No one had come through there. I said nothing to Michael about it and he did not ask to go through.

"What a place!" he said when we had finished. "So far as it goes, it's perfect. There's a lot to do yet, of course. Alexa . . ."

"Yes?"

We had returned to the large downstairs room. I walked

to the window and stared out over the valley, purposely keeping away from Michael.

"Oh, nothing. I was thinking of the might-have-beens."

"Don't do that," I said, with a lightness I did not feel. "Always a mistake."

"Yes. Well. Shall we go?"

I was glad that this visit was over. Following Michael to the door I glanced over my shoulder toward the picture, then quickly away from it again.

"If you decide to sell the house," he said, "you will let me have first offer, won't you?"

"For your client?" I asked.

"For my client, naturally."

"We'll see," I said evasively. "It's unlikely I'll sell this year, anyway. There's probate and everything, isn't there?"

"Yes, of course. I did not mean to hurry you." For Michael, he sounded almost humble.

Chapter 9

I T W A S L A T E afternoon when we returned to the Tramonto and I said goodbye to Michael. Though I still found him attractive, I had achieved an air of detachment during our time together, so at least I had matured enough to be able to control my emotions. But I had forgotten to ask him if he was going to the Jarvis home tomorrow and I had an uneasy feeling that if I met him on Noni's territory my detachment would vanish.

I talked to some of the hotel guests for a while, had a swim and changed in a leisurely fashion before going down to dinner. Lunch had been enormous so I was not very hungry, and by the time Randal Jarvis reached my table during his round of the dining room I had refused dessert and cheese and asked for coffee to be brought out on the terrace.

"Make it two," Randal said to the waiter. He drew out my chair and we left together.

"Did you enjoy your visit to Marsalforn Bay?"

"Yes, I did, thank you." Blandly, I added as we crossed the tiled hall, "There's an excellent hotel, the Calypso."

Equally blandly, Randal replied, "Well named, too. Calypso's Cave is not so far from it. Near to Ramla Bay. You've seen it, I suppose?"

"Never. Gozo is sometimes known as Calypso's Isle, isn't it?"

"That's right. I thought Michael might have taken you to the cave."

"No. I took him to the farmhouse instead."

I was surprised by Randal's reaction to this. An expression of stunned disbelief, followed by one of resentment, flitted over his face, but he only said, without any particular emphasis, "He would enjoy that."

When the waiter arrived with the coffee, Randal ordered brandy for both of us. "You will have one with me?"

"Thank you."

I watched without pleasure a cloud of flying insects performing a dance of death near the white-domed terrace lights, then turned to Randal. "You don't often drink alcohol," I remarked.

"Not often. But today has been one of those days. Carmela has not been well. A stomach upset. I sent her to bed." The absence of even one valued member of staff could create havoc. I sympathized with him. At my expression, he smiled. "Everything's under control now. I hope."

The brandy came, generous measures in balloon glasses, and when the waiter had gone I said, hesitantly, "I was . . . deeply troubled when I arrived. You know that."

"Yes."

"I feel much better now. It must be the peace of your excellent hotel."

"I'd like to think so, Alexa. But it is more probably the spirit of Gozo. It is a magical place."

"Yes, it is." I was thinking of the things I had seen to-day—the hot fields, the goats, the painted fishing boats moored near the *Francine,* the salt pans, the great churches with masses continually rising from devout worshipers. "But your hotel is a lovely place. I want you to know that I think so, because I must leave it soon."

He was dismayed. "You are going back to London? Or merely to Malta?"

"Neither. I have decided to move into my father's farmhouse." I took a sip of brandy and avoided Randal's eyes. "There is everything I need there, and to be honest, until his affairs are settled I haven't much money."

"But that doesn't matter. You are welcome to stay on here. You can settle your bill whenever you wish, a week, a month, a year from now."

"You're very kind, but of course I can't possibly accept what amounts to free hospitality."

Roughly, he said, "You cannot possibly stay in that farmhouse. It is most unsuitable for a girl alone."

"That is what Michael thought, too."

Randal flushed, then, almost visibly, collected himself. "Ah, yes, Michael. Let us not forget Michael. Tell me, did you decide today whether you want him back or not?"

I was angry. "That is not a matter for *decision.* I am not a child and Michael is not a toy to be reached for."

Randal sighed. "You are right of course. But please, Alexa. Don't go to the farmhouse."

"I have made up my mind to go. And the more everyone tries to put me off, the more determined I am."

"Are you always contrary?"

Dryly, I said, "Stubborn would be the better word."

I think neither of us wanted to quarrel. We began to talk of other things, and when Randal asked me if I would like to go for a walk later in the evening I replied, truthfully, that I had planned an early night. "I am going with Inspector Rapa to see the *Francine* tomorrow. My father's sloop," I added by way of explanation, but Randal appeared to know it by name. He nodded. "And in the afternoon, I am going to your father's house for tea."

Randal's composure cracked slightly. "Alexa, I wish you wouldn't get involved." He swallowed some brandy in a gulp, his normally calm gray eyes dark with anger.

I was astonished. "I'm only going to tea. Do you call that getting involved? And involved with what, for goodness sake?"

He stared at me, brooding, and I knew there were questions crowding his mind, but they remained unasked. His face was closed and wary. He was filled with simmering anger which I felt was directed at himself more than at me. His gaze shifted slightly and he glanced over my shoulder into a more brightly lit part of the terrace. When I turned my head I saw that he was watching Mr. Stark.

My expedition of today had thrust last night's wakeful vigil on the balcony right out of my mind, and I had forgotten about Stark's night prowl. I turned rapidly back to Randal. "Did you find out anything?" I asked in an eager whisper.

With an effort, he controlled his anger and relaxed. "Only that no keys are missing, or have been missing, so he has one of his own, presumably. I'd like to know where he got it from, and how."

"Are you going to do anything?"

"What can I do? Except keep a very close eye on him. I'll do that, I can assure you."

"I wonder where he went last night."

"So do I," Randal said thoughtfully.

I stifled a yawn. "Don't rely on my insomnia tonight. I'm sure I shall sleep like a log."

Randal rose when I did. "I hope that you do." He hesitated. "I wish you would listen to me, Alexa. Don't visit my father. And don't leave the hotel. Apart from anything else, there is going to be a change in the weather. The lane to that house of yours will be a muddy river if there's rain."

"I have Mr. Bartola's little car."

"And much good it will do you. Is there a telephone?"

"No."

He shook his head in despair, but said no more. I noticed that he had left half his brandy, while I had finished mine. No wonder I was sleepy.

When I got to my room, I pulled back my curtains, pushed open the balcony screens and went out for a last breath of air. A man was walking beyond the terrace. He took the path to Xlendi, and as he passed under a tall lamp which stood at the edge of the courtyard I recognized Stark. Tonight I was too tired to be interested. I lay down and was instantly engulfed in a dreamless sleep.

🐟.　　🐟.　　🐟.

I wakened early, conscious that today was to be different, with definite plans for morning and afternoon. First the *Francine*, and at the back of my mind there was the hope that I might find some clue to my father's death, though in my heart I think I knew that I would be disappointed.

The powerboat moored in the harbor at Marsalforn had been in the hands of the police for days now. If they had found no clue, it was likely that it held no significance.

Glumly, I thought over my conversation with Inspector Rapa. He had said there was no evidence of foul play, but had looked uncomfortable when I refused to believe that my father had drowned in good weather. In the Inspector's mind, too, there were doubts. I was sure of it. His efforts to reassure me had been kind, but futile.

Jumping out of bed, I took my swimming things from the towel rail where I had hung them and went for a swim before breakfast. It is glorious to start the day in cool, clear water before the sun is high. I had the pool to myself and stayed in longer than I meant to. When the two newly arrived couples dove in and began happily splashing and shouting, I left the pool and walked over the rocks for a closer look at the sea, my hair blowing dry in a soft breeze. I felt relaxed and ready to face the day: Rapa, the *Francine*, Edgar Jarvis and all.

Already, there was a powerboat streaking across the water with a wake like a white arrow frothing away from it, and behind, on tow, a water-skier—an anonymous stick creature in black rubbers, arms held horizontally in front, hands gripping a bar. From this distance it was impossible to see the towlines, and in all the bright sea this tiny figure was the only evidence of humanity.

I turned back toward the hotel, walking slowly, feeling beneath my feet the scored and patterned rock crowded with fossils. There were feathery seaweed patterns, larger grooves forming irregular, crazy designs and everywhere the whorls of shells and snails. My toes curled over them, feeling the warmth of centuries, the comfort of so much evidence of continuity of existence. No wonder Michael loved this island.

As I approached the hotel, I glanced up at the balcony of my room. I had left the screens open and my startled eye caught sight of a figure quickly withdrawing from the doorway. It was the act of a man or woman who did not want to be seen. I began to run, across the rocks, around the pool and into the hotel. There was no one at the desk and I flew past it; no elevator, so I took the stairs two at a time. I ought to have waited and called for help but my mood was of outraged anger. I wanted action.

There was no possibility of a chambermaid's being at work on the bedrooms so early. I had already discarded that idea. I glimpsed the startled face of a guest emerging from a first-floor bedroom but I did not pause. Panting now, I flung myself up the second staircase. The door to my room was fastened, but the key was in the pocket of my white robe. I put it into the lock. It made a great noise and for a moment I waited, quaking. There was no escape from inside the room. The next balcony was too far away for anyone but a fool or an acrobat. Resolutely, I turned the key and took a step sideways, away from the door. I don't know what I expected. Someone to rush out, knocking me over in the process? A thief, perhaps, angry and frustrated at finding only my simple gold chain. I had no other jewelry, and the chain was worth very little.

I was motionless, listening. The only sound was the loud insistent thump of my own heart, more agitated now than it had been while I was running upstairs. From within the room there was no noise at all. I pushed the door wide open. The usual square shape of a modern hotel bedroom with bath sprang into vision, and the gap at the hinge was wide enough for me to see that there was nobody behind the door. If anyone was still here, he or she was in the bathroom. That someone had *been* here was not in doubt. To back up the glimpse I'd had from the rocks there was now a full and sickening view of my bedroom in a state of complete disorder. It had been searched very thoroughly, with no attempt at concealment.

I left the door to the hall open and flung wide the bathroom door, leaping away from it and feeling ridiculous when I saw that the room was empty. Danger and crisis over, my knees began to knock and I felt sick. Quickly, before anyone could see, I closed the bedroom door and went out onto the balcony for some air.

Why, I wondered. Why, why, why? And what should I do now? I sat down, crossed my legs to stop the trembling and wagged the airborne foot up and down, watching it. My sandals must still be down by the pool. I had walked over the rocks in bare feet and they were still bare. I had felt nothing as I ran, but now I saw that there were some scrapes. No blood to speak of, just a dried trickle from one deep scratch on my ankle. I dimly remembered catching it against a protuberant rock as I began the marathon to the hotel.

I stared grimly over the balcony rail. The place where I had walked was in full view, clearly visible. The movement I had seen had probably been the searcher deciding to leave when he saw me returning. Or when *she* saw me returning. And always I came back to the why.

The correct thing to do, of course, was to telephone for the manager, Randal, and show him exactly what had happened. I was reluctant to do this but knew that I must. Getting up and feeling suddenly tired, I went into the room to see if my gold chain was still there. Again my nerves gave a twitch of alarm. While I was sitting out on the balcony, a note had been thrust under the door. I picked it up and read. If I'd needed proof that my father had been done to death, this gave it to me. It might not be enough for the law but it was enough for me.

There were only two words on the sheet of paper: "Leave Gozo." That was all. No reason, no threat. Just "Leave Gozo." It was printed in capital letters with a ball-point pen on a sheet of hotel notepaper, plenty of which was supplied downstairs, and as there was a small stock in my room it was safe to assume the same was true of other rooms. Not that the writer need be resident or have been into any of the rooms. A sheet could have been taken from the drawer right here during the search. I had not counted to see how many there had been.

The gold chain was still there of course. Robbery had not been the motive for this. Not ordinary, conventional robbery for something valuable. I revised my decision to show Randal the chaos and set to work methodically tidying my few possessions, folding and returning them to already opened drawers. I closed them and turned to the bed. The mattress had been dragged from it and hung askew, with the bed linen on the floor. The intruder must have been looking for something which might have been concealed beneath the mattress. He had been disappointed. I had nothing which could interest anyone. I knew nothing that I could disclose to anyone. I was frustrated, balked, bewildered and very, very cross.

When the room looked straight enough to have been merely occupied overnight, with the bed left open and my scattered things put in order on the dressing table, I took a bath and dressed. Instead of being early, I would now have to breakfast quickly and drive over to Marsalforn Bay immediately afterwards to meet Inspector Rapa at ten o'clock as arranged. But I would take this note with me and show it to him.

Randal was not in evidence that morning, to my great relief. His perceptive eye might have noticed that I was uneasy. Alternatively, he might know more of this affair than I did. Either way, it was easier for me to eat my roll and drink my coffee outside, hidden behind dark glasses and assiduously reading a book. Then I rose and went straight to the parking lot to collect my little Ford and drive to Marsalforn Bay.

It was slightly oppressive now that the sun was up— still, and with the hint of a storm in the air. The booths were busy in Xlendi Bay and I waved to Rosa as I went past, receiving a wave in return. Goats flowed over the rocks in their usual brown-black tide, a few strollers came down the road toward the bay and women were scrubbing clothes at the public washing place. Victoria was busy with Gozitans and tourists, both resident on the island and, I guessed, from Malta, as many carried baskets or boxes with packed lunches.

I turned left, bowled down the hill to Marsalforn Bay and parked near the police station. Nearby was a car that looked familiar. I looked, looked again, read the registration number and walked over to peer into the front of the car. It was my father's old MG. The slightly sagging driver's seat, the marks and scratches on the dashboard, the wear on the handle of the gear lever all spoke of my father's dear, familiar presence, not of his absence, and this unexpected confrontation shook me to pieces. I stood leaning against the car with my face turned to a blank wall, hoping no one would come along until I had gained control.

The visit to the *Francine* I was prepared for. I had steeled myself to it. I knew it would be difficult and had already erected my defenses, but this additional ordeal upset me to an appalling degree. I felt a hand on my shoulder and flinched away. It was dropped immediately but my lowered eyes caught the sand-colored uniform I was beginning to know so well, and I lifted my face to meet the sympathetic eyes of Inspector Rapa. I pushed fingers in behind my spectacles, wiping away tears, and smudged them into damp smears.

"I'm sorry," I said shakily. "I'm sorry. I was not expecting . . . to see the car."

"We shall have some coffee," Inspector Rapa said, and with one hand on my arm, above the elbow, he steered me into the police station and through to an empty office. Then he left me, ostensibly to order the coffee but also, I thought, out of tact. By the time he returned, I had got hold of myself and was ready for the inevitable questions. None came. Instead, I got some sort of an explanation.

"Your father's car was left parked near the harbor at Xlendi Bay. He must have sailed round the island and moored off Ramla. I thought it better to take the car into our custody and I mentioned, the other day, that we had it." He stopped walking about the room and sat down behind a desk. "We hadn't quite finished with the car when I saw you last. Investigations were completed last night."

Coffee came, in a pot, and was poured by a young policeman who glanced covertly at me. The china was thick and white, the coffee thick and black. I drank it gratefully and felt better.

"You say your investigation was completed last night, yet you must have had the car for some time. Why has it taken so long?"

"We dismantled it, searching. But don't worry, we have good mechanics." He was reassuring me as to its safety but I was not concerned with that.

"Searching for what?"

He shrugged. "We do not know, Miss Prescott."

"Drugs, I assume," I said with weariness.

"What makes you think that?" he asked quickly.

"Oh, isn't it always drugs, nowadays? Isn't that the thing which fetches most money and is most easily concealed in a car?"

The ghost of amusement narrowed his eyes. "Gold bars are popular, too. But heavy." Perhaps his little joke was intended to catch me off guard, for he quickly followed it with a question. "Do you believe that your father might have been concerned in drug smuggling?"

"Inspector Rapa, we are talking of your suspicions, not my beliefs. I *know* my father would not be concerned in drug smuggling, or any other kind of smuggling. I doubt if he ever smuggled anything in his life." Honesty made me add, "Unless, possibly, a bottle of brandy for his own use, a few cigarettes over the permitted amount. Nothing, but *nothing* else."

Inspector Rapa nodded. "That is what I would have thought."

I stared at him. "Then why the search?"

He shrugged again. "Routine."

"Surely taking a car to pieces is more than routine, Inspector."

"Not necessarily. It depends on what kinds of crimes are rife in the neighborhood. Smuggling is always a problem on islands."

"But you said you didn't believe my father was a smuggler."

"That is true." His eyes still looked tired. He, too, seemed to be slightly bewildered this morning. "But sometimes things are planted, to bring suspicion."

"You think something may have been planted on my father?"

"Might. Not may. We have searched the car and the *Francine* and we have found nothing. So presumably nothing has been planted. Or, if planted, it has been recovered by those responsible."

I put down my cup and leaned forward. "Please, Inspector Rapa, tell me why you think someone might have intended to implicate my father in such deep trouble. No one would do it without a strong reason."

He smiled, then, and said briskly, "We have no reason to think that he has been implicated in anything. The complete lack of evidence confirms that we were being overcautious. But when there is sudden death we policemen always try to see if it has a link with anything else. You understand that, I am sure? However, your father, so far as we are concerned, is completely in the clear. We are only sorry that he died in such tragic circumstances."

It all sounded very convincing, like any rehearsed speech, but I thought of my bedroom that morning and threw Inspector Rapa's reasoned, reassuring words out of my mind. Silently, I reached into my shoulder bag and handed him the piece of paper which had been thrust under my bedroom door.

"I found this early today," I said then. "I had been out swimming before breakfast. My room had been searched and left in utter chaos. Nothing taken."

It does not take long to read two words. He read them and lifted his head to stare at me. His lips were compressed. "So," he said, his voice sharp and cutting as I had never heard it before. "So, someone is beginning to show his hand. Who, Miss Prescott?"

I shook my head, helplessly. "And why?" I countered. "That seems to me to be more important than who."

He flung the note on his desk with distaste. "You may be right. But whichever is the prime factor this . . ." He pushed the paper with one finger. "This is a grubby little trick."

"No more than a trick?"

He sighed, wearily. "I cannot answer that. We shall test for fingerprints, naturally."

"But you don't expect to find anything helpful."

He admitted that was so. For a policeman he was totally unbureaucratic and I found that I liked and trusted him.

"Are you going to leave Gozo?" he asked.

"No. Not yet, anyway."

He nodded and I thought that he approved of my answer. "Be careful," he said. "At the very least, we know that someone would rather you were not here."

"Michael keeps telling me that I ought not to stay here."

"Michael Brent? He has your welfare at heart, I am sure, but he would not stoop to writing anonymous letters. Now, if you are ready, I suggest we got to the *Francine*. I think that there is nothing on the boat to distress you, apart from the fact that your father's last hours were spent there."

He gave orders for the note to be taken to his office in Victoria, photographed and processed, and we left, crossing the hundred yards or so of water in a police launch. We boarded the twenty-two-foot sloop and I examined everything in silence, remembering happy hours spent on this craft. Not very many hours. This smart boat was a fairly recent acquisition—he'd bought it not long before I'd gone to London to work. Everything was in perfect order, even the tiny galley. My father was immaculately tidy but while he had been out in the *Francine* he had *fallen overboard*. This tidiness was unnatural. The boat gave no sign of occupation.

"Have you straightened things up?" I said at last, looking at the Inspector.

"Yes. But I can tell you exactly how we found it. There was a fishing line overboard from the aft cockpit. In the galley the kettle had been boiled, we assume, because there was water in it and on the table a used mug which contained the dregs of black coffee. A jar of instant coffee stood on the table. There was a spoon beside it. The coffee was not sweetened. Did he take sugar?"

I shook my head silently.

"The only other article lying about was a pair of binoculars. But it was dark when he died. Could he see well in the dark? Or would he have been waiting for dawn?"

My mind was numb after trying to cope repeatedly with questions which had no answers. I tried to think. "He could see pretty well in the dark. But what would he have been looking for?"

There was no answer, of course.

I roused myself. "Was he alone? Do you know that?"

After a moment's hesitation, Inspector Rapa replied: "Part of the superstructure had been wiped clean of fingerprints. Which might indicate that someone had come aboard while the boat was moored."

My heart lifted with excitement. This was the first small indication that someone else might be concerned in my father's death. Slowly, I said, "So he might have been pushed overboard?"

"We have no evidence to that effect."

"And none to refute it."

"That is so."

I took a deep, shivering breath. "I have seen everything, Inspector Rapa. We may as well go now."

He nodded. "Is there anything here that you would

like to take with you?" He opened the cupboard doors in the galley.

"No. Unless, perhaps, the binoculars."

He took them from a drawer and handed them to me. "You don't want to use the boat?"

"No. At least, not yet. Later, perhaps."

The Inspector signaled to the young man who had brought us, and we went out into the bright sunshine to climb from the *Francine* into the police launch. The one small fact that part of the gleaming woodwork had been wiped clean seemed very important to me.

As we stepped ashore, Inspector Rapa said, "I will send your father's car to your hotel now, if you wish."

"That would be very kind of you," I said. "I can return the Ford to Mr. Bartola."

"He will call for it. That is the usual practice." He lifted his head and sniffed at the slight breeze coming off the sea—a dense, warm stirring of the air. "There will be a storm, I think. What are you going to do now?"

"I shall go back to the hotel. This afternoon I am going to visit Mr. Jarvis. He was a friend of my father's."

"Indeed? I did not know. I hope you will have a pleasant afternoon." He spoke almost idly and hooked one thumb into the shiny leather belt he wore. Then, suddenly, he remembered that there was work waiting for him in Victoria, shook hands with me, and left.

I looked again at my father's MG which was soon to be returned to me, got into the Ford and laid my father's binoculars, together with my bag, carefully on the seat beside me. The clock on the huge church began to strike twelve. Twenty-three hours ago I had been here with Michael. Now, I was alone. An accustomed state for me. I drove off.

Chapter 10

RAPA KEPT his promise. My father's MG was returned
to me at the Tramonto less than an hour after I returned. I
signed for it and gave it a perfunctory examination on the
young policeman's insistence that I must check that all
was in order, but I could not bring myself to enter the car.
After lunch, I told myself, I will arrange for Mr. Bartola
to collect his Ford and then I can drive the MG to Edgar
Jarvis's house. But I changed my mind, and after lunch
I went out to the parking lot and took the Ford instead. I
was not yet ready to use the shabby old MG, redolent of
my father's presence.

It was strange, this reluctance to enclose myself in car
or boat and make use of them, while I positively longed to
stay in the house. Contrary woman, I told myself crossly.
Or was it that I knew neither car nor boat would yield any

clues to my father's death? Both had been in the hands of the police. But then, the police had held the key to the farmhouse also, and had searched it—to find nothing, I supposed.

Frowning, I spun the wheel of the Ford, curving round the now familiar bends in the road down to the bay and realizing with dismay that I did not know where Edgar Jarvis's house was. He had not told me. Perhaps it was one of those places which "everyone knows"—except the person who actually wants to find it. I certainly could not go back and ask Randal. It would bring an explosion, and I couldn't really see him telling me anyway since he was so against my going. I would have asked Rosa, at the shop, but her place was shuttered. She must be taking an afternoon nap.

There were a few fishermen leaning against bollards and upturned boats, talking. They spoke no English and affected not to understand my halting Maltese when I asked for directions. "Edgar Jarvis," I repeated, with a rising inflection "Villa Melita?" And at that they exchanged glances, unsmiling, deadpan, suspicious. But finally one man, older than the rest, with thick hairy arms and a barrel-shaped body, pointed up to the hillside which rose behind the Hotel Tramonto.

I was puzzled. The Tramonto was on a dead-end road. Beyond and behind there was only rock. The man indicated not the way up to the Tramonto, however, but the road to Victoria, and mimed that I should take a right turn off the road before reaching the town. He jogged his clenched fists up and down, held as if on a steering wheel, and I grasped that he meant it was only a bumpy track. Then he curved his right hand around to the left and held it up like a policeman stopping traffic. Presumably he meant that I should stop there and would find the

Jarvis villa. It was a graphic instruction, easy to follow, and I admired his skill. "*Grazzi*," I thanked him in Maltese and I smiled in what I thought was my most winning way, but expressions of black hostility were fixed on the faces of all the men. Either I or Edgar Jarvis was not popular with the fishermen and I didn't see how it could be me, unless it had something to do with being my father's daughter. I hadn't been here long enough to give offense. And surely there wasn't a fisherman alive who would not get on well with Dad.

Swallowing unease, I got back into the car and followed those silent instructions. They were exactly right. I left the Victoria road just out of Xlendi, wound in between two farmhouses and along a bumpy track potholed and scattered with sand and stones which had tumbled from the dry dikes on either side of the road. Once I stopped the car and listened. There were larks singing, and I could hear a distant bleat of a goat or two. Nothing else. Heat thrummed into the car. It felt like a sauna bath but there would be no invigorating leap into cold water. I moved off, turning a corner, and found a flattened passing place with a few prickly pears struggling for existence alongside and room for a couple of cars. Further along the track there was another level stretch like a small lay-by but I wondered how often cars met on the road. I had seen no one, heard nothing. It was not an attractive route and so far as I knew it led nowhere, except to Edgar Jarvis's house, so there was nothing to bring the tourists. Perhaps Noni and her father met head-on occasionally. I wondered which of them would back up.

Another bend and I could see the Villa Melita—a pitched roof of green tiles, a long spread of white building with walled garden, carved stone balconies, blue and white candy-striped awnings on the lower windows and white painted shutters on upper rooms. As I approached, I caught glimpses of greenery trailing the top of the garden walls, and when I stopped the car outside the arched gateway to gaze in disbelief at the heart-catching loveliness of the place, I could even hear the ultimate, hot-country delight: the splashing of cool water. A fountain.

The gate, of wrought iron and with a heavy lock, stood open, and I edged the car through onto a large sweep of yellow gravel, raked and clean. At the side of the house I glimpsed a yard with two cars standing in the shade— father's and daughter's—with a man hosing suds off them. He was short, thickset and dark. My casual glance became a stare of searching intensity, and with astonishment I recognized him as the man I'd seen by the cliff path. Now that I faced him in a good light, I felt certain he was also the man who had seen me arrive at the airport in Malta and who had come to Gozo in Noni's car. He glanced at me now, his expression impassive, and went on with his job. I left my car and would have challenged him but Edgar Jarvis himself came out of the house to greet me, holding out a hand, taking mine, shaking it.

"I ought to have sent a car for you," he said. "I can't think why I didn't arrange it that way. It is a Godforsaken route up here—but not too dreary on arrival, eh?"

"Far from dreary. It is beautiful." I could not resist a backward glance at the man working with the cars. "I think I've seen your manservant before."

"Alfio Marcello? On such a small island, it is quite likely."

I wanted to add that I had seen him also in Malta, but decided against it.

Edgar Jarvis led me indoors. He was wearing pale-blue trousers and a matching cotton shirt which accentuated his blue eyes. The wealth of white hair looked healthily groomed and he was, of course, deeply tanned. A handsome man, I thought again, and wondered that he had remained a widower. His wife had died a long time ago, I believed, but he was vigorous and plenty of women would find him attractive. His surroundings, the trappings of a wealthy, leisured man, could be desirable too.

We went through a large hall with a pale tiled floor. The few pieces of heavy black oak furniture were probably Italian, but in the drawing room chairs were covered in soothing chintz and great vases of flowers stood everywhere. Sliding glass windows opened onto a terrace with garden beyond, and there was an irregularly shaped swimming pool at one side. Flower beds were filled with roses, black-eyed Susans, sunflowers and Michaelmas daisies, an incredible show for this baked island. There was even a lawn, but of camomile, I thought. The effect was beautiful, like a corner of England set down in strange Gozo. A spray was whirling and rocking gently, scattering its fine mist of life-giving water on the flowers.

A slim figure rose from a lounger by the pool and came toward us. Noni, golden and glorious with brief strips of purple fabric stretched tightly on upper and lower regions of her anatomy and hiding very little. Her skin gleamed with oil and every inch of her was perfection. She allowed me a good look before pulling on a pink robe.

I had to admit that for beauty she was in world class, but I managed to greet her with cool poise. We did not shake hands. I glanced past her but could see no one else. She read my thoughts, of course.

"We invited Michael, but he was unable to come."

I smiled, absently, as if her remark had not registered, but it was intended to jab and, for a moment, it succeeded.

Not in the way Noni wanted, though. I felt only relief that I would not have to face Michael here.

"If you would like to swim, I am sure Noni could lend you something," Edgar Jarvis offered, but I shook my head.

"I am swimming a great deal at the hotel. But your pool is lovely, and the garden a miracle. It must take a great deal of work to keep it like this. And a lot of water."

"Alfio is good with growing things and there is another man who helps. As for the water, I chose this site for the house after finding very deep wells—two of them." He turned. "Let us have tea indoors—the heat is intense today. It cannot be long before we have a storm."

I laughed. "Everyone keeps saying that, but I am beginning to think it will pass us by."

Edgar Jarvis looked up at the sky and his mouth was set in a somber line. "It will not pass us. And it will be severe. These Mediterranean storms can be terrible—terrible."

I was silent, remembering my mother. I had good reason to know that he was speaking the truth.

Edgar Jarvis, a perceptive man, changed the subject by saying, "I hope you are comfortable at the Hotel Tramonto?"

"Very. It is an excellent hotel."

"Good. Good." Something clouded his blue eyes for a moment. "Like many young people Randal was . . . unsettled for some time. He wanted to be a professional singer, you know, and trained for years, but of course . . ." He shrugged. "I'm glad he seems to be making something of the hotel." He did not sound convinced.

Afternoon tea was very much in the English mode. A silver teapot, hot-water jug, sugar and cream were brought in on a tray. The china was fine Wedgwood. There were tiny tomato and egg sandwiches, buttered scones, and little almond cakes. I might have been in any comfortable English country house, except for the maid—a dark, silent figure that I recognized from the Xaghra bar. She was the same woman who had been sitting with husband or brother, and who had responded to Randal's greeting only with a nod. Still unsmiling and dressed in black, she now had shoes upon her feet instead of sandals tied with laces.

"Thank you, Maria," Noni said, dismissing her, and without having uttered one word the woman withdrew. I saw no reason to mention that I had seen her before, so instead I remarked that I liked the pictures which were hanging in the room. One was obviously a view of the Citadel in Victoria, painted from across a pattern of farm fields, and all were landscapes.

"I'm glad you like them" Edgar Jarvis said. "They're all by Maltese painters. I amuse myself by trying to spot the young painter whose work may be valuable one day. Your father preferred prints, or good copies. He had an excellent copy of a Modigliani which I wouldn't mind owning, but I believe he sold it."

I took a tomato sandwich from the dish he was holding out to me, laid it on the small plate in my lap and reached sideways to take the cup of tea that Noni proffered.

"You did say cream and no sugar?"

"Yes. Thank you."

Edgar Jarvis offered sandwiches to his daughter, accepted a cup of tea with neither cream nor sugar and returned to his chair near the window.

"He hasn't sold it," I said after a moment.

I might have imagined tension in the air, but it seemed

tangible enough to me and Jarvis hesitated before saying easily, "Indeed? I thought he'd told me he'd . . ." He took a bite out of an egg sandwich and swallowed it before finishing, "parted with it." He ate another morsel quickly and added, "If you ever want a buyer, let me know. I rather like that picture."

I laughed. "All right. I can't say it is my taste so I may take you up on your offer."

He looked pleased and Noni looked politely bored.

An astute man, Edgar Jarvis sensed that Noni and I would not want to spend much time in each other's company, so after tea he offered to show me around the house and garden. We started with the garden and Noni disappeared upstairs—to change, she said.

The back of the house faced southwest and the sun was sending dazzling shafts of light through the branches of an olive tree. Part of the garden was in shade, but the swimming pool had been sited in full sunlight and the water shimmered invitingly. I was beginning to wonder how soon I could decently leave and return to the hotel for a swim. The offer of one of Noni's bikinis had not appealed to me and was not repeated.

Edgar Jarvis was a knowledgeable gardener and seemed to know the botanical name for everything, while admitting that he didn't do much work. "I potter a little, but I am not like your father. He was a creative gardener, creative in all kinds of things. Everyone will miss him . . . universally liked . . . If there is anything that I can do . . ."

To my horror, I found that I was feeling faint. The conventional words of sympathy came at me in waves, now loud, now soft. I hoped I was not being rude but it was either get out of the sun or admit my indisposition. Jarvis was being kind to me. If he suspected that I was not well he would try to detain me, make me rest, and I wanted to go. Particularly now that he had started to talk of my father. Seeing Noni with her father had brought back to me the memory of how close I had been to mine. It was obvious that she was a loving and much loved daughter, as I had been, and shamefully envied her because her father was still alive.

Standing in the shade I felt better, dismissed my envious fancies and glanced about me. We were in a yard at the side of the house and I recognized the place where Alfio Marcello had been cleaning the cars. Both vehicles were now in an open garage and Alfio was sitting perched on a low wall near the house. He had a knife in his hands and was paring his nails, but as we appeared he got to his feet and stood, silently, both hands at his sides. Jarvis nodded at him and he nodded back but did not move. I saw stone steps behind the wall, leading down to cellars, I assumed.

"What do you keep down there?" I made conversation to steer the talk away from my father.

"A generator, stores of various kinds, wine. Cellars are useful in hot countries."

I agreed, and made a mental note to explore the farmhouse further. It was bound to have cellars, surely. They would have stored olives and oil and wine there in the old days. And hidden their women when raiders came.

I thought with amusement that the servant standing by the steps looked as if he were on guard duty. Later, the thought was to occur to me again.

"Let us go in," Jarvis said abruptly. "It is too hot even in the shade."

We toured the ground floor of the house then, not hastily but not lingering too long either. I saw the dining room, which was entirely in shade, a long, narrow room with arched windows, each with a gauzy white curtain

154

as well as draperies of blue silk. It was an elegant room and I admired it.

There was a small sitting room, green and white, with a writing desk and, at a corner of the house, a study with an enormous leather-topped desk, a long refectory table and tall bookcases with lawbooks in them along with modern novels and biographies.

"There, that is all, except for the bedrooms." Edgar Jarvis withdrew and I followed him.

"I could not help noticing the lawbooks. Are you a lawyer?"

"A solicitor. Retired. Odd how one clings to earlier trappings."

I said, "The house is very beautiful. Thank you for showing it to me."

"A pleasure. You would like to freshen up?" He rang a bell and Maria came to conduct me upstairs, but Noni appeared above us.

"It's all right, Maria. I will show Miss Prescott where to go."

She was beautifully dressed in a soft, clinging white frock, with her hair brushed to corn silk and her make-up freshly and perfectly applied. Not that she wore a lot, only eye shadow and lip gloss. She looked as fresh as morning.

"I think you'll find everything you want in here." She showed me into a large bathroom, complete with dressing table and chair, and a range of cosmetics and tissues. There were ivory and silver tops to the containers and a very distinguished French name on the cosmetics. I could see why Noni looked as if she had stepped out of *Vogue.*

I washed my hands and from my handbag took a comb and lipstick, resisting the temptation to use an atomizer of a scent which I'd always loved but which was too expensive for me.

The window was open, a shade drawn over it to keep out the sun, and I realized that I must be over the yard where Alfio had been standing. Conversation floated up from below, a quiet voice at first, words indistinguishable but tones taut with anger.

I heard a reply from Alfio, stubborn, also angry. "It was not there."

A murmur again. Then: "No, sir. Nowhere in the house. I searched."

The first voice, Edgar Jarvis's, was raised now, and it said in tight fury, "Then who took it away? And who put it back? Had you any hand in this, Marcello?"

I heard no reply. They had moved away, perhaps, or dropped their tones, not wanting to be overheard. I certainly did not want *anyone* to know that I had heard their conversation, for I understood what they were talking about. They were discussing the Modigliani and its disappearance. Also its reappearance, evidently unknown to Edgar Jarvis until I mentioned it during tea.

My hands were perspiring. I ran the cold tap, making as much noise as I could, and put my wrists into the water to cool them. The high level of pent-up rage in Edgar Jarvis's voice was in sharp contrast to the urbane tones he had used with me. It frightened me. I wanted to get out of this house and above all I wanted no one to know that I might have overheard words not intended for my ears.

When I emerged from the bathroom I found Noni hovering near the top of the stairs. She looked hard at me, but I had recovered my composure and I asked, "Have you been waiting for me? I am so sorry."

She relaxed and led the way downstairs, trailing one brown hand on the banister. "Have you seen much of Michael?" she threw over her shoulder in an overcasual way.

"Not much. He took me out to lunch once. I daresay he told you. And I showed him the farmhouse."

"Did you?" She turned her head, quickly, to look at me as she spoke, but must have found my expression unreadable. I was becoming expert at hiding my feelings. More expert than Noni. She had known about the lunch, but not about the visit to the farmhouse.

Edgar Jarvis had recovered his charm, and he and Noni both came to the car with me, received my thanks with deprecating gestures and waved goodbye. As I drove out of the arched gate I felt as if I were escaping from some nameless threat. A visit which had begun happily and calmly had become supercharged with tension.

I wanted to drive fast but on that road it was not possible, so I kept going at a steady pace, putting distance between myself and the Jarvis house until I came to the second of the passing places. A car was parked there, and when I glanced quickly sideways I saw that it was a police car with two men in it. I had no way of knowing their business but remembered having told Inspector Rapa that I was to visit Edgar Jarvis this afternoon. Even the glimpse I caught was enough for me to recognize the young policeman who had brought the MG back to me, and I knew that he had recognized me also. Well, it was of no importance. I had been out to tea—an innocent enough way to spend the afternoon. Except that the last few minutes of my visit had made me wonder if the Jarvis family were other than they seemed. On the surface they were urbane, charming, moneyed and leisured.

Beneath simmered something which had nothing to do with peaceful retirement from business to a warm climate, a beautiful garden, a lovely home.

᠅. ᠅. ᠅.

I needed my swim that evening, for I felt sticky with heat, but I did not enjoy it as much as usual. Any therapeutic value was minimized by a mind seething with questions which had no answers. I looked for Randal but he was nowhere to be seen. Even when I came down to dinner he was not about, so I took dinner alone. A young couple who spoke French occupied a table next to mine, near a window. They were greatly absorbed in each other and scarcely had eyes to look about them. I felt a brief pang of longing for days I had known, submerged in my love for Michael.

I scarcely tasted my food. I felt hot and restless and very thirsty. A long glass of lime juice with ice tasted delicious. I had a second and skipped coffee.

As I passed through the hall I could see Randal in the small office to which Carmela retreated when she was not at the counter. I wanted to ask if she was still unwell. I wanted to ask a lot of things about the family Randal had so little to do with, but he seemed busy and harassed and he didn't look up. After a moment's hesitation I went out by myself.

I stood on the terrace, then walked round the swimming pool, wondering how to fill the next hour or so. It was too early to go upstairs. Not for the first time I thought that being in a hotel on one's own was a wretched business. I had seen so much of it in London. Determinedly bright ladies, touring alone and coping with tickets, foreign money, strange regulations. Men who seemed lost, perhaps recently bereaved and mistakenly thinking it would do them good to get away from familiar surroundings for a while.

Down in the bay it would be airless tonight, I thought, so instead of walking that way I would go out over the rocks, toward the sea, and catch whatever vestige of breeze there might be. There was a moon. I could see well enough.

The smell of salt was strong in my nostrils and became stronger as I got closer to the water. I ought to have changed my shoes—the ones I was wearing were not suited to walking on furrowed and seamed rock—but I managed well enough by avoiding the worst fissures and skirting patches of the strange succulent growing here and there, feeding on heaven knew what. The sky was crowded with stars so brilliant that they gave an incredible amount of silvery light. It seemed to fall on the island in a powdery haze, adding to the wash of moonlight.

I found a gently sloping ledge a score of feet from the edge of the cliff—not a high or menacing cliff, but not one I wanted to fall over, either. In the ledge there was a hollow which looked like a good place to rest for a while, so I sat and looked up at the sky. The powdery effect was greater now, and I realized that it was caused by a very slight haze. Was the heralded storm coming?

The sea was calm. Small waves were boring into funnels of rock below, rattling stones around, but the sound was not angry—rather desultory really, yet insistent, hypnotic. My thoughts strayed to the farmhouse. I would not feel any lonelier there than I did in the hotel. Tidying the house and looking after my own needs would give me something to do. As for the search for clues to my father's death, I had discovered nothing and yet was more convinced than ever that I still ought to try. I felt no anxiety to return to London.

Out on the sea there moved a small white triangle, the sail of a yacht making for the harbor at Xlendi Bay. Then came a subdued muttering throb and a powerboat made its way out, low in the water, not traveling fast. Once beyond the bay, the engine was cut. A few minutes later it started up again, roaring to life, and even in pearly starlight I could see the creaming wake—two wakes, one from the powerboat and one a measured distance behind it. A water-skier. They curved and swooped, out of sight, and I forgot about them. Not far away, I could hear the scrape of leather on rock. Someone else was not wearing suitable shoes for rock-walking.

A few yards to my left, a hunched figure dragged itself over the lip of the cliff and scrambled to full height. It was Harry Stark. We stared at each other, and during those few long seconds I became aware that his mood was in marked contrast to mine. Idly watching the sea, the two small craft and a water-skier, I had forgotten my troubles and fallen into a reverie. Whatever Stark had been watching had thrown him into an absolute fury, and seeing me there did nothing to diminish his anger. Indeed, it seemed to add to it. He started for me, growling something, then his voice roared out, "You again! You're everywhere, aren't you?"

I jumped to my feet, alarmed, wanting to get away but not knowing which way to run. If I made for the hotel in a direct line, such were the convolutions of the headland that inevitably I would cross his path. I hesitated, horribly frightened and not knowing why. Then I turned and began to run blindly along a ledge parallel to the clifftop. My mind was racing, trying to recapture what I had seen in daylight of this expanse of rock. I hadn't been over as far as this before, but I was sure the ledge curved toward Xlendi Bay. Further round, there might be more people and I would be safe. I ran, stumbling, out of breath through sheer fright.

"Come back! I want to talk to you!"

If talk was all he wanted, there was no harm in it. But this man frightened me. I did not know why, for though he was boorish, rude, a type I intensely disliked,, there was no reason for him to threaten me. I hesitated and half turned.

"Come back, you little bitch!"

In shouting abuse, he'd convinced me that, dangerous or not, I didn't want to be any closer to him than I was now. Especially out on rough ground in near-darkness. I ran as fast as I could. Then I paused for a moment to take off my shoes and cast them aside. In bare feet I could make quicker time even if it hurt.

"Stop! Alexa, stop!" It was a different voice, not behind me but to my right. Michael's voice! I paused, but the pounding feet behind me sent me running headlong again. Michael was far away, Stark close to me now, and all I could think about was getting away.

"Alexa, come back. You'll go over the cliff!" Nearer now, alarmed and authoritative, Michael commanded me. He had the expert knowledge of a geologist. If he said I was heading for a cliff, I was. I swerved toward him, sobbing in terror, and miraculously the sound of feet behind me died. Still running, I turned to look over my shoulder. Stark had gone. Disappeared! I was frozen to the spot, wordless, shaking.

Then Michael reached me, and immediately he put his arms around me, pulled me close against his hard, strong body and held until the shaking ceased. My physical and mental awareness had been concentrated on the nameless threat from Stark. Now it was on Michael and the old, familiar curves of his body as they fitted mine. His embrace, at first spelling only safety to me, became something I had longed for ever since seeing him at Mgärr Harbor. I wanted to press closer, but with an effort I broke away. He held only my upper arms then, staring down at me, his eyes moving over my face in a kind of hunger. His lips were slightly parted and his breath was warm on my cheek.

To break the spell I spoke. "I was being followed. Did you see?" I twisted my head to look over my shoulder, fear returning.

Michael nodded. "You poor darling." His voice was very gentle as he then said, "Who was he? A prowler?"

"No. No, it was not like that. He is staying in the hotel. He keeps talking to me . . . I was running away. Oh, Michael, if you hadn't come. Was I really heading for the edge?"

"Yes. Not at a very high point, but there's a chasm below that I wouldn't recommend for falling into. Come and see." He spoke lightly and walked me over the rock for a few yards, our steps falling into a rhythm that neither of us had forgotten.

It was a very nasty vertical drop and in my blind rush I would undoubtedly have gone right over, to fall twenty or thirty feet and probably break a leg or two in the process, at the very least. I shuddered.

"If you hadn't come, I'd be down there now." I was choking. To my shame, tears rolled silently down my face.

"But I did come and you're all right." Michael's hand touched my cheek, his fingers wiping dry first one and then the other, then curving round my chin. His other arm went round me. "Darling," he said.

"No!" I cried. "No!" I would be lost if we kissed.

"Yes," he said. "You want to as much as I do. You want to, Alexa."

I did. I did.

He pulled me against him again, and this time his body did not feel hard because I melted against it and lifted my hands to the back of his neck where the dark hair grew crisply, just as I remembered it. My fingers knew the nape, the bony lump above it, and my hands and arms knew the immense breadth and strength of his shoulders. It was a long time before sanity returned. Minutes of kissing and murmuring, of remembered joy and fulfillment and of longing. It was the intensity of my longing which brought me back to my senses. I wanted something that I could not have, or would not have, while it belonged in even a small part to someone else. I pushed Michael from me, staring up at him, at the blurred eyes, deep-set. Their hazel color was dark now and his mouth looked as mine felt.

He tried to draw me closer again and he bent his head to mine, but I kept myself stiff. I could not continue this without yielding utterly.

"Alexa, you still love me," he said, and his low voice was exultant. "You still love me, don't you?"

"I don't know," I said.

He laughed, threw back his head and laughed again. I could see a throbbing pulse in his throat. "Darling, you do know. Oh, you know very well, and so do I."

He hadn't said that he loved me.

"What about Noni?" I asked.

"My engagement is over. Finished." There was a carelessness in the way he spoke, as if it was something entirely in the past and of no importance. I was filled with a cold and immense sadness. Was this how he had referred to me when he went to Noni? In this same uncaring way? He was smiling down at me, expecting me to say I was glad, and his complacence roused in me a fury as intense as my earlier terror. Ever since coming to this island I had been manipulated.

I pushed Michael. It was like pushing a great rock and he did not move, but I thrust at him angrily, then stepped back out of reach. Bitterly, I said, "If your engagement is at an end, then you'd better make it clear to Noni."

"Darling, Noni knows. It was she who broke it off."

"I think she merely cracked it."

"Nonsense."

"Michael, it isn't nonsense and I won't be any part of your life while Noni is still in it."

I walked away then, leaving him. It was hard to do and it hurt. The thought of that drop still made my knees knock. Michael had saved me from hideous injury, perhaps death. Then he had given me something that I longed for—a reawakening. He had renewed emotion and hope, aroused all my most primitive urges. It would have been so easy to forget everything and respond. But I was not the Alexa he used to know. I was made of harder material now. A mirage was of no use to me. I wanted a real, solid, lasting love, or nothing.

I do not think Randal was in his office when I reentered the hotel, but if he was there I might not have noticed. I saw no one. I was in a state of exhausted preoccupation, and it was not until I entered my bedroom that I noticed my bare feet and remembered that I had kicked off my shoes out there on the rock. Well, I was certainly not going back for them.

Chapter 11

I WAKENED very early, before it was fully light, to a noise of distant clamor. There was another noise, too: wind. A growling wind, promising something sterner. I wanted to curl down into the bed and go to sleep again, but I was too cold. I got up to collect a warm blanket which I knew was in the bottom of the wardrobe, but the sound intrigued me and I pulled on my robe and went out onto the balcony.

The sea was heaving like a gray blanket with a restless sleeper beneath it, but it was not choppy. There were no white caps to be seen. The disturbance was coming from the bay, a rumbling, squeaking noise accompanied by excited shouts. Two or three figures broke from the hotel and ran toward Xlendi—young waiters, looking very different in jeans and thick pullovers.

I would not be likely to sleep again and I was consumed with curiosity. I pulled on white cotton slacks and a pink top and cursed that I hadn't had the sense to bring a sweater from England. My white wool coat would flap around and be a nuisance, but I would freeze without it so I put it on.

The front door of the hotel was unlocked, and when I reached a place on the path from which I could see the bay and harbor I found several other hotel guests watching and talking excitedly among themselves. I joined them, but after a while I wanted a closer look. I ran down the winding path, buffeted by the wind and hardly able to believe that this was the place where for days I had been trying in vain to keep reasonably cool. The overnight drop in temperature must have been thirty degrees.

An urgent shouting was coming from crowds of fishermen and villagers. Every man present was helping to pull boats out of the water and lay them up safely on land. I saw waiters from our hotel among them. The squeaking sounds I had heard on wakening came from an enormous winch, hand-operated, which was laboriously pulling a large, painted fishing boat out of the harbor and onto the quay. Even with half a dozen men at each side of the boat, muscles knotted with effort, it was a slow business and most of the shouting centered around this operation, with instructions and counter-instructions issued, contradicted, altered and finally obeyed.

The same kind of thing must have happened in Malta during my years there, unless the storm they expected was something far worse than usual, but I had not seen such safety precautions as these before. Already there were a score of boats neatly laid up alongside the road and it seemed as if everything that floated was being taken from the water. Brown, sturdy figures dressed in an assortment of old trousers, mostly blue, and thick jerseys of all colors ran about busy as ants, hauling, pushing, coiling ropes, piling nets and fish traps. Yet the sea down here in the sheltered bay did not look angry. It rolled a bit, but that was all. The wind was nowhere near gale force. If I hadn't been taught to have a healthy respect for the Mediterranean from an early age, I would have thought that the local population had gone mad. But in spite of myself I felt a curl of fear as I watched. In the sky, rags of cloud raced in from the north. In places there were solid banks, mountains of gray.

The earlier heat and humidity had led me to believe that if we had a storm it would be the sirocco, the *xlokk*, from the south, but this was the gregale, the dreaded Greek wind, the shipwreck wind. It was the gregale which drove St. Paul himself ashore in what is known still as St. Paul's Bay, Malta. It wrecked the ship in which he was journeying to his trial in Rome, and in Maltese eyes the momentous truth of that historic event is as fresh as if it had happened recently, instead of over nineteen hundred years ago. Devotion to St. Paul is profound; the islanders will tell you that never, since his stay on the island, has a snakebite been fatal.

A fragment of bone from the apostle's elbow is mounted in a golden arm and kept in St. Paul's Church at Rabat in Malta. I hoped now that faith in the power of the relic would protect sailors in this approaching twentieth-century storm. Meanwhile, Gozitan fishermen were doing all they could to protect their craft and everyone else's, and this harbor to the south of Gozo in any case would not suffer so greatly as Marsalforn, to the north.

"Alexa, what are you doing here?" A man in a thick-knit cream pullover and brown trousers broke from a group which had finished winching a powerboat ashore. "You're cold!" he exclaimed as he reached me.

I was shivering in spite of the wool coat which I hugged about me, but some of my shivers were of excitement at the air of urgency all about me.

"I came to watch."

The wind was blowing Randal's brown hair back from his face, giving it a sculpted look. My long dark hair was blowing forward as I faced him and I had to keep pushing it back, holding it, brushing it from my mouth. Randal was watching my movements and once he half lifted a hand as if he wanted to brush my hair back for me, but he dropped his hand again and took my elbow instead. "Come," he said, turning me around. "You're cold and I have to get back and help supervise breakfast. Half the waiters are out here helping, and who can blame them? The boat owners are fathers or uncles or brothers. I've told them they may stay until the job is finished."

"Will they take *all* the boats out of the water?"

Randal nodded. "Every one."

I shook my head in amazement, then said, "Well, you need not worry too much about breakfast. A lot of the hotel guests are out watching."

"Good. That will spread the load a bit. I can see myself doing some cooking today. One of the chefs has joined the sea-rescue party at the harbor."

"How is Carmela? I saw you in the office last night."

"Carmela is at the hospital in Victoria. Appendicitis."

"Oh, no!"

"Yes. But she's all right. They operated last night and when I telephoned they said it was quite straightforward."

Not a word about the inconvenience to himself. He was a kind man, I thought. And if he had been unsettled in his youth, he did not seem to be so now. I wondered if he regretted becoming an hôtelier instead of a singer. Except when he talked of his father, he seemed to be happy.

We passed the other hotel guests and many of the staff who usually looked after them. The Islanders' priorities were firmly with their families in this time of crisis, and Randal appeared to think this was natural and right. I felt a glow of warmth toward him and when we entered the hotel, regaining our breath in the still hallway out of the wind, I smiled when he said, "See you later," and instead of going to my room I hung my coat in the hallway and followed him down the passage which led to the kitchen.

There was a tangy smell of coffee and the big Cona machines were healthily full and hot. The sole remaining chef was cracking eggs with one hand and beating them with a wire whisk held in the other. He greeted Randal with a shout and a broad grin, which widened as he caught sight of me following behind. Randal swung around. "What are you doing here?"

"That's what you asked me at the harbor. *Then* I was watching. This time I'm here for the action. What can I do?"

Randal did not argue. He handed me a large white apron and pointed to the grills and toasters. Orders sang out over the kitchen from the two waitresses who were the only ones left in the dining room. Orders which were picked up by kitchen staff and chef, repeated and acted upon. Written slips were spiked, and those who had their appointed tasks were managing to fit in other duties as well. I loved being back in an atmosphere I knew well.

Randal was everywhere at once, pouring orange juice, collecting coffeepots and filling them, stacking trays and carrying them out himself. I could hear his cheerful voice explaining to those guests who had not gone outside what was happening and why. "Nothing to worry about," I heard him say.

During a lull, he took a tray of croissants from the oven, put two on a plate and brought them to me, together with a cup of steaming coffee. "Here, eat while you work."

"Only if you do."

I don't know what made me say it. The stricture made something personal of my helping hand and I had not meant to be personal, but I knew he was under strain and would have a great deal to do. It seemed important that someone should make him eat and no one here would be likely to take it upon himself to do that. Carmela might have, but Carmela was in the hospital.

Randal stared at me. He had peeled off his thick pullover and was wearing a cream linen jacket over his dark trousers, so that he was dressed for the dining room as well as the kitchen. I thought again how efficient he was at his job, and how happy he seemed, and I wondered why his father should have any doubts about him.

"All right," he said slowly. "I'll eat too." He brought two more croissants and poured another cup of coffee. Then, glancing over his shoulder at me, he said, puzzled, "It's a long time since anyone asked me to have something to eat . . ." He sipped his coffee and grinned suddenly, his gray eyes sparkling. " 'Only if you do' sounds much nicer than 'Will you take breakfast now, sir?' "

"Well, I rather liked your 'Here, eat while you work.' "

Neither of us said anything more. We ate our rolls and drank our coffee quickly, the scalding liquid burning our throats, and with another exchanged smile we went about our business, working quickly until everyone had breakfasted.

"There's still someone to come." I eyed a numbered disc which still hung on its hook on the wall.

Randal glanced at it. "Our friend Stark," he said. "Sometimes he misses breakfast."

I had almost forgotten, in the mad rush, the events of the night before. Not Michael, of course. I had not forgotten Michael, only banished him temporarily to the back of my mind. But the horror which led up to his passionate embraces had been forced right out, and now, remembering, I felt as if I had lost color. Perhaps I had, for Randal said quickly, "You don't like him."

"No."

"Did you know him before you came here?" The worried frown was back between Randal's brows, the wariness again clouding his eyes.

I shook my head. "I had never met him before he arrived here."

"Keep away from him," Randal said urgently. "He's dangerous."

I recalled the night before. While running away from Harry Stark I had courted danger and been saved only by Michael. Which in itself, perhaps, would prove dangerous for me.

I forced a smile. "I'll try to keep away from him because I don't like him," I answered. "But why do you think he's dangerous?" What I really wanted to know was why Harry Stark should think *I* was a threat. I remembered his angry shout on the cliff: "You're everywhere, aren't you?" It was coincidence that we should keep meeting, but he did not think so.

The kitchen staff were eating their own breakfast at a small table in the corner. We could not be overheard. Carefully choosing his words, Randal said, "I know some of his associates. They're an unscrupulous lot. You're a nice girl, Alexa. I would not like to see you getting mixed up in their affairs."

I thought it better not to answer, for he might be alluding to his own father and I had no wish to be drawn into a family quarrel. "Randal, if there's nothing more to do here, I'll go and pack."

"Pack!" he said, horrified. "But you can't leave now that the storm is so near. You *must* stay here where you'll be safe."

Again I thought of last night. I would have to stay in the public rooms of the hotel to feel safe. My bedroom, the rocky headland out there, both had unpleasant associations for me now, and Stark had earlier accosted me down by the bay when I was with Randal himself. It was the members of the Jarvis family who attracted Stark's venom and the Jarvises could look after themselves. I would feel safer and happier in that peaceful, solid old farmhouse which had withstood a hundred storms in the past and would withstand a hundred more. "I'm sorry," I said. "There are reasons . . . I must go this morning, as I planned."

"Then let me come with you."

I laughed. "Goodness, no! You have your hands full here, but if you could just let me have my bill I'll settle it before I leave. Oh, and one more thing . . ."

"Anything."

"Could you telephone Mr. Bartola for me and say that his car is here to be collected? Inspector Rapa tells me that is the usual way. And the police have returned my father's old MG so I shall use that now."

"Certainly I'll attend to that for you." Randal still seemed as if he wanted to persuade me not to go, but he did not say any more.

I packed in no time, leaving the hotel room cloaked once more in impersonal comfort. Individuality, I thought, that's what hotel bedrooms lack. Perhaps it could only be supplied by an occupant, but occupants seldom stayed long enough to provide it.

Randal was at the desk when I went down and to my relief he had prepared the bill. I'd thought I was going to have an argument about it. "You could leave for Malta," he said as he receipted it. "The ferry is still running. I just checked with Bartola."

I shook my head, then looked Randal straight in the eye. "Everyone I talk to is anxious for me to leave Gozo," I said crisply. "But I am not going to leave. Not until I am ready and that won't be for some time yet. Tell them that."

"Tell whom?" He was more angry than surprised.

"Anyone who asks." I hadn't had much sleep and I was becoming snappish, but I controlled myself. "I'm sorry about Carmela," I offered. "I hope she will soon be better."

"I'll pass on your good wishes."

"What shall I do about the car?"

"I'll deal with that for you."

"But I owe something."

"I owe you something for helping out in the kitchen this morning." He softened slightly. "It was so good of you to give such practical help."

"No trouble. I was trained in all departments and the kitchen is one of my favorites. Such drama!"

He laughed then. "Yes, often there is. Today was relatively calm in spite of the crisis."

In my experience, hotel staff, like other human beings, often responded magnificently when there was a real emergency but were quite impossible in the face of constant pricks of annoyance by even one difficult guest.

"Or because of it!"

"Yes, perhaps because of it." Randal knew what I meant.

Suddenly he bent and picked up something from the floor behind the counter. "I found these early this morning, out on the cliff. They're yours, aren't they?" He was holding the shoes I had kicked off in such terror the night before.

I caught my breath and swallowed, my throat dry. "Yes, they're mine. Thank you." It was a wooden response and I knew it, but if I tried to explain why my shoes had been left outside all night I would become emotional. I felt that the choice was between being boorish and saying too little, or being indiscreet and saying too much, so I chose the former. I took the shoes from Randal and thrust them into my case, again thanking him. He watched me, then came round the desk to pick up the case and my father's binoculars. I lifted my coat and handbag.

Randal looked at me with a kind of grim reassurance, as if he were trying to show that he wouldn't hold it against me that I'd given no explanation for leaving my elegant shoes lying outside on the rocks all night. Probably he thought that I'd had an amorous encounter, and if so he was not that far wrong. Only there'd been another encounter first.

"What about the hired car?" I asked, still pressing, still unhappy about not paying for it.

"What a fuss! I have telephoned. They'll collect it this morning. I'll settle it for you and let you know what you owe me."

"If you forget, I shall ask Mr. Bartola," I warned him, but he only laughed.

The wind had dropped slightly, but the sky was still sullen and I felt edgy and depressed. Though secretly I was not looking forward with all that much pleasure to being alone and cut off if the storm proved to be a bad one, I had been so stubbornly independent about going to the farmhouse that I could not back out now. The other thing needling me was that I'd expected to hear from

174 ☙

Michael this morning and there'd been no word at all. I could not bring myself to ask Randal if there had been any telephone calls. He would know at once who I was thinking of. There was no one else on the island who might telephone except the police, and police messages were not forgotten. Not that I was likely to receive any more of those. My contact with the police had ceased now.

Randal stowed my case on the back seat of the car and laid the binoculars on top of it. "Will that do?"

"Yes, thanks." I threw in my coat and handbag, and got in myself. "You've been very kind." I held out my hand.

Randal took it. His grasp was firm and secure. "If I could do more, I would," he said. "Will you remember that?"

"Yes, I will, thank you."

He stood back and thrust his hands deep into the pockets of the brown trousers. A small gust of wind flapped the cloth back against his legs and I realized that he was too thin. He looked very fit even when tired but his slenderness was in sharp contrast to Michael's muscular strength.

I drove off with the wind coming chill through the open window, thinking as I wound down the hill that Randal had not even asked about my visit to his father.

At the bay an extraordinary sight met my eyes. Boats by the score, all shapes and sizes, covered the ground in serried ranks, lashed together and to the trees along the waterfront. The water of the bay was empty. There was something weird about it.

As I took the last bend into Xlendi, the church clock struck eleven. I was cold. I thought of putting my coat on, but a coat was a nuisance driving. Deciding to stop at Rosa's to buy a warm sweater, I parked outside her shop, collected my handbag and got out.

"Ah, you leave Gozo?" Rosa came to greet me and threw up her hands as she glanced into the back of the car and saw my case. I thought she seemed pleased.

"No. I'm not leaving Gozo."

"But the last ferry will run soon, before the storm comes."

"I thought the storm had come this morning, but now it is quieter." I looked up at the gray sky. It had a brooding quality, and it seemed as if the little island were crouching, waiting prepared for whatever disaster might assail it.

Rosa looked up also, her experienced eye taking in more details than I knew anything about. "The storm will come tomorrow," she pronounced with conviction. I did not doubt her.

"Then I shall want a warm sweater," I said.

"Ah!" She flung delighted hands together in a mighty clap. "Come! Come in and see what I have."

She led me into the deep recesses of the shop, where one small lamp was burning fitfully against the gloom. I thought that going in there in order to *see* was a contradiction in terms. Well, no matter, I could take the sweaters to the door to have a better look.

"First, a cup of tea to warm you," Rosa said, and I gratefully accepted, thinking only of the hot drink and forgetting the local addition of quantities of sweet condensed milk. It was hot all the same, and I was glad of it.

Sipping her own tea, Rosa turned over one after the other of a pile of sweaters, all of which, she assured me, were my size. There was no sizing on them as we know it, but I judged that she was right and pulled out two or three—one white, one deep purple and a very thick one the color of clotted cream.

"Did you enjoy going to the beautiful house of Mr. Jarvis yesterday?" Rosa asked. The expression on her seamed face was unreadable.

"Yes, I did." Again I felt a stirring of unease. It seemed as if my movements were always known. "How did you know I'd been there?" Even to myself I sounded aggressively suspicious.

Rosa spread her expressive hands. "But of course I would know. Maria told me. My daughter. You have seen her here at night, knitting." Rosa pointed to the dark corner of her shop. "Maria tells me everything."

Holding a sweater in one hand, the cup of tea in the other, I linked up in my mind *three* times that I had seen Maria: here, at Edgar Jarvis's and in the bar in Xaghra. So *that* was why she had seemed familiar in Xaghra. I had seen her here earlier.

Rosa read my thoughts. "And you have seen her in Xaghra with her brother Joseph. My Joseph. He has a farm near Ramla Bay. He is a good boy." Pride glowed in her eyes and then the glow faded as she added broodingly, "But he, too, works for Mr. Jarvis sometimes." She scowled. "He does not talk about it." She flapped her arms like a black crow and changed the subject. "He worked for your father, too."

"Doing what?" I was astonished.

"Making the garden, cleaning stone, everything. He is a good boy. Not clever, but good."

I decided that Joseph might be a useful man to know, and asked for his address. Laying my cup down I fished pen and notebook out of my bag and wrote down a stream of instructions which did not add up to an address but presumably described where Joseph could be found when asleep. It was a hut near a rock shaped like a man's head, near the end of Ramla Bay and ten minutes' walk up into the fields from the shore. I gathered he worked late and early, and did not sleep much.

"I expect I shall see him around," I said philosophically, and she nodded. As I put my pen away, I saw one of Mr. Bartola's cars going past, two men inside, up toward the Tramonto. He was losing no time in collecting his car and I wished I had waited and paid for it myself. I knew I would have to argue with Randal again about that.

I started to try on the sweaters, which slipped easily over the top I was wearing and felt very comforting. The mirror was adequate, if no more, and I could see that the woolens were beautifully knitted and, as Rosa had predicted, the right size.

"Does Maria enjoy working for Mr. Jarvis?" I asked. I had often thought how unhappy she looked, and I was curious.

Rosa gave another of her expressive shrugs. "Enjoy? For a woman, what is enjoyment? How to find it, without children?"

I was puzzled.

"Alfio Marcello is her husband, so she is with him in employment. It is her duty. But there are no children and Alfio, a Sicilian, blames my Maria." Rosa crossed herself, adding with a sigh, "Certainly he has fathered children with others. Poor Maria. It is God's will, but poor Maria."

Yes, poor Maria, with her huge, sad eyes. I murmured something in sympathy and picked up a hip-length sweater in bright gorse-yellow, with great, twisting cables from neck to hem. As I struggled into it, my head emerging through the neck, I saw the car which had been mine for three days going by, driven by Mr. Bartola's assistant, followed by the newer car driven by Bartola himself. In spite of the cold, the top was down and Mr. Bartola's shiny bald head with its fringe of black hair was clearly visible. He waved to a man who was working on one of the fishing boats.

"This one," I said to Rosa as I saw myself in the yellow sweater. "I'll have this one and I'll keep it on. How much?"

"For you, ten pounds."

I forked out without arguing over the price, I was so thankful for the warmth.

"Miss Prescott."

"Yes, Rosa?"

"You go to catch the ferry for Malta?" She was looking into the MG, at my father's binoculars.

"No. I'm going to stay at my father's house."

She frowned, deeply disturbed. "Don't go, Miss Prescott. Don't go to that lonely place. Leave Gozo."

"Rosa, did you put that note under my door? Did you?"

I imagined that she had changed, reverted to the sinister crone I had first seen in her, and I stepped closer, demanding an answer to my question.

"What note? What door?" Angrily, she shook my hand off her arm and hurried, muttering, to a door at the back of the shop. She was going to leave me here!

As she opened the door I was surprised to see a pretty, walled garden. But Rosa was surprised by something else and she gave a shriek of fear. Alfio Marcello was standing there and clearly he had been listening. Without a word, his eyes burning with anger, he pushed past both of us, went out into the street, collected a cup of coffee from a neighboring café and seated himself on an upturned boat near the entrance to the shop. From there, he watched us with a scowling, unwinking gaze.

Rosa came back into the shop, slamming the door to the garden and plunging us both into half-darkness again. She came to stand near me by the roadway, hands on hips, and screamed Maltese words at Alfio that I could not understand. "*Mur 'L Hemm. Kemm int cattiv!*" He glared at her, still silent.

She turned to me. "He is always watching, always waiting and spying."

"But why?"

"For Noni! For Noni!" She flung up her hand and rolled her eyes upward.

Alfio shouted something, his tongue loosened at last, but she made a gesture of contempt at him and leaned closer to me. "Mr. Brent wrote to you in London, no?"

"Yes."

Intensity burned in her eyes. "He wants to buy the house, no?"

"Yes. For a client."

"For himself, for a client, what matter? He wants you to stay away from Gozo. But Noni tell him that the letter he wrote to you will *bring* you to Gozo and he is a fool. She is cunning, that one." Rosa was stabbing at my collarbone with a clawed forefinger, emphasizing the words. "So when Noni go to Valletta, shopping, she send Alfio to Luqa, to watch for you."

"*Every* plane?" I simply did not believe it.

"No no no. Not every plane. When she go shopping in Malta. So you will not arrive without her knowing." Scorn deepened her voice. "You see him? At Luqa?"

"Yes, I did, but . . ." At the time, I'd thought that the man seemed to be watching for me and yet I could not imagine why, or how he would know me. I still did not know why Noni should set a watch for me. Jealousy? I thought not. She was too confident, too sure of herself.

"How would Alfio know me?" I ridiculed. "He'd never seen me before."

He heard that and with an insolent smirk left his perch on the boat to walk over to us, taking something from his pocket as he came. It was a photograph of me, one I had given Michael. I was so shocked that I reeled, but then I snatched at it, furiously angry. Alfio laughed, pulled it out of reach, thrust it back into his pocket and walked away, but not out of earshot. He was anxious to hear our conversation.

"I don't understand," I said to Rosa, helplessly. "Why should it matter to them whether I come to Gozo or not?"

Rosa felt she had said enough. "Who knows?" she muttered. "Who knows?" And she shuffled into the darkness at the back of the shop. I would get no more from her, especially with Alfio watching. I was afraid of him.

Cold, in spite of my brave new sweater, I drove off. Near Victoria the steep road was partially blocked and made completely impassable by a throng of excited people. I braked the MG, parked and left it, then walked up to the crowd. There had been a road accident. Through a small gap I saw with chilling horror that the car I had been driving right up until today had been hit by the back of a runaway truck. The truck was an ancient vehicle, with rust showing through faded blue paint. The owner had galloped downhill after it, having burst out of his greengrocer's shop. He was loudly protesting his innocence to the shaken driver of the car and to Mr. Bartola who was supporting his employee. The car was badly damaged and had been slewed sideways with the front crushed in.

"What is he saying?" I asked a bystander, a shopkeeper who might, I thought, speak English.

He did. "He says the brakes are good, that someone released them and ran away. An *Englishman*." He snorted. "Is it likely?"

I looked at the car and at the driver, mopping his cut forehead, and I began to shiver. Only the police, and Randal, and Mr. Bartola, had known in advance that I was giving up the car this morning. Someone thought I would still be driving it and had waited near a truck habitually parked outside that shop at the top of the hill. I had seen it there myself, on previous occasions.

Oh, it was likely. It was very likely indeed that someone had released the brakes when my hired Ford came into view. I knew without any doubt that this malevolent act had been directed at me, but I could not begin to guess whose hand had released the brake.

Chapter 12

QUICKLY, I SEARCHED the faces in the crowd, trying vainly to recognize someone who might attempt to injure me. I saw no one I knew, except for kind, concerned Mr. Bartola and the unfortunate driver of the car which had been mine.

I pushed my way toward them and asked if there was anything I could do to help. I was incoherently saying how sorry I was, which led the poor man to feel he had me to soothe also.

"No, no, Miss Prescott, there is nothing. Do not concern yourself. It was an accident and Rico is not badly hurt. How fortunate that you were not driving the car, eh?"

"For me, very fortunate." Feeling sick and faint, I walked slowly back to sit in the MG until the narrow road was cleared. My presence in Gozo must be a threat to someone, so I was in danger. Yet, as far as anyone knew, I would not be likely to stay for long. Why should anyone care?

Then I thought of Harry Stark. *He* felt threatened by me. He had said as much. And in some way he was linked with the Jarvis family.

There was no sign of the road being cleared, although a police car had arrived. I got out of the MG again, in need of air, and decided to buy some food.

A shopping basket would be useful, so I started with that—locally made, pretty and cheap. From the outside, food shops on the island looked small and dark behind their curtains of plastic strips, but inside they were well stocked with everything imaginable. I flinched from the flies wheeling in great clouds and confined my purchases to food which was packaged or could be washed. I confess I felt some self-contempt for my squeamishness but I knew that if I took home unwrapped food it would not be eaten, so I played safe. Butter and cheese, crackers, tinned soup, fish and ham; canned orange juice, instant coffee, fresh fruit I would peel. That was enough. I would not starve.

As an afterthought I bought two flashlights—one handbag-size, which I slipped at once into my bag, the other a large one which would stand on a table. It seemed likely that somewhere in the house there would be an oil lamp, but I wanted to be prepared. The idea of being in total darkness from early evening did not appeal to me at all.

In a lighter-hearted mood, swinging my new basket, I returned to the car and found that the road was clear. The battered Ford had been pushed to the curb and only mild interest was being shown by passers-by as they glanced at it. The truck had gone, the owner doubtless having decided that there were safer places to leave it than outside his shop. I felt sorry for him and for Mr. Bartola but thankful for my own escape. The attack must have been designed more to frighten than to do permanent harm, but I felt a momentary qualm at the thought of driving down the narrow lane to the isolated farmhouse. An attack there would gather no crowd. I shook off my dread and drove off, up the hill and through Victoria.

For a change, I went via Marsalforn Bay and stopped the car for a moment or two to watch the gray, heaving seas. The storm was worse here than on the southern side of the island because of the wind direction. The harbor was totally empty, with scores of boats of all sizes tilted on the quay, many of them lashed down. The hotel where Michael and I had lunched looked as if it had been barricaded with boats and the *Francine* lay snugly between two larger craft. I was grateful to the local fishermen who had drawn all boats to safety without stinting time or labor. After seeing their work at Xlendi, I was beginning to appreciate the islanders' uncomplicated attitude toward life. In Malta, people were more sophisticated and I doubted if so much care would have been taken with other people's property. On the other hand, absentee owners of Malta moorings might not like to have local fishermen handling their craft.

I went on, passing the sign that said "To Ramla Bay," and on impulse backed up and drove down there. Sooner or later I would have to see the bay; why not now?

The road swerved steeply downwards but the first glimpse of the bay even on this sunless day was breathtaking. How I wished I had come here before the weather had broken. It must be a wonderful place to swim. Then I thought of Father's lifeless body washed up on this very beach and I shivered in spite of my warm sweater.

I stopped the car beside two or three others and sat looking. The sand was indeed red and the bay was well named Ir Ramla l-Hamra, The Red Beach. The sand was fine and stretched to my right in a great shallow curve, backed by small farm fields dry as dust. There were two or three tiny square huts and these, I realized with surprise, must be the "farmhouses." One of them would belong to Joseph, Rosa's son, but though I looked closely at the fields, searching each of them, I could see only one man working, an elderly man, judging by his stiff movements. He was surely not Joseph.

There were vineyards—some of the best wine in Gozo came from here—and up on my left there climbed a steep path, ridged and cobbled, with a sign pointing to Calypso's Cave in the cliff. Was it true that Calypso, legendary queen of Ogygia, kept Ulysses with her here for seven years? Gozitans believe that Gozo is Ogygia.

I fell to watching the waves crashing in onto the beautiful beach and falling back again. Out on the open sea there was tossing water, running fast before the wind. A few spots of rain fell on the windshield and I set the wipers going.

There were no swimmers, only one or two holiday visitors walking near the water on hard-packed sand. There was a barefoot Gozitan at the edge of the fields, his eyes lifted to the sky, a dun-colored dog at his heels. He was carrying a gun and doubtless hoping to shoot small birds for the pot. I did not know whether to pity him for the poverty of his existence or envy him for the richness of having only one problem—the next meal. It is good to leave the easy Western environment for a while. Life falls into perspective. But not death, I thought with a memory, sudden and vivid, of my father's smile, his joy in sailing and in the sea which had taken from him his wife, and finally his life.

The sea can be a brutal companion but man is more brutal. I thought of the superstructure of the *Francine*, part of it wiped clean, and had no doubt at all that my father had been pushed into the sea and perhaps held under until he drowned. Sighing, half distraught with worry, aware of how seriously I took the whole thing now that I had allowed it to surface in my mind, I began to turn the car. If my father had been pushed, he had been murdered.

Murder! Murder! Murder! A sea gull wheeling and crying seemed to be calling the word above my head. I had to use a lot of noisy accelerator to climb the steep hill, up and away from Ramla Bay, and I was glad of it.

Under a gray sky and with a whining wind blowing through the archway to stir the twisted boughs of the olive tree in the courtyard, I had to admit that the farmhouse did not look so attractive. I comforted myself with the fact that I knew the walls to be thick and sturdy, capable of withstanding any storm, and I could see no sign of intrusion. The door was closed, the corner where the motorcycle had been parked, half-hidden, on my first visit held only stunted bushes and a prickly pear, and I could hear no sound but the grumbling, menacing whine of the wind. It made me depressed and fearful. At any moment it might burst into fierce attack, whipping off tiles.

I unlocked the great front door and made two trips into the house—one to carry my suitcase and the basket of food, the second with handbag, coat and my father's binoculars. Then I thankfully shut out the storm. It was remarkably quiet, with the kind of hush that is held within the thick stone walls of a deserted church. I crossed the living room to the new window to look out over the windswept valley, using the binoculars. There was no living soul to be seen anywhere.

As I turned to put the binoculars safely in a desk drawer, a shaft of metallic light, somber without the golden tint I had grown to love, fell full on the Modigliani and lit up the strange, ovoid face. I walked over to it, longing to ask questions of the seated figure. It is a mark of a great painting, I think, that one should be curious about it, unsatisfied, hungry for more. I looked, and looked again. Surely there was something different about the picture!

Cold tendrils of fear curled up my spine, spreading across my shoulders, chilling the back of my neck so that I swung around, expecting I knew not what—but something alien, an intruder, an attack. All my senses were stretched and alarm bells were ringing in my head.

This Modigliani which hung above my father's desk was not the picture I had seen before. The brushwork was good, the apparent simplicity identical. The passive acceptance of the painted woman was the same—*everything* was the same, except for one of her eyes. In the picture I had seen before, it had been crosshatched, giving an oddly defensive expression. This eye was just an eye, the same as the other eye, painted with great clarity but little detail, the iris round as a marble between almond-shaped lids. I seized the frame, lifted the picture off the wall and stared at it more closely. I was not mistaken. I was *not*. But all the same I wanted confirmation and only one person could give it to me. Michael. Last time I had been in this house he had been with me. We had looked at this together. He too would remember the criss-cross strokes on that other eye.

But how had anyone been able to get into the house to make this substitution? By the same means as he or she had gotten in to rehang the picture, I supposed. And with my nerves jangling I ran upstairs to check the heavy bolt that secured the door to the unrestored part of the house. It was in position, as I had surreptitiously noticed when Michael and I had made the rounds of the house together. But I was, if anything, more uneasy than ever. I checked the windows but none had been forced so far as I could see, and the front door would need a battering ram to make it yield. *Or a key.*

I went to the window and gazed out, unseeingly, into the courtyard. I was remembering the time when I'd been on the balcony outside my bedroom at the Tramonto and had seen Harry Stark let himself in, apparently with a key. If he or anyone else had a key to this house I would not want to stay here.

Shaking off my fears, I decided that at night I would push the heavy old chest against the front door and put a wedge under my bedroom door. Anything would do—a piece of wood, a sloped piece of stone. I would be secure enough if I took care.

I went downstairs again, wishing that my father had had a telephone installed in the house. I *knew* that the picture was a different one, but I wanted confirmation from Michael. Then, at least, I would have something to tell Inspector Rapa.

I ran out to the car, backed through the archway, drove to a call box in Xaghra and asked Enquiries for Michael's number. I got it and called his house. He was out. I might have known he would be. But someone answered, a daily help presumably, and in strongly accented English she promised to tell Mr. Brent that I had called and that I wanted to see him. After I'd hung up, qualms assailed me.

I hoped he wouldn't jump to any wrong conclusions over my call. If he did, I thought grimly, I would have to disillusion him. I still meant what I had said to him last night. I did not want a place in Michael's life if Noni were still a part of it.

The afternoon flew by in a series of discoveries, not all pleasant. I tried all the taps first, wondering why on earth neither Michael nor I had done so after the discovery of the well. Michael had told me that the water might not yet be piped into the house and he was right. The taps were dry, the downstairs lavatory—the only one in operation—merely a chemical closet. This last was the worst disappointment for me.

Still, water for washing and drinking could be brought from the well, and I decided to bring some into the house right away. Out into the chilly courtyard I went, and rinsed out the bucket from the well, throwing the water on the ground. Immediately I felt guilty. How wasteful of me! How did I know how much water was in the well or whether it would go dry? If enough rain fell, the underground caverns always present in limestone would fill again, I supposed, and there had been a few spots of rain already this morning. There would be more when the storm broke.

I poured one bucket of water into a clean plastic bowl I'd found by the sink, filled a kettle and a pan, and then brought the bucket indoors again, refilled from the well. All this gave me a ridiculous sense of pioneering achievement. I laughed at myself for it.

When I had unpacked the basket of food, I put the large torch on the kitchen table and had another look in the cupboard beneath the sink where I'd found pan and kettle. There must be a means of heating them. There was. A cooking stove of the kind used by campers, one burner only, but with a cylinder of gas. This discovery cheered me greatly. Without the stove, my instant coffee would have been somewhat superfluous. I also found two bundles of plain white candles, three boxes of matches, some soap and other cleaning materials. Nothing whatever in the way of food, which puzzled me. Apart from this one small cupboard there were only shelves, and these held a box of assorted cutlery and a few pieces of china brought from our Malta home. I remembered the pattern of yellow flowers from my childhood.

Still nagged by the total absence of food, I went to the wooden chest where I'd seen linen and blankets and took some clean sheets, a pillow-case and an extra blanket upstairs. Swallowing a lump in my throat, I stripped off the sheets my father had slept in and remade the bed, then returned downstairs, ready for something to eat. But first I would push the chest over to the front door. With a kind of barricade there I would feel safer if someone did have a key. At least there would be noise to alert me as he tried to force the door.

I'd moved the chest only a couple of feet when I stopped, staring in astonishment at a trap door beneath it, eighteen or twenty inches square. There was no dust in the cracks, or very little. This must have been in use right up to my father's death. Perhaps even since his death. Would it be possible for someone to open this from below, get something underneath the chest and lever it over the floor from beneath, afterwards getting it back in place again? The chest stood on four feet, really angled corners which raised it about six inches from the ground. It *might* be possible, if the flagstone was not too thick. There were two rings in it. I hooked my middle fingers into them and slid the stone to one side with no trouble at all. It was newer and thinner by far than the surrounding stones, and rested on a ledge reinforced with a metal rim. A metal-runged ladder led downwards into a cellar but I could see only the top two rungs. A faint draft reached me, clean and sweet-smelling.

I was nervous, which made me angry. It was not in character for me to be so jumpy. I kept the thought of my father in mind, walked briskly to the kitchen for my large flashlight, blessed the impulse which had made me buy it, and shone the bright light down into the cellar. There were stone shelves, wooden cupboards and wine bins. Immensely relieved at this evidence of domestic normality, I went backwards down the ladder to investigate more thoroughly.

The flashlight revealed a half-burnt candle on a stone shelf, with a box of matches beside it, and I lit the candle. The soft glow was pretty, but it cast leaping shadows. I set down the flashlight, still on, and made the rounds carrying the candle in its scarlet enamel candlestick. To think I had imagined there was no food in the house! The stores here made my basket of groceries look like K rations. There were tins of everything. In the wine bin were at least three dozen bottles of local wine and I found two whole cheeses on a stone slab, with a third which had been started. This last was wrapped in foil and perfectly good, but a loaf which I found in a large stone crock was moldy and the sight of it brought tears to my eyes. I pictured my father enjoying this same bread, unaware that he would not live to finish the loaf. It was more touching and sad than anything I had come across. He was so impeccably tidy, my father, that in a way he had left too few traces of his daily life. But here was something that he had bought, and used, right up to the day of his death, and I wept to think that he should have been snatched from vigorous life so suddenly and so cruelly. I wiped my cheeks quickly with the back of my hand, blew out the candle, picked up the flashlight and went on a tour of inspection.

There were cellars under the entire house, and at the far end of the L-shaped building some stone had fallen in so that a draft came through above my head. I judged that this hole would lead to the arched arcade, and would be hidden by the pile of prepared stone that I'd seen outside. At my feet there were two rollers, small sections of tree trunk, smoothed off and about six inches in diameter. With the trap door slid aside and these placed under the chest, it could be moved sufficiently for someone to gain entry. This, then, was the route used by the intruder. Well, I might not be able to prevent entry but I could make it more difficult. I took away the rollers and a neat pile of stone which made the drop from above easier.

Tired, but much more tranquil, I climbed back out of the cellar, closed the trap door and was immediately in a quandary. If I pushed something underneath the heavy chest, the trap could not be opened from below. Only if there was a gap could new rollers be maneuvered into place. On the other hand, if I jammed the trap door shut in this way I could not use the chest to barricade the front door and there was no other piece of furniture heavy enough. After a few moments' deliberation the trap door won, and I brought three flattish pieces of stone from the garden, laid them on the flagstone, and pushed the chest on its four feet back into place. The idea that Harry Stark or anyone else had a key to this house I put firmly out of my mind. It was most unlikely. Cheered now, and realizing that I was hungry, I ate some of the food I had brought with me and put the kettle on for coffee.

Outside it was dusk, that indistinct, hazy period between light and dark when shapes are distorted and nothing is clearly defined. I heard no sound but the wind, blowing fitfully. Still no rain and I was glad, for tomorrow was the day of the horse-racing in the streets of Victoria and I intended to go. When Michael had supplied confirmation that the picture above the desk was not the one we'd looked at earlier, I could also try to see Inspector Rapa. Whether the information would mean anything to him or not I had no idea, but I hoped it might be a fragment of jigsaw.

It was very dark in the courtyard. I pressed my forehead to the glass of the windowpane but could see nothing except an arched luminosity where the entrance to the courtyard lay, the dim blackness of the other wing of the house and the tips of the olive branches etched against the sky. Crossing to the other window, I stared out over the darkened valley. On the far hillside I could see a few lights where there were houses, and beyond, a string of yellow beads, streetlights far away leading into Victoria. Only their height made them visible. In daylight the road could not be seen from here.

Still using my flashlight, I stuck two candles to saucers and put one on the table and one on my father's desk. I was about to try reading by candlelight when I heard the engine of a car. Michael? Would it be Michael? I realized then that my feeling of restlessness was partly one of anticipation. Subconsciously, I had been waiting for him, but now I resisted the temptation to fling open the door. It might not be Michael, and here in such isolation I intended to be cautious.

The car engine died and someone knocked on the door. I went over to it, and with one hand on the enormous key, the other on the latch, I bent my head to listen.

"Who is it?" I called.

"Michael." The voice sounded amused, and when I

unlocked and opened the door he said, "Were you expecting someone else?"

"No. No one." I felt uncertain, relieved to see him yet disturbed momentarily by the speculative glance he gave me. He lifted his arms but I evaded them. "You have to believe me," I said, making a joke of it, "this isn't an assignation. It's a request for help."

He was still for a moment, his face expressionless. Then he smiled, ruefully. "I suppose I'm not too surprised. Sorry I couldn't come sooner but I didn't get back until half an hour ago, and I found an extraordinary note written by my housekeeper. Her spoken English is minimal, written English microscopic, but she conveyed the meaning."

"What did she say?"

"Please be looking at Miss Prescott tonight."

I laughed.

"So here I am, looking at you. And by candlelight, darling Alexa, you are even more enchanting."

"Thank you." I moved further away and said, "How about a cup of coffee?"

"How about coming out to dinner with me?"

"No, thanks. I've had dinner, actually."

"*Here?*" He looked about him in disbelief.

"You'd be surprised at how well stocked I am."

"Ready for the siege?"

"What siege?" My heart beat painfully as I thought of the hole into the cellars.

"The storm. You might be marooned, you know."

"Oh, that! Well, I won't starve if I'm marooned."

Impatiently, Michael said, "Alexa, you refuse to take the gregale seriously, but you can't have forgotten entirely what it did in Malta. Here, believe me, it's far worse because of fewer communications. You've chosen to take yourself right out to the back of beyond and at this time it's a perfectly idiotic thing to do. I can't understand you."

I started a hot rejoinder but really it wasn't fair to snap back at Michael. There was a lot of truth in what he said and my decision to be here on my own for a while could have been postponed until after the storm. My lack of money I was not prepared to disclose to him. So in the end all I said was, "I shall be all right, Michael. This house was built to endure. I'm sorry that I can't offer you dinner here but I'm not really experienced at cooking on a campstove."

My tone was placatory and his expression softened. "That's all right, darling. There's some food waiting for me at home, as a matter of fact, so the coffee you offer will be fine. While we're drinking it, you can tell me why you wanted to see me."

"Let me tell you that first! It's the picture!" I caught his arm and dragged him over to the desk, lifted the candle and held it high so that the light fell on the painting. "Look hard at it, Michael. Can you see anything different?"

The muscles of his arms were rock-hard, as if tensed, but his laugh was relaxed and he shook his head. "Alexa, you know I'm not very good about pictures. It looks the same to me."

"It's almost the same. There's just one thing different. Look at the eyes!" My excitement was mounting.

He leaned forward, then took the candle from me and held it closer, looking from one eye to the other. I waited, almost holding my breath.

When he turned to me, holding the candle between us so that the light fell on both our faces, his expression was perfectly blank. "I'm sorry, darling. I don't know what you mean."

The disappointment was shattering. I had so hoped to have the confirmation I wanted, without any prompting from me. "You thought the picture was good," I reminded him. "Please, look at the eyes again."

He did so, but only to shake his head again, and when he looked at me there was puzzlement in his eyes. "What is it?" he asked. "I can see it means a lot to you, but what is it?"

I took a deep breath. "In the picture we looked at before, one eye was crosshatched—the eye on the left. Don't you remember? Michael, *can't* you remember?" It had been a very noticeable feature of the portrait. It seemed impossible that he should have forgotten it but slowly he was shaking his head again, and when he spoke his words were like a douche of cold water.

"Something as strange as that I couldn't have missed, surely. Alexa, aren't you confusing it with some other picture you may have seen? A real Modigliani, perhaps?"

Michael did not remember that eye, and what was worse, he implied that I was mistaken about it. I would get no confirmation from him. But I was not wrong. I knew it. This was not the picture we had looked at together on his previous visit.

I turned, and shielding the flame of the other candle with my palm I picked it up off the table and went into the kitchen to boil the kettle.

I was in a turmoil of confusion. Michael was a very observant man. His training as a geologist plus his author's eye was a formidable combination. I did not believe he hadn't noticed that eye.

The picture now hanging above my father's desk was a

substitution. Someone had been in the house between my first visit and the second, when the picture in the upstairs room had been moved to the place where it now hung. Today I'd found a way into the cellar from outside the house—and the rollers for the chest. Oh, yes, someone had been coming and going here. But who? Surely not Michael himself, who was now denying that he could see anything different in the painting. No, not Michael, I thought. But he knew more about it than he was willing to disclose.

He followed me to the kitchen. I had only half filled the kettle to conserve my store of water, and it was coming to the boil. I mixed coffee for two, stirring vigorously. "Sugar?" I asked, tonelessly.

"Yes. One spoonful, please." His voice was gentle. "Darling, I am truly sorry. I have disappointed you in some way, but isn't it possible that you are mistaken? I mean to say, how *could* it be different?" He frowned. "No one else has a key?"

"No one."

"There you are, then. I expect at some time you saw a picture with an eye such as you describe, and your memory of this one played tricks." He spoke as an indulgent father would speak to a young child, bracing and soothing at the same time.

We moved back to the sitting room, and I indicated a chair by the table and put his coffee down. Mine I carried to the window seat. "You're probably right," I said, but my voice lacked conviction.

"What other explanation could there be?" he asked in a reasonable tone. "There isn't another way in, is there? A back door which is unlocked?"

This time I made my voice completely confident. "No," I said. "No back door. I must have been mistaken."

Michael sipped his coffee, his eyes resting on my face.

"And if you had *not* been mistaken, what then?" he asked.

"Wh–what then?" I stumbled over the words. If Michael could not confirm what I had seen, I was not going to give him any more information. I would not tell him that I thought someone had substituted this picture for the other, and that in some way the incident might be connected with my father's death. It was all too nebulous. And Michael was too close to Jarvis *père,* who talked to me of pictures. When I was alone, I would try to recall every word that had been exchanged on the subject during my visit to the Jarvis home. A knock on the door startled me so much that I spilled my coffee and was conscious of a small scald on my knee. At my nod of consent Michael himself went to unlock and open the door, and I heard him say ironically, "Come in. I suppose you want to see Alexa?"

I was still sitting on the window seat, half in shadow, staring at the door, when Randal Jarvis entered. Ducking his tall head and glancing about him, he could not see me beyond the two pools of candlelight. But I could see him clearly, and the displeasure that furrowed his brow. I rose and said, "Hello. Come in and have some coffee."

"No, thanks," he said stiffly. "I'm sorry for intruding. I thought I ought to see if you were all right."

"I didn't hear your car."

"I left it outside the gateway."

"You didn't come here *only* to see if Alexa was well, did you?" Michael's remark was more of a statement than a question.

"Not exactly, no. But Alexa's safety and well-being concern me very much."

"Really?"

Randal turned abruptly back to me. "I'm sorry," he repeated. "I did want to talk to you, but it can wait.

Again, my apologies for intruding." He was simmering with anger, and obviously thought that Michael and I were enjoying a planned cozy evening. As Michael was half engaged to Noni, Randal's fury was understandable. He went quickly to the door, let himself out, and was gone before I could say another word. I felt totally inadequate, and for no good reason guilty, and I was cross when Michael laughed.

"It isn't funny!"

"I think it is. Alexa, darling, come here."

He came toward me, warm purpose in his eyes, but I quickly said, "No!"

"Why not?"

"Just—no." I said, my wearily stubborn tone convincing him that I meant it.

"Then I may as well go. It hasn't been exactly a successful evening on any count, has it?"

"No, it hasn't. I'm sorry for bringing you all this way on a rotten night."

"That's all right. Any time. But one thing I ought to say . . ."

"Yes?"

"If you're alone here, and Randal comes again . . ."

I stared at Michael, who was searching for the right words to make his point. In the end, he finished with a lame anticlimax. "Don't let him in," he said.

"Why not?"

"I just think you shouldn't. Be on your guard with him, Alexa."

And then he too had gone, and I was alone in my father's house with a gust of cold air chasing shadows round the room. I ran over and turned the key.

Chapter 13

WITH THE COOLER atmosphere I slept soundly and woke early with my thoughts on Michael. I had a vague feeling that I had been dreaming about him and about the picture, but I could remember nothing about the dream.

How ridiculous, I thought crossly, to have wanted Michael's backing on the picture. *I* knew it was not the one I'd seen previously. Why bring anyone else into it? *Especially* Michael. I was exceedingly irritated with myself and vowed that in the future I would act on my own without seeking advice from my friends, but if I saw Inspector Rapa I would tell him about the substitution in case it was relevant to his investigations.

With unease, I realized that if I had not telephoned and left a message for Michael, I would have been alone when

Randal called and would have let him in without hesitation. It would not have bothered me. Jarvis or no Jarvis, I felt safe with Randal. He had been kind to me at the Tramonto; when I left he had offered his help if ever I needed it. But I wondered why he had called here last night and why Michael had warned me against him.

I got out of bed and padded over to the window to look out. The stone of the sill felt cold under my palms. There were enormous banks of gray cloud crumbling and tumbling around. It would not be long, surely, before their burden of rain became too heavy to hold and a deluge would fall upon parched ground. Before that happened, I wanted to be in Victoria. Today was Independence Day, the twenty-first day of September, celebrated as usual with the horse-racing in the street. I did not want to miss it.

I washed in cold water in the kitchen, pouring from a bucket into the sink, and thought with fleeting regret of my luxurious bathroom at the Hotel Tramonto, with hot water, clean towels and good soap. Then I dismissed sybaritic memories and boiled a kettle of water for coffee. It tasted good and I ate buttered crackers with it. I was wearing trousers and the thick yellow pullover bought at Rosa's shop, but I put on my coat before going out. It was much, much colder.

As I opened the heavy door, grit stung my ankles, blown by the wind. I looked down to see where it had come from and moaned aloud in terror. Fear was washing over me in an icy cascade. I felt numb with shock. The step beneath my feet was covered an inch deep in sand, damp red sand, carefully patted until it formed a level, firm beach. Spread-eagled on it, face downwards as if tossed there by an angry sea, lay a doll. It was wearing white trousers and a yellow sweater, and it had long, dark hair. It was me, this doll, *me*. Drowned and abandoned on the same beach as the one where my father had been found. It was a warning—a terrible, threatening warning. But who would take the time and trouble to arrange a vivid and nasty tableau with such artistry in the darkness of a stormy night?

Shaken with horror at the sick malevolence of it, I went back indoors, slamming the door behind me. I walked about the room with arms folded and hands clutching my elbows, trying to pluck up my courage to go and sweep away the beastly mess.

If someone meant to frighten me they had certainly succeeded, but I would not be my father's daughter if I allowed myself to be scared off the island by any kind of threat.

When I had calmed down, I decided to leave the sand picture as it was and stepped carefully over it. As long as I was not being watched *now*, no one would know whether I had been upset by the doll or not. After I returned from Victoria I would decide what to do about it.

I went out again and looked carefully about me but could see no one. Nor had I any feeling of being watched. I leveled the sand where I had kicked it earlier, and hurried to the car. It was covered in fine dust, and having backed out onto the rough road I could see that sand was sifting from the fields through collapsing walls and blowing along the surface of the track.

The streets of Xaghra were deserted. People were staying indoors because of the weather, I imagined, but I had underestimated the importance of Independence Day. The bleak aspect of the countryside was in sharp contrast to the scene in the main streets of Victoria. The ferry from Malta must still be running, for local population flocking into the town had been augmented by day-tourists. The island was *en fête* and gray skies did nothing to dim enthusiasm. Wherever one looked there were smiling faces. This was a day for enjoyment.

I edged the car slowly through crowds strolling in the road. For once, curbside parking was impossible, so I drove to the lot near the bus station, left the car there and went on foot to Racecourse Street. The races would not start until after lunch but there were horses about, groomed into glittering beauty and parading for the admiration of the crowd. Some were harnessed to gigs and curricles, and their owners, dressed in tight trousers and frogged jackets, saluted friends with shouts and waving whips. I bought coffee from a bar and drank it outside, perching on the stone ledge of a magnificent building.

Officials and town dignitaries were watching the scene from a large terrace over a portico, and there were priests with them. At a balcony opposite was a family party with a perfect view. Someone lifted a hand to me in salute and I waved back. It was Inspector Rapa, out of uniform and looking not in the least like a policeman.

I finished my coffee, returned the cup and saucer to the bar and bought some little almond cakes, deciding to walk around nibbling, like so many others.

Horses and riders were local and, to the islanders, well known, so there was brisk betting with money changing hands in street and café. Even the poorest of peasants, with wrinkled brown skin and toenails thickened from working in the soil barefoot, were making wagers with good-natured laughter. The contrast between these people and the men and women on the balconies of their town houses, richly dressed and elegant, was very marked, but I could detect no muttering of unrest or any sign that those thronging the pavements were other than perfectly happy.

A small spattering of rain caused everyone to look up-wards. There were a few shouts of welcome rather than disappointment, but the rain passed again with no more than a two-minute sprinkle having fallen.

Walking without purpose, putting off time, I turned a corner and found myself entering a square I had seen before. The square was crammed with people in slow promenade, talking and laughing, eating nut cakes and ice cream, scattering crumbs to be snatched up by strutting pigeons. As I returned to Racecourse Street and took up my position at the edge of the pavement, I saw Maria with her brother Joseph. There was no sign of Michael or any of the Jarvis family but I caught a glimpse of Stark, wearing a thick, high-necked brown pullover. He was three or four yards away, standing at the back of the crowd. I thought of moving further away from him but decided it would merely attract attention, and in any case he did not appear to have seen me.

As the hands on the church clock moved toward start-ing time, excitement grew and intensified. I wanted most to see the gigs and curricles, but was told they raced last of all.

There came a roar from the crowd. The first race had started and I forgot everything in the tangible force of excitement which took possession of the huge crowd—and me with it. This was like nothing I had ever been involved in before. Drama and primitive emotion caused the crowd to move as one body, surging forward and back, roaring encouragement, moaning disappointment, laughing, shout-ing, jumping up and down. I was a part of it, totally iden-tified.

The course was uphill and I was lucky enough to be in a good position, about fifteen yards from the finishing post. Horses galloped toward us, spurred into action, straining tendon and nerve. As they flashed past there was a thunder of hooves, a glimpse of rolling eye and flaring nostril, a flecking of foam blowing off satiny sides, and the race was over. The jockey-for-a-day who had won was beside himself with joy and rode round in circles to wild applause, his mount rearing and prancing. Money was paid out and another race began.

Spectators swayed out into the road like a multicolored ribbon, falling back only as the racing horses drew near. There were no fences of any kind and it seemed a hazardous way to watch, but the crowd was orderly. Miraculously, for four races, no one was hurt except a jockey who fell off, to his own mortification and the crowd's good-natured amusement.

I suppose I was lulled into forgetfulness by the air of general bonhomie, or perhaps I could not believe that I was in danger on the island, in spite of all that had happened to me. I'd had a horrid encounter with Stark on the clifftop, followed by the affair of the truck smashing Mr. Bartola's car, and today there had been the shock of finding a macabre decoration on my doorstep. Yet I had no inkling of approaching danger, no thought that there was anyone around me other than Gozitans enjoying their Independence Day.

With the crowd, I surged forward at the fifth race to see the approach of galloping horses—nine of them. They were large animals, powerful and moving very fast. The crowd fell back in time, as on previous occasions. I was drawing back with them when a jostle pushed me off balance, and then I felt a vicious push in the small of my back and fell forward into the road. Instinctively, I thrashed violently and tried to fling myself away from hooves which seemed now to be above my head as a horse reared and its rider fought to retain his seat. I covered my head and face with my arms, shutting out the awful sight of rearing animal, threshing hooves and sparks being struck from the road.

I wanted also to shut out the sounds—screams of horror from the crowd, the thudding of my own heart, the shouts of the jockey, the terrified whinnies of the poor horse and the straining creak of leather and metal as the bridle was hauled and jerked. It was a bedlam of sound and the jockey could not save me now from those pile-driving hooves. The murderous attack had been well timed.

Those brief moments when I hovered on the verge of injury, perhaps of death, seemed endless. Then I was aware of someone leaping past me. I opened my eyes and saw feet in brown leather shoes, then hooves coming down inches from my head, prancing, rearing, prancing again in a fight for balance. The screams of the crowd turned to shouts of relief and admiration. I rolled over and looked up. The rider was pale under his native tan. The man restraining the horse, a huge animal still too close for comfort, was Michael Brent.

Having stopped the horse and saved me, Michael was searching the crowd with cold, angry eyes. He did not once look down at me and he brushed aside the compliments of those who crowded round to thump him on the back. Willing, kind hands reached for me, women murmuring in sympathy, but I lay there in a shaking, demoralized heap, totally unable to get up and deeply ashamed of my continuing terror. The danger was over and I wanted to stand up and thank Michael, yet I could not utter a word. I knew this was a further attempt on my life. It had failed, so there would be others. I had no proof that it was Stark who had pushed me, but by all the laws of probability it must be he.

At last I responded to lifting hands and was hoisted to

my feet, knees knocking. "I was pushed . . ." I said, dazedly. "I was pushed . . ."

"No, you fell." Michael's attention was on me now, his voice crisp as he continued, "I saw what happened. You stumbled. You might have injured this man and his horse very badly." He spoke severely and I stared at him, outraged. His annoyance did more to restore my composure than any amount of sympathy might have done. I was still in one piece, thanks to him, but I had been close to death and through no fault of my own. Whatever might have happened to horse and rider was nothing compared to what would have happened to me if those hooves had come down on my head and body.

I felt the color coming back to my face as anger rose in me. Firmly, I said, "I'm grateful to you, but I assure you I was pushed." Then my knees buckled and I would have fallen if I hadn't been held up by the crowd. A policeman arrived, busily concerned with getting everyone back on the pavement, but he was not a man I knew. Before I could make a complaint I heard Michael say, "She is a friend of mine. I will take care of her. She fell and is very sorry. Come, Alexa." He began to walk me along a narrow alley, away from the crowd who did not hear my protests and who would forget about me by the time the next race began.

I was still shaking and I felt sick, but I'd retained enough presence of mind to look about me as we left the crowded street. Stark had vanished.

After a minute or two I stumbled. "Wait, please wait." I leaned back against a massive stone building and gazed across the narrow roadway at another. There was an arched doorway and a closed door, solid wood, iron-hinged and iron-studded, centuries old. I thought, They knew how to keep enemies away in those days.

Aloud, I said, "It was that man again. The one on the clifftop. Stark. He *pushed* me. You must have seen him, Michael. You must. How could you say that I fell?"

"I was walking by. I didn't see anyone special, only a commotion, and when I forced my way through the crowd, there you were on the ground, with that damn great horse threshing its hooves over your head. Alexa, my car is just along here a few yards. Let's get in. You've gone white again."

We reached the car. Michael helped me in and got in himself. "Are you all right?" he asked gently. In contrast to his attitude in the street, he now seemed kind and concerned. "Apart from bruises, I mean."

"I'm all right." I took a deep, shuddering breath. "You saved my life and I am grateful, but now I would like to go, please."

"Go where, Alexa?"

I did not know where I was going. The choice was between going back to the farmhouse and that ghastly step or returning to the Tramonto where Stark was staying. I could not view either course without shuddering.

"I can take you to your car if you'll tell me where it is, but then where will you go?" Michael must be reading my thoughts. He had been good at that in the past.

I was silent. My fists were clenched in my lap, and as I looked down at them a large hand slid over, lifted both of mine and held them in a strong, comforting grasp before releasing them. The gesture had been made slowly and with infinite gentleness, and it was as if with one hand Michael had drawn much of the tension out of me. I felt myself relax.

"Oh, Michael, I don't know where to go." I slumped, sighing, laying my head back against the car seat. "I don't know what is going on. I'm so confused."

"Gozo is a strange island. Your imagination is working overtime."

"It wasn't imagination when I felt myself being pushed."

"And it was that same man again—Stark? I wish I had seen him."

I myself had seen him only in the crowd, but it would be stretching credulity too far to imagine there could be two people pursuing me with such evil intent.

Lightly, I said, "I suppose he isn't the client you mentioned, the one who wants to buy the farmhouse? With me out of the way, he might get it."

"Good Lord, what an idea! He's obviously out of his mind. He must be. Which brings me to a decision."

"What decision?"

"You must go to Malta." As I stirred and began to demur, he put an arm around my shoulders. "Yes, Alexa, you must. It's the obvious solution. You'll be safe there. Meanwhile, I'll tell Inspector Rapa what's been happening and he can investigate this man Stark. You can come back here later, if you wish." He glanced at his watch. "But we shall have to hurry. The ferry is due to leave soon, and there won't be another until after the storm. Some of those day-tourists are going to be stranded."

In a quick movement, he drew me close and kissed me. It was not the emotional embrace we had shared at the clifftop, but it was not a brief kiss either. When he lifted his head, Michael whispered, "I ought to thank Stark. He brings you closer to me."

It was true. My pulse raced but as we drove out of town by a circuitous route Michael took to avoid the crowds, I came to my senses. "Michael, this is ridiculous. My car is in Victoria, and I have no clothes—nothing but what I stand up in. I can't possibly go to Malta."

He turned to glance at me. "There must be some of your things left in the Malta house. And there are taxis, and buses from Marfa Quay almost to your door. I can let you have some money if you're short. There's no problem at all, and I'm damned if I'm going to let you stay here as a target for some maniac."

He sounded angry and determined. I knew Michael in these stubborn moods. No amount of arguing would make him change his mind, and in a way it was sweet to have decisions made for me. Yet I felt uneasy. Meekly, I was sitting at his side to be driven to Mgärr. I still did not want to leave Gozo, but I was being given no choice. As the car sped on under a lowering sky, I reflected that I hadn't even seen the sulkies and gigs racing. The crowd would be watching them, at this moment perhaps. I thought of Stark again, and shivered.

The road down to Mgärr Harbor was steep, with a sharp bend to the right. Until we had taken that curve we could not see the sea, or the line of cars waiting to board the ferry. Michael braked hard to pull in at the end of the line. I gasped, staring ahead of us down at the water, and Michael's mouth became set. It was only too evident that the ferry would not run. The police were frenziedly trying to sort out the chaos of cars attempting to turn back.

The car ferry was lashed to the quayside and here, too, small boats were out on dry land, though this was a calm, well-protected harbor compared with Marsalforn or even Xlendi.

"The sea . . ." I gasped in a strangled voice. It was running through the straits in a great, high wall, green and opaque and mountainous, iridescent and sinister. I had never seen anything like it in all the time I had spent in the Mediterranean area. I looked toward Malta and could see nothing but water, spume and rain. The other island was blotted out. It was terrifying.

A policeman was making his way from car to car explaining that the ferry would not run again until the storm was over. He was wearing a waterproof cloak over his pale uniform and made his rehearsed statement at regular intervals. "The hotels will be pleased to accept overnight guests. There is no danger. Have no fear."

By now we were boxed in by cars which had followed us to Mgärr. A curtain of rain swept in from the sea and fell with a rattle like machine-gun fire.

All attempts to push me off this island had now failed. Here I was and here I would stay, like everyone else, until the storm had passed. I began to laugh.

"It isn't funny," Michael said irritably. He fell silent, brooding, and when the traffic was disentangled he turned the car and went back up the hill and away from Mgärr.

Chapter 14

"I SUPPOSE you wouldn't come to my place for the time being?" Michael asked tentatively.

It was not difficult to imagine what Noni would think of such an arrangement, and in any case I did not want to go. I said, "No, thanks." With amusement, I added, "It would have put you in a spot if I'd said yes, wouldn't it?"

He raised an eyebrow. "Useless to deny it, but I might not have minded the spot."

Torrential rain was forming a muddy yellow stream at the roadside, a stream which was steadily widening. Wind buffeted the car in vicious gusts, shaking us in our seats and whirling debris into the air. I thought of my little farmhouse, crouching in the hollow, huddled around court-yard and olive tree. The dirt road to it would quickly turn into a river and the sand picture on the step might be even more realistic, smeared by the elements. I was reluctant to let Michael see it—he would ask endless questions and I was tired, my bruised body beginning to ache all over. I longed to lie down but knew I would have nightmares about that rearing horse.

"I don't want to go to the farmhouse at present," I said as casually as possible. "So would you drop me at the parking lot in Victoria, please?"

Michael answered without hesitation. "Certainly, if you'll promise to return to the Tramonto."

"The Tramonto? I'm not going there! It's where Stark is staying."

"*Was* staying. If you're right in thinking that Stark pushed you in front of the horse, surely he will have checked out." Michael was full of a confidence which I did not share. "Think about it," he added. "*If* Stark pushed you, he does not know that you didn't go straight to the police about it. If you'd done that, he'd assume that the police would head for the hotel immediately to question him. On the other hand, if Stark is innocent and had nothing to do with your fall . . . well, there's nothing to fear at the Tramonto. It's the place where you'll be safest."

"I suppose you're right." I still felt reluctant. "I'm not thinking very clearly—my head hurts." I tried to pull myself together. "But I hardly have much choice in the matter, so it had better be the Tramonto."

"Why don't I take you there, instead of leaving you to drive yourself from the parking lot?"

"No, Michael. It's Dad's car I've left and I can't bear to think of it out in this weather."

"You're being sentimental, Alexa."

"Of course I am," I said. "Oh, Michael, I loved him so very much. He meant so much to me. And now it's too late."

Michael drew a quick breath, and in a husky voice he said, "I know. That's one thing you don't have to tell me."

Victoria seemed to whirl with traffic and torn awnings, with people huddled in doorways or braving the driving rain and trying in vain to hold up umbrellas. While I watched, three umbrellas ripped inside out, flapped, broke and blew away like giant multicolored butterflies. The horses had disappeared and cars sent waves of rain water spraying from their wheels. The Gozitans, always happy, walked in the rain, turning their faces to the sky, laughing and calling to each other that soon they would need a *dghajsa*, a rowboat, to take them home.

Michael stopped by the parking lot and I hurried from his car to where I had left the MG. He followed me, apparently oblivious of drenching rain, and leaned down as I got into the driver's seat. "Should I come with you?"

"No, of course not. I shall be perfectly all right. Call me. And Michael . . ."

"Yes?" His hazel eyes, holding mine, were strangely remote.

"Thanks for everything."

"Don't . . . There's nothing to thank me for." He sounded almost angry, and with a kind of half salute he loped back to his car. When I drove out to the street and turned left for the road to Xlendi, he was still parked, watching. Perhaps he thought I would go to the farmhouse after all, but in this weather the hotel, whatever problems there might be, seemed far more attractive.

Xlendi was frightening. The water, normally blue and emerald, and clear as a spring in the deep bay, was clouded with debris and sand churned up off the bottom. Water surged up the fjord from the angry open sea, crashed over the harbor wall and ran foaming in the street, leaving piles of stones and seaweed under the trees.

Above all, I was struck by the noise of the wild weather.

Boats of all shapes and sizes, pulled up onto what had been dry land, were being washed by the waves. Sea and sky had merged in smudgy shades of gray, and the few people who were outside hurried about their business with none of the camaraderie there had been in Victoria. Here, the stormy sea was too close for comfort.

I crawled up the hill to the Tramonto and turned into the parking lot. It was almost full; I had to search for a space and the one I found was a long way from the hotel door. Randal must already be inundated by refugees from the storm, and here was I—another lost soul. As I got out of the car, my muscles positively twanged. I had fallen harder than I'd realized in Racecourse Street and was beginning to stiffen up, but I took to my heels all the same.

To hurry inside out of the rain is instinctive, but futile when it is so heavy that water reaches the skin in seconds. I entered the hotel and stood dripping on the beautiful black and green tiles. In astonishment I looked about me. The spacious foyer was packed. Crowds of people of all ages were sitting in every available chair, on the staircase and even on the floor. Some were agitated, others calmly reading. They watched the sky and racing storm clouds, or just sat with an air of resignation, staring at nothing— waiting, I supposed, for the gregale to stop blowing, or more immediately for a meal or a drink to be prepared. Any hotel would find it hard to cope with an influx of these proportions. Independence Day had brought these people as day-visitors from Malta, but they would be staying for longer than a day, I thought.

Apprehensively, I glanced toward the desk, but there was no sign of Randal. The last time we had met he'd been thoroughly displeased at finding Michael at my house, and now I was going to have to throw myself on his mercy. I had no wish to drive off into the storm looking for somewhere else to stay, knowing I might come across Stark—unless Stark was still here. My heart lurched at the mere thought of meeting him again. Wincing as my bruises made themselves felt, I took off my sodden coat and hung it with some others.

"Alexa! Thank God! I've been out of my mind, worrying about you." Randal had come up behind me, pushing through the crowds from his tiny office. As he spoke, he put a hand on my shoulder, turning me to face him. "You're soaked!" He half laughed. "But of course you're soaked. Who isn't? Come into the office for a moment. Where is your luggage? You must change."

The words were tumbling over each other as he uttered them. I'd never seen him so . . . spontaneous, except perhaps when we had prepared breakfast together on the first day of the storm. At the moment his guard was completely down, and the thought crossed my mind that if I was not so set against fresh involvement I might enjoy getting to know Randal Jarvis better, in spite of Michael's veiled warning.

I found myself being hurried into the office. Unwittingly, Randal was hurting my bruised arm and shoulder, and I bit my lip. He closed the door behind us and the babble of voices died to a low murmur. I had not uttered a word, and when I looked at Randal I noticed that he was white under his tan, with a pallor that gave a deathly tinge to his face from hairline to chin.

"Randal, are you ill? What is the matter?" I lifted a hand toward him and my gesture broke through his reserve. With an incoherent murmur he pulled me into his arms, held my face in the hollow of his shoulder and put his cheek on the top of my head. Then I felt his mouth at my temple, my forehead, my cheek, and finally, when his hand had lifted my chin, he bent and laid his mouth closely on mine. It was a strange, bewildering kiss—a vow, a benediction and a declaration all at once—and I had never known anything like it. I was not sure if it had anything to do with love. Michael's kisses had been all passion and possession and I'd known how to respond to them. This was a subtle embrace.

Reluctantly, Randal released me and took a pace toward his desk. "You must think I've taken leave of my senses," he said abruptly. "I went to the farmhouse to try to persuade you to come back here . . ." He broke off. "That was the reason why I arrived last night, by the way, and found you with Michael. I wanted you to come back here where I thought you would be safer. Then, I was thinking of the storm . . ."

"I see. Thank you," I said, feeling utterly inept. Randal was obviously under strain.

He shifted a pile of letters on his desk, thumped a heavy glass paperweight on top of them and said angrily, "Last night I was surprised to find Michael Brent with you but it was none of my business. Today . . ." He shook his head and stared at me. "Today, I was shocked out of my mind by that horrible mess on your step. Or haven't you seen it?"

"Of course I have seen it and the message is all too vivid." I indicated the clothes I was wearing. "My father was washed up on the sand at Ramla Bay, dead. I suppose I am threatened with the same fate."

Randal glanced at my new yellow sweater and nodded, grimly. "Oh yes, the doll is meant to be you, all right. But I doubt if the arrangement was a threat."

"What else could it be?" I was astonished.

"That sand-picture is island work. What native of Gozo would harm Commander Prescott's daughter? It's a warning, Alexa, not a threat. But it's a warning you should heed. Whoever put it there was in no doubt that you are in danger."

"I never thought of it that way. As island work, I mean." I spoke slowly. "I was just . . . frightened."

"I'm not surprised." After a pause, slowly he added, "Alexa, were you alone when you saw it?"

He had come out with it at last. Coldly, I answered, "Certainly I was alone. I found it this morning. Michael stayed last night for only a short time—though you have no right to ask."

He lifted his hands and dropped them at his side. "True. I'm sorry." It was no more than a muttered apology, and as if he had suddenly remembered his manners he pushed forward a chair. "Sit down. I'll send for some hot coffee. Or would you prefer tea?"

"Coffee, please." It would be more bracing and I needed something to keep me going. "I suppose my old room has been occupied by someone else?"

"I'm afraid so." He pressed a bell by his desk.

I smiled, shakily. "I haven't any luggage anyway. Maybe you don't accept guests without luggage."

"I make exceptions. I could let you have Carmela's room, if that would do?"

"Would you really? It would be marvelous." My spirits lifted but then I remembered my attacker of the afternoon. "Has that man Stark checked out?"

"Yes. This afternoon. Why do you ask?"

"No special reason."

Randal made an impatient sound, half snort, half imprecation. "It is, of course, the kind of question that one does ask in an intensely nervous voice, without having any special reason. Alexa, you must take me for a fool."

"No, I don't!" I was indignant.

One of the young waiters came in, looking understandably harassed, and Randal ordered coffee, adding when the boy had gone that I ought to get out of my wet clothes. "But I was forgetting, you have no luggage." The ghost of a smile crossed his lips. "I can find you a bathrobe to wear while we dry out your things. Now, tell me why you asked about Stark."

I didn't want to talk about this afternoon to Randal so I said. "Nothing to tell. Did you ever find out how he got hold of a key?"

"He 'borrowed' a front-door key from one of the chambermaids one day. Doubtless he had a copy made. I'm afraid I fired the girl."

"Why did he want it, do you suppose?"

"Presumably so that he could come and go, undetected."

"I had got that far myself," I said, dryly. "But to do what?"

After a moment Randal said, "I don't know."

I was not sure whether to believe him but it was the only answer I got. At that moment, the waiter brought coffee and an urgent message from the chef. Randal poured coffee for me and with a word of apology he left, saying he would be back soon to show me to Carmela's room.

I was grateful for the hot coffee. The drop in temperature, my damp clothes, reaction from the events of the afternoon—all contributed to make me shivery. This quiet respite in the small office was exactly what I needed. Randal's desk, very tidy, was made of English elm, the whorls of pattern in the pale wood showing through a simple glass top. One wall of the room had a row of filing cabinets along it, another was given over to bookshelves. There were two chairs: a comfortable leather armchair with high back in which I was sitting, and a similar chair without arms, behind the desk. Both were a warm tan and the floor was black and green tiled like the foyer. Walls and ceiling were washed a plain matt cinnamon. It was a beautiful office. The effect was elegant and I felt soothed.

It would have been pleasant to blot out all thought of strange happenings and near accidents, but also dangerous. When I had poured a second cup of coffee, I forced my mind to start reasoning.

Somewhere at the center of the mystery there was the Modigliani, for the painting which now hung over my father's desk was not the one I had first seen in the house. Edgar Jarvis himself had mentioned the picture to me— oh, so casually—but I had overheard from the upstairs bathroom of the Villa Melita his far from casual conversation with Alfio Marcello in the yard outside.

I remembered the hostility Stark had shown to me down by the harbor, a hostility born of a mistaken assumption that there was a connection between me and Edgar Jarvis, whom he referred to as "the old fox." For good measure he had called Randal the cub and me a vixen. Nice man. If I personally was not a danger to him, perhaps he wanted revenge on someone through me . . . Whichever, I seemed to be the target. My thoughts went round in circles but always I came back to the exchange of one picture for another, the only happening I knew about which might have some significance, some bearing on the violence I had suffered.

I began trying to link my father with Edgar Jarvis. Michael knew both men well, yet he had claimed to know nothing of that picture. If he was telling the truth, there must be someone else. At last, after sifting through every single person I had met or been told about on the island,

I came up with Joseph. He had worked for my father, and occasionally for Mr. Jarvis as Rosa had told me. Also, his sister Maria worked for Edgar Jarvis and she was an unhappy woman who might confide in her family rather than in Alfio.

I had to talk to Joseph but I might find it hard to locate him. His farmhouse, as described by Rosa, would by now be waterlogged in a low-lying field, and the thought of negotiating the steep road to Ramla Bay did not appeal to me. I looked through the window at the violence of the storm, ever increasing, and knew that I would be going nowhere this evening.

"I'm sorry for leaving you." Randal was back, looking at me in concern. "You must have some food. When did you last eat? But first I'll show you to Carmela's room. I've had a robe put in there for you, and a chambermaid will take your clothes to have them dried."

I got to my feet in a movement which was far from fluid.

"What is the matter? Have you hurt yourself?"

I longed to tell Randal all that had happened but mulling over my problems had made me uncertain. I did not know whom to trust, and deciding on discretion at this stage I said, "It's nothing at all—a pulled muscle."

"Plus damp clothes I should think. I have neglected you disgracefully. Come along." He took my elbow and turned me so that we walked together from the office and away from the crowded foyer. We went through an archway and up a small flight of stairs to staff bedrooms which were above outbuildings at the back of the hotel and at right angles to the main building. Carmela's room was at the end of a row and it had a bathroom next to it. I thought with longing of hot water. It had been an interminable day. I found it hard to believe that it was only a few minutes before six o'clock. Apart from how I felt, the sky was so dark that it seemed much later.

Randal lit a candle which stood on the dressing table. "Sorry about this, but the electricity has failed. I have my own generator but must conserve it for freezers and cooking. We immobilize the elevator and use candles for lighting excepts on stairs."

I became aware of a throbbing noise coming from underneath this wing. "Is that the generator?"

"Yes. It will go off in two hours."

I was looking about me. The candle flame flickered in a draft from the window. The bedspread was white, and a white terrycloth bathrobe lay upon it. The only picture was a small Madonna, and there was a plain wooden crucifix over the bed.

"Will it do?" Randal's smile was quizzical.

"Oh, please . . . It's charming and I'm so grateful to you."

"Nothing to be grateful about. I'm glad you came back." Randal spoke briskly and touched my cheek gently with one finger, the emotion he had shown when I arrived completely expended. By the door, he hesitated. "Alexa, I'll repeat the question I asked downstairs. Is there something wrong? You moved as if you'd suffered more than a pulled muscle."

How much did he know? I wanted to blurt out everything but it was out of the question. Edgar Jarvis, I thought, might be in trouble with the law. Randal could scarcely be indifferent to his father's fate. In a crisis, he might find himself deeply involved.

"I fell, in Victoria." At his exclamation of concern I hastily added, "Nothing serious. I'm all right now. Really."

"You don't want a doctor?"

"Good heavens, no!"

"Well, have a hot bath. By the time you've finished there, your clothes should be nearly ready for you. The drying rooms are still warm. See you at dinner."

He left, and I had scarcely stripped off my clothes and put on the robe when there was a soft knock on the door and a chambermaid with strongly Arab features said, "*Jekk joghbok*"—please—I bring them back soon."

The warm water was soft as silk. It drew pain from my body and relaxed sore muscles, so that after a long soak I felt much better. I toweled myself, briskly where possible, gingerly over the sore places, put on the robe and slipped back into the bedroom. My clothes were not there but I did not have long to wait before the same girl returned them, not only dry but with the trousers beautifully pressed. "*Grazzi*," I thanked her warmly.

A low-powered electric light bulb fed from the generator shone in the foyer but it was the only one I saw. In the dining room, on each table, there was a candle in a flowered candlestick. The room was suffused in light, the flames shimmering like topaz. Extra tables had been brought in to seat stranded visitors. The meal was simple and delicious and the flying waiters, genial as always, got through the extra work with amazing efficiency. They seemed to be taking pride in rising to this occasion of crisis.

There was no room for Randal to sit down that evening but he joined me for a few minutes as I was leaving the room. "Feeling better now?"

"A new woman." I answered his smile and there was a moment of intimacy between us, without any words. We were both, I am sure, remembering my return to the hotel that afternoon, Randal's anxiety, and the embrace.

"I want to talk to you about that sand-picture." His resonant voice was soft. He put a hand under my elbow and steered me to his office again. It was in total darkness, but he shone a pencil flashlight which he took from his pocket, and then lit a candle on his desk. We both sat down, he behind his desk, I in the chair I formerly occupied.

"You must keep an enormous stock of candles!" I observed.

"We do. Not that this happens often, but when it does, the only areas with electricity are those which can be served by the hospital supply, in Victoria."

"Then Carmela will be all right. I hope she won't mind my having her bedroom."

"She will be pleased," Randal said simply, and I knew he was right. Carmela would always be pleased to help someone.

"You said you wanted to talk about the sand picture?"

"Yes. I was trying to think who might have arranged that artistic but disturbing warning. Have you any ideas? Could it be Joseph?" Randal's gray eyes were serious as they locked with mine.

I had already thought of Joseph as the link between my father and Edgar Jarvis. What more likely than that he might also have tried to warn me, if I was in danger.

"I think it might be Joseph," I answered. "I understand his farm is near Ramla Bay, where the sand is red."

Randal nodded. "He is a simple, good man, Joseph—and he was devoted to your father. The method of warning was unorthodox and I think unfortunate, but I believe he meant well."

"I was scared rigid when I saw it." I laughed ruefully.

"So was I," Randal said soberly. He stretched a large hand across the desk, palm upwards, and after only a moment of hesitation I put mine into it and felt strong fingers close around mine.

He came around the desk, and without letting go, drew me to my feet. "I have to get back. I'm sorry. But, of course your work is the same and you understand . . ."

"Of course. And can I do anything to help?"

"Certainly not. Your eyes are the proverbial two holes burned in a blanket—very beautiful, shining holes," he added. "But you need rest."

We were standing very close and we looked at each other long and searchingly. As if compelled, I lifted my face, Randal kissed me gently, and we said good night.

Chapter 15

I SLEPT SOUNDLY in Carmela's bed, safe and warm. The last noises I heard at night and the first the next day were the howl of wind and the lash of rain at the window. The sea was a muted roar, and in the morning, a clangor of church bells called the islanders to prayer. The storm had not abated.

In my borrowed robe I went to the window. From here the view was inland, over wind-swept rock and torn fragments of succulents. The landscape was smudged, the colors running and blurred. The very rocks looked battered—what had happened to dusty fields and dry stone walls I dared not imagine.

Breakfast, in the chatty atmosphere of the crowded dining room, was cheerful and my own troubles receded in an atmosphere of holiday adventure. The relaxed interlude gave me courage to start my search for Joseph and I decided to begin by asking Rosa where he might be found.

Since there was no sign of Randal this morning, I was able to leave the hotel without having to answer any awkward questions. Dressed in my standard wardrobe of trousers, yellow sweater and coat, I drove slowly down to the bay, the zigzag road almost unrecognizable under a coat of sludgy mud, pebbles and debris. The bars and Rosa's shop were open but almost empty. I stopped the car, got out and was riveted by the sight of a lightweight motorcycle propped beside Rosa's doorway, with a sheet of polyethylene over it to keep off the worst of the rain. There was no gun, of course, but I felt sure it was the same make, if not the same cycle, I had seen in my garden on that first visit to my father's farmhouse.

There was no need to ask where I could find Joseph. He was there in the shop with his mother and he looked very uneasy when he saw me. I decided to leave the matter of the motorcycle and I asked him first about the red sand on my step. I opened my coat.

"Red sand and a doll dressed like me in a yellow sweater," I said in a hard voice. "Who dressed the doll? Maria?"

Joseph nodded—not shamefacedly, almost eagerly.

Rosa bridled aggressively. "Why do you speak like that to Joseph? He is a good boy. He help you, Miss Prescott."

"Did *you* know about the sand on my step, Rosa?"

"Yes, I know. We decide together how best to warn you without . . . without anyone knowing." Consternation touched her, making her frown. "You were frightened?"

"How would you feel, Rosa, if you got up one morning and found yourself drowned on your own doorstep?"

Murmuring a brief prayer, she crossed herself. "*Skuzani.*
We did not mean . . . Joseph and Maria, they would not
hurt you. We wanted to warn you."

"I know," I said gently, and sighed. "I know that now,
Rosa. When I'd had time to think who might have done
it, I stopped being frightened."

A beatific smile spread over her old face. Joseph's
bright, anxious eyes looked from one to the other of us.

"Joseph, I need your help again. Could we speak privately? About the picture?"

He shot a swift glance at his mother. The picture was
something she knew nothing about, I could tell instantly.
Talking in rapid, staccato Maltese which I could not follow, Joseph escorted his mother to the doorway at the
back of the shop. Protesting, she went through it. I walked
as far away as I could, to the front of the shop. I knew
only too well that from behind the back door even normal
speaking voices could be heard inside the shop. I remembered Alfio's threatening mien when Rosa had opened
the door and found him there, listening.

Every now and then the angry sea tossed a wave over
the harbor wall where it washed about, hissing, before
falling back into the sea. I gazed at it in silence with
Joseph close beside me before I could think how to begin.
Finally I asked, simply, "How did my father obtain the
picture which hangs above his desk, Joseph?"

As if he wanted to clear his mind or conscience of the
whole thing, Joseph answered promptly, "I bought it for
him."

"*You?*" Other questions hung in the air.

"Oh, I did not buy it with my money. Fifty pounds is
too much for me." (And too little for the picture, I
thought.) "Commander Prescott gave me the money to
buy it when I told him that there was a man in the Villa

Melita who had a picture to sell. Maria told me that, you understand. But please, Miss Prescott, do not tell anyone about it. Maria is not supposed to speak about what happens in the Jarvis house. It would be very bad for her. Alfio would be very angry."

"If possible, Joseph, I will tell no one. But I have to know more, because of my father's death, you understand."

"Yes," he said, unhappily, reluctantly.

"So how did you get the picture?"

"There are two men hiding in the cellar. They come out only at night."

The cellar at the Villa Melita. I pictured Alfio Marcello as I'd seen him by the stone steps, paring his nails, watching, keeping guard.

"*Two* men? And one of them had a picture to sell?"

"Yes." He nodded his dark head. "One man stays there all the time. He is the one who paints, copying other pictures. He is very clever. The other, he came two, three weeks ago. Before, when a man has come, he has not stayed so long."

"Then this has happened before, Joseph?"

"Many times."

"And they always hide?"

"Yes."

"When they leave, where do they go? To Malta?"

"I do not know. Only one man leaves. He goes at night, in Mr. Jarvis's boat. The painter stays. He is often drunk." Joseph spoke without censure. "Alfio is supposed to take their food to them but sometimes Maria carries the tray, with Alfio to keep watch."

The place sounded like a motel, I thought. Edgar Jarvis must be trafficking in stolen pictures or art forgeries, or both. I thought fleetingly of Randal, who had become so angry when he heard I was to visit his father.

"Joseph, tell me more about how you bought the picture for my father."

"Well, one day the painter offered Maria a picture for fifty pounds. Maria told me. She say, 'Where would I get fifty pounds?' And for such a picture! Not the Madonna, not a beautiful picture of the sea or boats, but a picture of a woman with a face like an egg. She did not want it. But when I told Commander Prescott about it, he said *he* would like a picture if I could get it without Mr. Jarvis knowing. I told him it would be easy and he gave me the money for Maria. She bought it for your father from the painter and hid it under a tray to get it out of the cellar. Then I took it from the Villa Melita to your father's house on my motorcycle."

"I see. And after my father died, what then, Joseph?"

"Mr. Jarvis found out about your father having a picture and questioned Maria, but she lied to him and said she knew nothing about it. Then Maria told me she heard talk that Alfio would come and look for the picture, so when your father died, I hid the painting." Joseph took a deep breath and continued. "Then when I saw you come to the island, I thought I should put the picture back, for it will be yours. But you came while I was in the house, before I hang it. I ran away, leaving the picture in that room upstairs. Later I came to put it back on the wall. I thought you would not have noticed it the first time."

I did not disillusion him. While the picture was out of the house, in Joseph's care, the police would have entered, looking for clues to my father's death, and found nothing unusual. And according to the conversation I had overheard between Alfio and Edgar Jarvis, it was during this time that Alfio had first searched the farmhouse. He must also be the one who had later changed the pictures—though none of this explained why anyone would sell an original Modigliani for fifty pounds. Nor was there an explanation yet of my own dear father's involvement in such matters.

"Joseph, you used to go into the house by that hole in the floor of the arched patio, where the stones had fallen in?"

"Yes."

"Did my father know?"

"He knew. It was better that way. I did not want to have a key, for I might lose it, but sometimes when your father was out in his boat, if I had a little time, I would work inside the house on the stone."

"Who else knew of the hole, Joseph?"

"No one else."

"Not Maria, or your mother?"

"Oh yes, my family. No one else."

"Someone else knew, Joseph. Alfio, perhaps?"

He looked uneasy and scuffed a sneakered foot on the stone floor. "Maria would not *want* to tell him, but sometimes it is difficult for her."

"This secret, I think, would have been impossible to keep." I spoke gently. "So she did not keep it. Later, my father's picture was exchanged for another. You knew that, didn't you, Joseph?"

"No! I did not know!"

It was too pat, too prepared, too indignant.

"You knew," I repeated. "I want you to tell me why, and how, it was done. If you cannot, I will go and ask Mr. Jarvis."

I would do nothing of the kind, of course, but I would not let Joseph know that I, too, was frightened of Edgar

Jarvis and no longer believed that he had been a friend of my father's.

"No, you must not ask him! Please, Miss Prescott!"

"I have to know, Joseph. Either you tell me or I go to Mr. Jarvis. It is very important. More important than you know."

"That is what Alfio said," he responded angrily. "But I did not help him to change the picture. I would not. So if the picture was changed, Alfio must have changed it." He kicked a pebble out into the street. "I wish Maria was not married to him."

Certain now that Alfio had killed my father, I said sharply, "How did my father die, Joseph?" He knew something, I was convinced of it.

"I do not know."

"Then who does know? Who *does* know?" My voice was urgent and rising.

He shot a nervous glance toward the door at the back of the shop, then looked outside at the dirty road, the few huddled people in other doorways, the rain-swept, heaving sea. There was no one near us. "I am telling the truth, Miss Prescott. I do not know. But Louis saw the man, that night."

"Wh–hat?" I could scarcely believe that in spite of all the police activity on this small island, someone should have seen what happened and not told the police. "Louis is the man who has the bar in Xaghra, is that right?"

Joseph nodded. "He was near Ramla Bay late that night. Your father's boat was moored. Commander Prescott was fishing, I think. Louis saw a skin-diver swimming out to the *Francine* and going aboard. Later he dived off, and in the moonlight Louis saw a man still aboard. He thinks it was your father. The man leaned over to the far side, then his legs went up in the air, and he fell overboard."

I was silent, swallowing hard, trying to digest what this meant.

"Perhaps he was pulled overboard," Joseph said reluctantly.

"Yes, perhaps he was." I pictured the scene—the diver pretending to be in difficulties. Would that be how it was done? My father leaning over, or diving in to help, being held down by his clothes, so no telltale bruising, but the two, threshing in the water, reaching the bottom so that my father's fingernails got dirty as he scrabbled for a grip on the rocks which would give him some purchase to lash out with his feet. Horrible. Horrible.

"Did the swimmer come ashore?" I felt as if I were listening to someone else asking the questions, so detached did my voice sound.

Joseph nodded. "He came ashore, and ran past the place where Louis was lying in a hollow."

"Then Louis *saw* him?"

"Yes. But he did not know him. Louis does not go out much. He is in his bar. Once a week he goes out, in the evening."

"I can't believe that he did not recognize the man."

"It is the truth. Louis is a friend of mine. He would not lie to me. I go always to his bar." The vehemence rang true.

"Then why did he not tell the police what you have told me now?"

Joseph was unhappy at this question. "He was with a girl. He does not want to marry her, but her parents are of the old ways, very strict. If they know he has been out with her alone, after dark, they would go to his parents. He would have to marry her."

"Then why didn't *you* go to the police, Joseph, and tell them this?"

"Louis is my friend. The police would have known who had seen it."

It was all so clear-cut to Joseph. Loyalty to a friend came first. Yet, perhaps it was friendship that kept Louis from telling who had been on my father's boat. Perhaps he was protecting Joseph's family from the terrible consequences of identifying Maria's husband as the man who had killed my father.

Slowly, I said to Joseph, "If I bring a man to Louis's bar this afternoon, at about three o'clock, do you think he would be willing just to nod to me if it is the man he saw that night?"

Joseph thought hard, frowning with the effort of concentration. Finally, he said, "I think he would. You will not bring the police?"

"No, Joseph, I will not bring the police."

There would be no need for the police today. The island was cut off. The man could not get away. If he had swum to the *Francine* and gone aboard, as seemed likely because of the wiped-off superstructure, it was someone who was known to my father. Alfio must have been acting for Edgar Jarvis on some matter to do with the picture, though I could not say so to his brother-in-law, Joseph.

I must try to get a message to Alfio at the Jarvis house. I hoped that he would not be able to resist meeting me, if only to find out how much I knew. Then perhaps Louis, faced with the murderer and the victim's daughter, would feel compelled to identify him.

I thanked Joseph for his help and went back to the car. I drove to Victoria, bought a writing pad and some envelopes, and wrote a note which said: "Meet me in Louis's bar in Xaghra at 3 p.m. today." I signed it "Alexa Prescott." I gave no reason, no explanation for my request. Curiosity would bring him, I thought, and I drove back to the rough road which led only to the Jarvis house, the Villa Melita.

The surface of the road was sticky with mud and there were no fresh tracks, so no one had come from the house or approached it that morning. How I was to get the note to Alfio without anyone else knowing, I could not think. I parked my car in the second of the two passing places, facing toward the track, and sat there for nearly half an hour of indecision, the note lying on the seat beside me. I was in luck. A grocery van came jolting along, heading for the house. As it drew level, I got out of the car, note in hand, and was immediately deluged with rain. However, I proffered the envelope to the driver, together with a one-pound note, and asked him to give the letter to Alfio Marcello without anyone seeing. "Can you do that?"

Fortunately, he spoke English. "It is easy. Alfio takes the boxes of goods from us."

Overjoyed with this success, I scarcely noticed that another car had pulled up alongside mine. The engine noise was drowned by the rattle of the grocery van and the roar of the wind; only the slam of the car door reached me. I turned, and found myself face to face with Harry Stark. The van had gone. I was alone, my knees shaking, my feet seeming to sink into the slimy mud. I tried hard not to show my terror, but I was desperately frightened. Stark marched toward me, shaking his bull head. I backed off a little.

"Why the hell didn't you leave Gozo when I told you to?"

"Was it *you* who put that note under my door?"

"Who else would it be?" He had stopped in the middle of the track, knowing he had cut me off from my car. "You are in this up to your pretty neck and you didn't come from Marseilles, so where *did* you come from?"

Even if I had known what he was talking about, I could not have answered. For the first time in my life, I was aware that the tongue can indeed cleave to the roof of one's mouth. Mine had. I felt sick. Stark just stood there, shoulders hunched toward me, hands hanging at his side a little away from his body, ready to spring, and grab. He seemed totally unaware of the rain and I wasn't thinking about it much, either. I watched those hands.

"Did you come from Marseilles?" I asked, to keep him talking.

"Don't pretend you don't know. You're a lot closer to Edgar Jarvis than you make out. And that son of his is in it too, I bet. Well, I want my cut. If I'd been paid in Marseilles, I wouldn't have come to this God-awful place. And as soon as I do get paid, I'll be off by the first boat. Until then, if I keep you with me . . ." His voice had become softer, more malevolent. "If I keep you with me, my lovely little bitch, perhaps they'll pay up that much quicker."

He lunged, then, to cover the two yards which separated us, but I had already decided what I would do when he moved, and very quickly I leaped sideways and twisted my body, curving away from the grabbing hands. I had counted on my lighter weight to help me stay upright on the muddy surface. If Stark, with his bulk and girth, went off balance, he would slip and be bound to go down. He was not in good condition. It worked. With a curse, he fell and I ran. He shot out a hand and touched my ankle but did not manage to grasp it. The position in which I had parked my car, facing the track, saved me. I jumped in, started the engine and tore away. Stark had to turn his car, but in my rear-view mirror I could see that he had done so very quickly. When he started down the road after me, the grocery van had still not reappeared. No one knew that I had come here and was now being followed by Stark. I stood on the accelerator and bounced down the hill as fast as I dared.

No use returning to Xlendi, a dead end by a lashing sea. Instead, I went up the hill toward Victoria but turned left, skirting the town and heading along a good road toward Gharb. In my mirror I could see that Stark was still following—and gaining on me. As I sped along, I saw that the road narrowed ahead. At the same moment, a horse-drawn cart turned out from a farmyard right in front of me, splashing through an enormous pool. There just *might* be time for me to squeeze past it. If so, I would gain a few minutes, for Stark could not hope to pass the cart until the road widened again. I put my foot down and managed to slip through. On one side, my wheels must have been within inches of the cart; on the other, they slid perilously close to the ditch. But then I was through and gaining speed, the farmer shouting angrily after me and waving his whip. I could not blame him.

The road improved and I was able to drive much more quickly. Along the banks behind the ditches, large yellow boulders were scattered, washed out of collapsing drystone walls by the torrential rain. Fields lower than the road were under water. The sunny island I had found when I arrived had changed completely and I felt that I had changed just as much. I was ruthlessly determined to finish the job I had started, to find out how my father had died, but I was frightened by Stark's determined pursuit, the more so when I saw that he had passed the cart where the road widened and had begun rapidly to gain on me.

"I've got to get off this road," I told myself. If I took a right turn I would be clearly visible across flat fields, but there was a turn to the left. I took it, clinging to the wheel. Rain was rattling on the roof of the car and streaming down the windshield. The wipers could not cope with it, but through a sheet of water I saw a sign There was no time to read words, but from having studied a map of the island I realized that this must be the way to the Inland Sea, Il-Qawra, a pool formed by the falling-in of once subterranean caves.

If I had known this precipitous road I would certainly not be plunging down it now, pursued by Stark at a madly dangerous pace, as if in a nightmare. I felt that I had no control over the car at all. The narrow track was a river, a torrent, with a base of yellow mud. On either side of me the land fell steeply away so that I was driving along a slippery knife edge, barely wider than the car, between two deep depressions. Far below me lay Il-Qawra, pewter chopped with white. On a fine day if would be magnificently blue, but not today. With horror I saw that the track leveled briefly to a narrow bridge before plunging on downward.

I got over the bridge somehow, hauled the car out of a skid and found myself in worse trouble. A huge, moving tide of brown, black and white was crossing the road only yards ahead of me. A herd of goats!

The animals sprang up onto the track from the left and ran across it to jump down again at the right, drawn by some instinct which told them that there was more to eat, or better shelter, at the other side. By some miracle I slid and roared through between tossing horns, rolling yellow eyes and scurrying hooves without hitting anything, but I was fighting the wheel all the way. More goats were coming. Even in the wet mud they made a thundering noise. I tore my eyes from the track to look quickly in the mirror and saw Stark reach the second wave of animals, plough into them with a sickening noise, hit a rock and rake from side to side.

Still I could not control my own vehicle. I tried to use the brakes but abandoned that tactic when the car went into another skid. Then I was at the bottom of the hill and could see a stony patch beside the road. I pulled onto it, stopped the car and jumped out.

Above me Stark's car was still weaving, out of control, wheels locked and sliding. As I watched it skidded toward the lip of a ravine, hovered for a moment and then tipped over. Almost in slow motion, it crashed and somersaulted to the bottom, one wheel and bits of metal flying off as it went. It came to rest upside down. The hideous noise of crushing metal ceased, the echo died and there was only the rain and running water and the bleat of frightened goats. No one got out of the car. Stark could not have survived.

Chapter 16

I STOOD THERE, shivering, trying to pluck up the courage to climb down to the wreck and investigate. There was no one else to do it. The few huts around the Inland Sea seemed to be deserted, and what other visitor would endure a journey to this place in such weather? I was standing in a kind of bowl, but high cliffs did little to shelter the inland water which was fed through cave and tunnel from the wild seas beyond. The wind whistled round the deep hollow and soared, screaming, over the hillsides. I looked back at the steep road I'd come down and shuddered. My own escape had been miraculous.

Along the track and at the lip of the ravine, dead goats lay in grotesque positions, their blood mingling pinkly with rivulets of rain water, forming red pools where there were hollows and slowly overflowing. For a moment I thought I would faint, but instead nausea overcame me and I was violently sick. Afterwards I pulled myself together and began a slow and careful descent to the wrecked car. The climb down satisfied my conscience but was a wasted journey. One did not need a trained eye to see that Harry Stark had a broken neck.

To return to my car I picked my way along the valley bottom toward the Inland Sea and followed the rough road to where I had parked. That way was further, but safer. In all that time I saw no other living soul, and I was faced with driving back the way I had come. A daunting task. I sat behind the wheel and thought about it.

On the opposite hillside a mottled river was flowing upwards, leaping and jumping, not stopping for a moment. I looked from the goats to the hill I would have to climb, a yellow ribbon glistening with water and blood, twisting up and out of what in happier times would be a splendid place to explore.

I decided to race my car hard at the hill and roar up without slowing or even thinking. Mercifully, I met nothing and whizzed up past rough country and a field or two and into the town of San Lawrenz, where I stopped the car. Exactly like a waterfall, rain was cascading off an enormous church. I watched it in a detached way until my pulse had slowed to something approaching its normal pace and my knees had stopped behaving like castanets. Then I restarted the car.

Drained, I drove slowly back to Victoria, thinking of the ordeal still to come: the necessity to call the police about Stark, my proposed visit to Louis's bar and my note to Alfio. I hoped Alfio would turn up and yet I felt afraid—dreading that he would come, scared that he would not. The police could sort out the business of the pictures but I was obsessed with the need to know how my father had died and by whose hand. This story of Louis having seen someone might be a trap. The gentle Joseph—how could I be sure he was to be trusted?

I drove to the police station to make a statement about Stark's death. Inspector Rapa was not in so I told the sergeant on duty that I had "happened to see" the accident at the Inland Sea. He was kind and concerned for me but clearly bewildered that any visitor should dream of going to such a place in this weather. He offered medical assistance, which I refused. I signed some forms and went out again into the rain.

Now that I had reported the crash, the horror of it receded a little and I became obsessed again with the prospect of my confrontation with Alfio Marcello at Louis's bar. So much depended upon it. No police, I had said, but it would be good to have somebody with me. On impulse, I went to the post office and searched in my purse for the letter Michael had written to me after my father's death. I had noted his telephone number on the envelope when I'd called him from Xaghra, and now I dialed it again, reflecting that when I was in trouble it seemed to be Michael I turned to. But then, up until very recently, there had been only two men in my life—my father and Michael Brent.

Michael answered with an impatient growl I recognized as meaning that he was writing and did not want any interruptions. Explanations would take too long, so I said merely, "This is Alexa," then brushed aside his greeting and the warmth which altered his tone of voice. "There's something I have to do this afternoon and I think I need help."

"What is it?" He sounded willing, but cautious.

"I can't discuss it on the phone. Would you meet me at two-thirty in Louis's bar in Xaghra?"

"Well—sure, if you want me to. I don't know the bar but I expect I can find it."

"It's in the big square, near the church."

"Okay. I'll see you there."

I felt enormously relieved at the prospect of having someone with me and drove back to the Tramonto as quickly as the sheeting rain allowed.

🐦.　🐦.　🐦.

It was sheer misfortune that Randal was in the foyer when I got back to the hotel. I was filthy with mud, soaking wet, and I had the shakes again.

He caught his breath. "Where in God's name have you been?"

"I went for a walk," I said lamely.

"A *walk*. Is that why you're as white as a sheet and trembling? Alexa, why won't you trust me? Because I'm a Jarvis? Haven't I shown you that I have very little to do with my family?"

There was no one about. The multitude of guests were in the dining room. I could hear the murmur of many voices and the clash of cutlery on china.

I said, "Randal, why should it even cross your mind that my muddy state could have anything whatever to do with your family? That chip on your shoulder makes you jump to some very odd conclusions." Close to tears, I hurried to Carmela's room, half expecting Randal to follow me. But he didn't—at least, not at once.

In the bathroom I washed up and sponged my muddy trousers. The yellow sweater was at least clean, if damp, because it had been covered by my coat. When I returned to my room, I could smell wet wool and also good strong coffee. Randal himself had brought it up and was standing by the window. Beside the coffeepot was a plate of chicken sandwiches.

"You must eat something," Randal said in a coaxing voice.

"I'm not hungry. But I would like some coffee. It—it was kind of you to bring it." I spoke stiffly.

He looked at me and said nothing, then walked to the door. I hoped he was leaving, but he stood there watching me as I took out the small hairbrush I carried in my handbag and brushed out my hair.

"You look terrible," he said. "Worse than last night, and that's saying something."

"Thank you," I managed.

His tone changed. He sounded choked. "And you also look very beautiful. You always do."

I turned quickly to look at him, startled, saying nothing. I was aware of a pulse beating strongly in my throat.

"What's going on, Alexa?" he asked at last, and I knew it took an effort for him to speak calmly.

I turned away. "I don't know." I sounded breathless.

"Tell me. Damnit, I may be able to help. Tell me!" His voice shook, filled with irritation and tiredness. I thought of the strain he was under, with his hotel overflowing, inadequate electricity, perhaps difficulty in obtaining food. Carmela who did so much for him was away ill. And yet he found time to try and help me when he thought I was in trouble.

"I'm sorry. It is kind of you to ask, but . . ." I shook my head. I could not tell him. Whether or not he liked his family, it would not be right to put him in the position of judging them, taking sides against them. To my horror, tears spilled over again. I laid the hairbrush down and it slipped from the dressing table to the floor with a clatter.

I put both hands over my eyes but my cheeks were already too wet for me to be able to hide the fact that I was crying.

Randal took two strides across the room, and with an exclamation he put his arms around me and held me against him. "Tell me," he said. "Alexa, tell me. Please." His deep, murmuring voice held nothing but a yearning tenderness.

So I told him that today Stark had chased me in his car. "And he's dead," I sobbed. "He's dead."

"Dead! How? Where did this happen?" He spoke in little more than a whisper.

"I was coming down the road from your father's house . . ." I began.

"*My father's* house? What were you doing up there?"

"Nothing. I can't explain."

"Did you see my father?" Randal was angry again.

"No."

"Or Noni? Did you see Noni?"

"You don't understand, Randal. I didn't go as far as the house. Only to the road. Stark followed me from there."

"Then *he* was on his way to the house?"

"I don't know. I only know that he's dead. He followed me to the Inland Sea and went off the road." I shook my head, trying to get rid of the memory. "It was horrible."

"The Inland Sea! In *this* weather? For God's sake, why go *there*?" Randal was astounded.

"I didn't know where I was going. I'd never have gone down there if I'd known what it was like . . ." I pulled myself together. "I've told the police."

"The police." Randal seemed to fasten on to the last two words, utterly horrified. He had not been greatly concerned about the death of Stark but the thought of the police shook him. Yet they would have to know of such an accident.

Randal's hands were cold on my shoulders, even through the gown. Then they moved to the back of my neck. He touched it almost absent-mindedly, one hand sliding under the fall of my hair. His brilliant gray eyes were dark and full of a powerful emotion I knew had nothing to do with me.

"Alexa, you have helped me, you don't know how much." He pulled me against him and kissed me, his mouth firm, then hard, on mine. "I have to go and see Noni," he told me gently. "Don't go away."

I did not answer. I was going to Louis's bar in Xaghra and Michael would be there, but I did not mention that to Randal.

The pot of coffee was still steaming on the tray when I heard the engine of Randal's car roar into life by the garage behind the hotel. I poured a cup and drank it, and ate some of the sandwiches after all. I was still eating when someone knocked on the door. I opened it and saw Inspector Rapa, his burly frame filling the doorway.

"I was told I would find you here. Do you mind if we have an unofficial talk in your room?" He seemed apologetic. "There is nowhere downstairs where we could be private. I would not want to use the office in Mr. Jarvis's absence."

I looked beyond the Inspector.

"I have no one with me except a driver. I left him in the car. Do you mind?"

"No, of course not." I opened the door wider and closed it behind him. His uniform was streaked with rain on the shoulders, and he flicked at it and laid his flat hat on the dressing table. His dark eyes were alert as ever but his face was pale and lined with exhaustion. On an island suddenly beleaguered by storm, police duties must have multiplied. "Please sit down." Indicating the one chair, I perched on the end of the bed.

"Thank you." He sank down and looked at me, sighing. "You had a very bad experience at Il-Qawra. Thank you for reporting to the police station. Do you need medical attention?"

I said no. "Your sergeant offered, but I'm all right."

"Would you tell me what happened, in your own words?"

I told him, and he said, "It was brave of you to climb down and make sure that Stark was dead. But why, I wonder, did you go up the road toward the Jarvis house on a day like this? Were you visiting?"

"No, I . . . no reason, really."

He waited for me to amend this statement, but I said nothing. The less I revealed for the time being, the better my chances of finding out what I wanted to know. I had told Joseph that there would be no police at Louis's bar this afternoon and I must not do anything that might frighten the two men.

The Inspector broke in on my thoughts. "Do you think that Stark followed you to the road to the Jarvis villa? Or was it coincidence that you met there?"

"Inspector Rapa, I don't know, but Stark seemed to assume that I had some connection with Edgar Jarvis."

The policeman shrugged. "Since he found you at the Tramonto, he would naturally believe you to be connected with Randal Jarvis and his father . . ."

"But Randal says he has nothing to do with his father!" I exclaimed.

"Do you believe him?"

Slowly, I answered, "I think I do."

"Nevertheless, Stark may not have believed it." The Inspector looked at me for a moment and seemed to make a decision. He nodded and said, "Miss Prescott, we have learned a good deal in the past few days about Edgar Jarvis and his activities. According to information I have obtained, Stark came to Gozo following a trail which led him to Jarvis, who he apparently believed had betrayed him. It must have been a shock for him to find that *Randal* Jarvis owned the Tramonto. Stark would not know that Randal had opened his hotel more than two years before his father came to this island—a year before his father even took up residence in Malta, in fact. It was natural enough for Stark to assume the two men were working together and to include you when he saw you with each of them in turn."

I digested this. From Stark's point of view, it was reasonable. Then I asked a question which had been haunting me. "Was my father really a friend of Edgar Jarvis's?"

"No," said Inspector Rapa, his eyes kind. "Oh, they talked occasionally, but friends—no. Your father was an honorable man, Miss Prescott. Edgar Jarvis, it would seem, is not."

"Then what is he?" I asked, thinking I knew the answer but wanting to be told. I was tired of mysteries.

"A smuggler."

"Of pictures?"

With sharpened interest and in surprise, he said. "You know about the pictures?"

"There was a Modigliani in my father's house. If not an original, then a very good copy."

Rapa's face darkened. "My men searched the house. They found no pictures." He spoke sharply.

I explained, then, about the picture I'd first seen, and

about the substituted copy, and how Joseph had hidden the first picture, then taken fright and put it back.

"So when we searched, it had been removed from the house. A pity. It might have helped us. It certainly, now, raises new questions about your father's death."

"An ill wind, Inspector. Alfio Marcello missed the painting too—at first."

"That one! Yes, Jarvis would tell him to recover it, when he found that an original had been passed to your father as a copy. That secret transaction must have made Jarvis frantic. Did Marcello use Joseph's method to get into the house?"

"The hole in the cellar." I smiled sadly. "No doubt you wish my father had sealed it."

"Naturally, I wish he had taken more care of his property—and of himself." He was cool, all policeman again.

"Do you think my father knowingly bought a stolen picture?"

After a moment, Rapa said, "If he did, he had his reasons. Anything he found out, he would have told me about, I'm sure, if he had lived. He may have stumbled onto something accidentally.'

"And as a result he was silenced?"

"Miss Prescott, you must believe me. I have told you all the facts I know, to this point, about your father's death. As for the affair of those hiding at the Villa Melita, Stark's presence has hampered me. I wanted my net to catch him also, but now"—he shrugged—"there is one less. Also, because of the storm, there is other urgent work to do. But no one can get away from the island. It would be suicide to try." He rose and went to the door, moving wearily. "Miss Prescott, I must ask you to keep away from the Jarvis home."

"I have no intention of going there again." I spoke with feeling.

He nodded and left. Bitterly, I thought of how totally involved he was with Edgar Jarvis and the smuggled pictures. He did not care about finding out who had killed my father.

Chapter 17

I DROVE to Xaghra through the eye of the storm, aware that the weather would worsen again, grateful for the lull. When I drew up in the square there was no sign of Michael's car outside Louis's bar. Now that I had set this meeting up and the moment had arrived, I was anxious to get it over with. Too impatient to wait for Michael, I went into the bar, pushing aside the plastic curtain, my eyes searching the gloom for Alfio Marcello. He must have received my note because he was there, sitting with his back to the wall in a position halfway between door and bar. Near to him sat Joseph, who greeted me. Louis was behind the bar, looking a little nervous, I thought. He did not give me the prearranged signal of a nod. Had he thought better of it?

"Good afternoon," I said to Louis, and when he answered his smile was a shade less anxious.

"A *kinnie*, Miss Prescott?" He began to pour one.

I was aware that I ought to approach Alfio, with whom I had made the appointment, and reluctantly I did so. Still Louis gave no sign. He was pouring *kinnie* for me, frowning in concentration. Behind me I heard the rattle of plastic strips in the doorway and Michael's voice saying, "Alexa?"

Louis froze, half-empty bottle in one hand, half-filled glass in the other. His eyes rolled from Michael to me and he nodded. Alfio was very still, a look of intense surprise on his face at seeing Michael there. I felt a fierce stab of pain deep inside me, welling up and bursting into a fountain of horror.

In utter dismay, shocked beyond belief, I forgot my promise that Louis should only have to indicate with a nod that he recognized the man.

"No!" I cried. "No, you must be mistaken!" I moved to Michael's side. My hand clutched his sleeve. I wanted no doubt in my mind. "Did Michael Brent drown my father ? Did he? Did he?"

Pandemonium broke out. The customers in the bar milled around, shouting and screaming, knocking wooden chairs to the ground with a thunderous noise. The hubbub was indescribable. Joseph launched himself at Michael to hold him, but Michael grabbed my arm with one hand and with the other shoved Joseph off his feet so that he collided with the others. I found myself firmly held, spinning to the door.

"No!" I shrieked. "No, Michael. Let me go!"

Out of the corner of my eye I could see Alfio, Joseph and Louis trying to get to me but it was useless. Michael was stronger, more ruthless, quicker. I was his prisoner and I found myself tossed into his car like a bag of feathers. While he ran round and jumped into the driver's seat I tried to open the door, but he had pushed the catch down and I was unfamiliar with his car. I failed to get away and in a moment we were crazily screeching around the square, out of Xaghra and along the main road to Victoria.

"Michael, *why* kill my father?"

"You don't believe those . . . *peasants?*" He thrust the word out with vicious contempt.

"Why should they lie?"

"Drama. They live by it."

"And what do you live by? Money? Greed?"

"Greed? What about your father? Buying a picture for peanuts and refusing to part with it when the mistake was discovered."

"What mistake? That the picture was an original instead of a copy? And after you'd killed him, was that why you wanted to buy the house? Were you really buying back the picture? I suppose the price of a Gozitan farmhouse, half restored, would be a lot lower than the price of an original Modigliani."

"You should have sold the house. Then none of this would have happened."

I turned and pummeled his arm with my fists, too overwhelmed to care whether I caused an accident. "None of this? None of this? You think I cared about *anything* when my father was dead? You had already killed him!"

Michael swerved momentarily when I hit him. He seemed to have no sense of regret, or shame.

"You know my father would not be party to fraud!" I cried.

He turned then and looked at me. Brutally, he said,

"Most men have their price. He was too stubborn. Now shut up."

I had thought Michael would be taking me to his own house but instead we went up the track to the Jarvis home, and as we swerved across the gravel, rain pelted down again with increased force. Edgar Jarvis himself opened the front door, his face pale, the thick white hair ruffled. I had never before seen him other than well groomed. He looked . . . diminished.

"I was expecting you. What do you want?" He asked the question of Michael, his eyes only flickering toward me.

"Noni. And that picture. Everything else is blown here."

An ironic smile lifted the corners of Jarvis's mouth but his eyes were anguished. "You're too late, I'm glad to say. Noni has gone."

"Have you sent her to sea in this weather?"

"I'm not a fool."

"Then I'll find her. Give me the keys. Throw them."

Michael held out his left hand, and with the right he pulled something from his pocket. I drew a breath of horror. It was a small gun, glinting blue in the stormy light. And it was no toy.

Jarvis glanced down at it, his eyes somber. "So," he said. "You'd kill *me* now? First Alexa's father, now Noni's." With irony, he added, "Perhaps you prefer fatherless fiancées."

"You knew how my father died?" My voice was shaking.

Edgar Jarvis shook his head. "Not until a few minutes ago. Alfio telephoned from Xaghra. Art theft, forgery and the safe escape of those who steal and copy, these are my business. I admit it. And I am successful because others are covetous. But murder and violence are *not* my business. Believe me, I am very sorry about your father."

He had a strange dignity about him as he spoke, and I believed him.

"The keys." Michael snapped the fingers of his extended hand.

"No." Edgar Jarvis took one step backwards. Michael leveled the snub nose of his revolver and the older man had time only to say, "You wouldn't . . ." before he was shot down, to lie on his own doorstep with blood forming a spreading stain on his chest. He coughed once, twice, and was silent, still.

For seconds I stared at his body in disbelief. Lashing rain hissed on the gravel. We were in the shelter of the porch, all of us. Then Michael moved toward me.

"I should have left you to Stark on the clifftop. You know now what you saw that night, don't you? A dummy run with the Jarvis cruiser, designed to flush out Stark. And when I came for Stark, *you* were there between us and I had to play Sir Galahad. I'd thought I was cured of loving you, Alexa, but I wasn't. Then at the horse races I might have left you to die when Stark pushed you. I couldn't. But now . . ."

I began to scream.

"Stop it!"

I couldn't stop. I would be killed now, I knew that. Michael lifted the gun. I looked right down the barrel, and then, instead of shooting me, he clenched a fist and hit me.

It must have been only moments later that I came round, for Michael had the keys and was dragging me down the cellar steps. "No!" I began to struggle. I knew there were men hiding in the cellar. The prospect of being locked up with them was as terrifying as the gun.

"Alexa, I ought to shoot you. I almost *want* to. If I

256 🕭

didn't know that I can get away without that, I would do it."

His breath was fanning my cheek. One arm was clamped around the upper part of my body, holding my arms to my sides. He dragged me forward and to the cellar. Our feet splashed in water. "Think yourself lucky," he muttered as he unlocked the door and thrust me inside.

I landed in the arms of a man with hot, garlic-laden breath. Another pushed forward, trying to reach the door, but he was drunk and stumblingly awkward. We all fell in a heap in the floodwater on the floor, the men swearing, I biting my lips to keep from screaming. I was frightened but determined not to show it, and thankful for light thrown across the cellar by a polished brass lamp. We stood up, wary of one another.

One man spoke with a French accent, the other used some Italian. Neither was young. The drunken Italian had black hair but the face beneath it was mapped with wrinkles. He was fat, and his hands and clothes were stained with paint.

The Frenchman, well dressed even in this cellar, was slim and lithe. He had close-cropped, grizzled hair and neat, controlled movements, and he was suave as he surveyed me. He was chewing, with small nibbles which twitched his jaw now and then. A perpetual habit, I imagined. He reached for a towel and dried his hands.

Presently, he threw the towel to me and began to laugh. The smell of garlic came strongly across the cellar. "Don't be nervous, little one. You are more in danger of drowning than of being molested."

"Sì, sì." The Italian bobbed his head, too drunk to do other than agree.

The water was rising fast. I pictured the cellar steps,

channeling rain downwards in a stream which far exceeded the volume of water escaping through a small grating. The eye of the storm had passed and even from down here we could hear the renewed deluge, like stage rain, rattling immoderately onto the gravel.

"Jarvis is okay," the Frenchman said to me in a rough attempt to comfort. "He will let us out. We shall get away in that boat of his."

I swallowed and was silent, remembering the body of Edgar Jarvis lying in his own front doorway in a spreading pool of blood. Better to say nothing about that.

"What have you done to be made to join us? Who are you? Come, sit on the table and keep your feet out of the water."

We all sat on the table, an ill-assorted row of bedraggled human beings, and after a moment's hesitation I said, "I am Alexa Prescott."

It conveyed nothing to them.

"You sold a Modigliani to my father," I said to the Italian, "through Maria."

"Ah." He began to chuckle, a wheezy sound. "Did he know it was an original?"

"I think he did."

"Then he made money."

"No. He died. Is that what you wanted?"

"*Mama mia!* No! No, *I* wanted to get away. *He* is here by his own wish, hiding." He jerked a thumb at the Frenchman. "I am a prisoner, making copies for those greedy . . ." The thumb jerked toward the ceiling and he used an unprintable Italian epithet. "I thought . . ." He lapsed into silence, contemplating what he clearly saw now as a disaster.

"He thought that if he released an original for a very

small sum of money, questions would be asked of Jarvis and Jarvis would at once smuggle both of us to North Africa instead of keeping this *cochon* to paint more copies." The Frenchman spoke with weary irony. "But Jarvis delayed, believing he could get the picture back."

"He did get it back."

"He did?" The Italian was startled, then angry again. "So Signor Jarvis lied to me. He lied and kept us here and then the storm came." The man flung up his hands. "So we are all trapped."

It was a suitable description for our plight. We were locked in a cellar, with water rising. Either we would drown, or someone would release us and the men would be caught.

The water gurgled and lapped under the door, and as the legs of the stout table became sodden, they creaked. I began to shiver. The Frenchman was still impassive, the Italian was weeping maudlin tears and muttering half-remembered prayers.

It was extraordinary how little sound penetrated through the stone and the thick wooden door. Nothing more distant than the top of the steps seemed to exist. We could hear rain on gravel and the sound of water trickling and seeping and that was all. We fell into a kind of stupor of despair, I think. I was watching the water rise against the opposite wall and knew that when it reached a certain mark it would be level with the top of the table, because the table had evidently at some time or another been against that wall and had marked it.

We were roused from torpor by the sound of cars on gravel, then voices at the top of the steps. We leaped into water which was over our knees, and plunged toward the door in a mad frenzy in case we would not be heard.

We hammered and shouted and screamed in three languages and I think that by then the men did not mind who rescued them.

When the door opened, I saw Inspector Rapa. Four other policemen stood on the steps, and hovering in the background was Alfio Marcello. I stumbled up the steps, emerging slowly from the floodwater. Dimly, I was aware of orders being given and of my fellow prisoners being led away by two of the uniformed men.

"What made you come here *now?*" I asked Rapa, unable to believe my good fortune at being rescued.

"Marcello telephoned from the bar in Xaghra and asked us to come."

I said, "He also called Edgar Jarvis to warn him, but it was no use."

Rapa's eyebrows shot up. "You know that Jarvis is dead?"

I thought that the utter horror of that killing would be with me forever but I kept my voice steady as I said, "I saw it happen."

"Then who shot Jarvis, Miss Prescott?"

"Michael Brent," I told him, and thought of the days when I had said his name over and over in a chant of joy, thinking of myself as his future wife.

After a long moment, Rapa said, "You've had a lucky escape."

I answered, "Yes."

Chapter 18

WE WERE ALL drenched, standing there at the top of
the cellar steps. I could see the door forced back, and the
water level at the fourth step from the bottom.

Inspector Rapa turned to the two policemen and ordered a search for Michael. "He can't leave the island
until the storm clears, but keep a watch on all roads. I
want to be kept informed, if you please."

As they went, I asked, "Do you think they'll find him?"

"They're very thorough." He was looking at me speculatively. There would be questions he wanted to ask, explanations I must give. And I was suddenly so very tired.

At that moment, Randal came round the corner of the
house, pale and shaken, grim-featured, walking quickly.
His face flooded with relief at the sight of me. He came
straight to my side and gripped my hand.

"Miss Prescott, will you go with Mr. Jarvis to the Tramonto?" Rapa spoke with kindness. "Any further questions can wait until tomorrow. The storm will be over then." To Randal he said, "Treat her gently, Mr. Jarvis. She saw your father killed. Thank you for coming to identify the body."

Disregarding the thanks, Randal said to me, "You *saw* it, Alexa?"

I nodded, and answered his unspoken question. "It was Michael. He killed my father, too."

"Dear God!" Randal breathed, and taking my arm he walked me to his car. Very gently, he brushed the wet strands of hair off my face and saw the bruise on my chin. "That, too?" he asked quickly, and his gray eyes were dark with anger.

"Yes. Before locking me up. I don't . . ." My voice broke and I had to try again. "I don't know why he left me alive when I'd seen him shoot your father."

Randal's arms went around me then, and in a husky voice, with his cheek resting on my head, he said, "Michael also loved you, Alexa."

He held me close, then released me, gripped my hands hard, let them go, and started the car. I knew he must be thinking now of Noni and I asked where she was.

"In my room at the Tramonto. When you told me about Stark and the police, I knew that someone must be investigating my father's affairs at last. It was bound to come. I persuaded Noni to leave the villa, but against her will, I'm afraid."

We bumped down the track, shivering in our wet clothes. "Randal, are you an accessory?" I asked, and my anxiety for him was profound.

"I suppose the police will decide about that. Technically, perhaps I am. My father lived in such style, you see.

Greater style than a 'retired' lawyer could possibly manage
—unless there were other sources of income." He slowed,
and drove through a deep pool. "I told you there were
contributing factors to my giving up singing."

"I remember."

"You'd better know it all, Alexa. I toured, of course,
singing. And when my father was disbarred for a fairly
minor misdemeanor, he felt ill-used. From then on, he
thought the law-abiding world owed *him* a living. He
wanted Noni and me to join him in a venture he and his
brother started in Marseilles. At first, it was legitimate—
an art gallery, some copying, which is not the same as
forgery."

I nodded. I knew that so long as a copy was not passed
off as an original, there was nothing against it.

"Eventually, they dealt in stolen paintings and all the
rest. Noni joined them. She didn't seem to mind, but I refused."

I thought about Randal, the young idealist, starting out
on his own career as a musical artist, about the years of
study and practice and, at last, engagements and travel—
all to end in nothing.

Randal's hand moved from the steering wheel to grip
mine for a moment. "My father thought I was priggish.
He asked me to carry pictures with me on my tours. I'd
have been a good cover for him, but I refused." A look of
pain passed over Randal's face and he paused a moment
before speaking again. "Then, one evening, a painting was
left at a concert hall in Paris where I was appearing. It
had arrived by hand but no one remembered who'd
brought the parcel. I recognized the painting, a small
Cézanne which had been stolen from a private collection
in Versailles—the robbery had been reported in the papers.
I rewrapped the canvas, posted it back to the owner

anonymously and went to Marseilles to tell my father what I had done. He was furious. That was when I got this." He touched the small scar on his jaw.

"You mean your own father hit you?" I was filled with compassion.

"Not all that hard. He was wearing a ring, otherwise there would not have been a scar. But he hit me, yes, and we quarreled violently. After that, there were no more parcels left at concert halls for me, but I couldn't relax, couldn't be sure he wouldn't try again or that his 'career' would get him into terrible trouble. So I gave up singing, managed a small hotel in Sussex for a while and decided that I liked the life. I borrowed from a bank and came here to start up on my own."

We were driving into Xlendi and the whole town seemed to be strewn with the wreckage of the storm.

"Why did your father follow you here?"

"God knows! Actually, I don't think he followed me at all. The Malta apartment was a tax haven, for he retained his British nationality. Then he decided that quiet Gozo presented possibilities for his current venture of ferrying art thieves out of Europe and across to North Africa. This I learned from Rapa today." Randal's voice was bitter.

"Noni didn't tell you?"

"No. There was a pact between us that we would never discuss my father's affairs."

"Then you didn't know what your father was doing here?"

"No. I kept well away from him and he from me." Randal frowned. "But of course I suspected he was continuing his old tricks, if that makes me an accessory."

"Suspicion and knowledge are not at all the same thing," I told him with great firmness.

He glanced at me, and I could imagine how I looked,

sopping wet and shivering. But Randal's expression was full of tenderness and wonderment and he said, "Dearest Alexa." Then he added, "You must be so shocked and so cold."

I thought of Edgar Jarvis, lying dead. A disbarred lawyer who claimed to have retired. He was colder than I. Then I recalled my own father, and Michael who had killed them both. He was still alive, somewhere on the island. Such a small island. I knew it would not be long before the police caught up with him, and I had no regrets.

Randal and I entered the hotel by the back door, hand in hand, dripping all over the floor.

"Well! Orphans of the storm. How touching!" Noni looked as beautiful as ever, unaffected by weather or emotion, standing in the small hallway. She was wearing a light wool suit of pale blue and a matching silk scarf. Her blond hair gleamed and by her feet was a small, expensive traveling case.

"What are you doing?" Randal was very angry.

She shrugged. "As you see, I'm waiting for a taxi. Sorry, Ran, but the redemption scene is not for me. Being poor but honest does not appeal, nor does going to jail."

"But Father is dead. You know that! I told you before I went up to identify him."

For a moment her eyes looked bleak and her lovely mouth quivered. Then she said, "That's partly why I'm leaving. I was too involved, Ran darling, unlike you. Gozo isn't healthy for me any more."

I assumed that she was planning to join Michael and felt that I had to warn her. "Noni, you don't understand. It was Michael who shot your father. And he killed mine, too."

Noni stared at me for a long moment. At last she said,

"You don't like me, Alexa, but I did you a favor a year ago, didn't I?"

I was shaken by her calm. "Did you know that it was Michael who killed your father?"

"No. Not for certain. But he was capable of . . ." She took a deep breath. "Of *anything*. That's why he attracted me so much." She looked at me with contempt. "He had qualities you could never appreciate."

"Had?"

She shrugged. "He's in the past for me now, whether he's caught or not."

"And where do you propose to go now?" Randal's voice was harsh.

"Tunis? South America? It's best if you don't know, Ran, darling. Here's my taxi. Be happy." She flipped the fingers of one hand at him and was gone, flying through the rain and into the taxi.

"She'll get away," I said to Randal, partly to comfort him but with conviction also. Noni was a butterfly. She would find a bed of roses for herself somewhere. It was Michael the police were looking for, and once he was caught and the storm died, powerboats and pleasure yachts would go to sea again and Noni would be aboard one of them.

"Don't look so terrible." I lifted a hand to Randal's face.

He pulled me against him. "Alexa," he whispered. He bent his head and we kissed and kissed again, clinging together, glad to be alive.

At Randal's insistence I had a hot bath and went to bed in a pair of his pajamas, ridiculously large. He brought me some hot soup and a small, delicious mixture of meat and vegetables, and then he left me. When I had eaten, I lay down, convinced that I would not sleep, but it was after nine o'clock the next morning when I wakened. I lay for a moment, puzzled by the silence. It was quiet outside. The storm was over. The sun was shining as it had when I arrived in Gozo, expecting to see my father's grave, hoping to find out how he died. How long ago it seemed!

I ran to the window, and in spite of all the horrors my heart stirred at the sight of so much rain-washed beauty, and the thought of Randal, who must have been up for hours. I dressed quickly and made my way to the dining room.

"Where is everybody?"

The young waiter I had spoken to smiled, his dark eyes gleaming. "Some by the swimming pool, others all gone."

I could see the middle-aged couples back in their favorite chairs by the pool, and one or two others.

"Breakfast on the terrace for two, Tomas," Randal said from behind me, and received a beaming "Yes, *sir*."

We were alone and Randal kissed me before we walked outside into fresh, moist air and hot sunshine. He looked calm and his eyes were serene. I thought that perhaps he had faced his family catastrophe in anticipation scores of times before it actually happened. Now he could face his own future. Inspector Rapa would question both of us, but with compassion.

Randal took me to the balustrade and we looked out over garden, swimming pool, rock and glittering sea. "In four days," he said, "the island will be covered in green, no longer bare and barren."

"So quickly? Won't the seeds have been washed away?"

"No. You will see three inches of growth in a few days." He turned to face me, drew me around also, and we looked at each other in silence.

He had a remarkably strong jaw and I liked his bony nose, the mouth which could be firm or tender, or quirk up at the corner, the eyes warm as fire or cold as a stormy sea . . . In four days, I was thinking, I could be back in London. It seemed very remote, the hotel, and my job.

"I ought to go back to London," I said. "My business here is finished." I panicked suddenly and wanted to run away.

Randal knew how I felt. "My absurd darling," he said, laughing at me gently. "You *must* see my island of the seven hills turning green. It's a kind of miracle."

Hesitantly, then more confidently, I smiled. "If there's to be a miracle, I think I must stay and see it."

"I shall be closing the hotel soon for a few weeks. I could come to London, my beautiful Alexa, if you would like that."

I felt a pulse beating in my throat. How could I have thought that I did not want to be involved with anyone again? I was involved already.